burying the lede

the

lede

Trisha & Grayson Mysteries

Corrina Lawson

BURYING THE LEDE

CORRINA LAWSON

CITY OWL
PRESS

BURYING THE LEDE
Trisha & Grayson Mysteries, Book 2

CITY OWL PRESS
www.cityowlpress.com

Cover Design by MiblArt. All stock photos licensed appropriately.

Edited by Tee Tate.

For information on subsidiary rights, please contact the publisher at info@cityowlpress.com.

Print Edition ISBN: 978-1-64898-524-9

Digital Edition ISBN: 978-1-64898-525-6

Printed in the United States of America

To Jenny, who saw the first draft of this book and said, "You have a fabulous character and no plot," and then proceeded to help me fix that. Teachers are the best.

CHAPTER ONE

THE ANGELIC TOPPER on the Christmas tree leaned precariously to the right, a festive disaster waiting to happen. Great, a dead-on metaphor for her relationship with Grayson.

Trisha Connell stepped back, hands on her hips, to survey the tree in full. Boxes of tinsel, lights, icicles, and a few cheap ornaments sat nearby, waiting to be used. She'd wanted to have it fully decorated as a surprise but now? Not a chance, she decided, and removed the angel, leaving the branches bare again. They could decorate it together. That was supposed to be romantic, so everyone said. Her experiences included a ton of shit, but holiday decorating wasn't on that list.

Tree. Romance. Christmas, blah, blah, blah. Ho, ho, ho!

She retreated to the kitchen and dumped a week's worth of her letters and magazines for sorting on the marble countertop of Grayson's fancy kitchen island.

She flipped through the mail, ignoring the ads, flyers, and magazines, seeking the check that would pay next month's rent. She discovered a Christmas card from Joe, her former editor. There was another from Kimba Sue. How did the woman find the time when buried in her new job as the *Herald*'s crime reporter? Perhaps Trisha should reciprocate. Get into the

Christmas spirit, whatever that meant. Maybe she'd purchase a red or green leather jacket to wear instead of her black one.

A postcard caught between junk mail slipped out and floated to the floor. She grabbed it in mid-air.

From Florida.

Grayson.

A sailboat decorated the front. She turned it over. Stamped November 28, 1984. The same day he'd left.

Been sailing & thinking of you. See you soon, Patricia.

Aww…

Oh, damn, now he had her being all mushy. Next, he'd be sending her flowers and chocolates for Valentine's Day, and *she'd like it*. Fuck. Anyway, if he missed her that much, maybe he should have invited her to Florida. No, never mind. Had she really wanted to be cooped up on a family vacation where his ex was also invited?

She finally found the check from that history magazine. As hoped, it was big enough to pay rent. Enclosed with the check was a request from the editor to pitch her again. Who knew a history magazine would pay so well for a feature on the elevated steps in the Bronx?

Finally, all that remained was a single white envelope with no return address. Uh-oh. Another one of *those*. She dug out the other letters from the depths of the backpack. The typewriter font on the new one matched. No return address, but they were stamped by the same post office in Upper Manhattan.

Trisha set the new one aside and tapped her fingers on the marble counter, deciding what to do now. The first three letters had been full of Bible quotes about vengeance. A cut above her usual hate mail yet oddly unsettling. What Biblical call for punishment had the asshole sent this time? She probably should just toss them all and forget about it.

Except she was pissed and wanted to find the person responsible. That meant opening the envelope and hoping to find a clue about the sender.

She slit the flap with her finger.

Hell!

Sudden pain sliced through her hand. Blood poured out of her fingertip and pooled into her palm. Dark red drops splattered onto the envelopes of the Christmas cards and oozed onto Grayson's marble counter. She seized her wrist, raised it over her head, and fumbled for the sink. What the heck had just happened?

She spotted the answer: a blood-covered razor blade peeked out from the half-opened envelope. *Motherfucker.*

Blood dripped from her palm into the stainless steel sink. *Fuck.* She needed to wrap it, but bandages had to be in the bathroom, and she'd be damned if she dripped blood over the expensive carpet between the kitchen and the bathroom.

She closed her eyes, swallowed hard, and counted to ten to avoid thinking about the last time she'd been cut with razor blades. She still carried those scars.

Trisha shoved her injured hand under the water and fumbled for a dish towel. She wrapped the towel tight around it, ignored her dizzy head, and scooted for the bathroom. Once there, she washed the cut in the bathroom sink, poured half a bottle of hydrogen peroxide over it, and wrapped it with a washcloth.

A deep slice, enough for stitches. This was more than just threats now, it was action. That probably meant a police report, if only to create a paper trail if things got worse. Could take hours. Fuck.

———

Trisha called the local precinct from a pay phone in the ER's waiting room. The desk sergeant took her name and said someone would get back to her. She provided her number and Grayson's and told him she'd be at Mercy's ER for the next couple of hours, in the unlikely chance anyone wanted to take her statement there. Fat chance with such a minor injury, especially on a holiday weekend.

Thankfully, it only took an hour to be seen and stitched up. She gingerly slipped her jacket back on over the bandage on the finger. She could run by the precinct in person and have the report filed before Grayson came home tomorrow.

But when Trisha walked back in the ER waiting room, Lieutenant Dorothy Gilbert and Detective Harold Newman of the NYPD's major crimes unit were waiting for her.

"Connell. Heard you had a problem," Dorothy said.

Grayson and Dorothy were friends. Trisha might buy the lieutenant checking up on her because of that. But her partner Newman too? The guy actively disliked her.

"Damn, Lieutenant, how does my sliced finger rate a visit from *two* major crimes detectives?"

Dorothy drew out a notebook. "Do you want to tell me what happened or not?"

Newman simply glared.

"Fine. Be mysterious." Trisha flopped into the hard, featureless chair opposite Dorothy, squinting from the bright overhead lights that were feeding a developing headache. "We doing this here?"

"Unless you'd rather go to the precinct?" Newman suggested.

"No." Trisha grimaced at the idea of being surrounded by so many cops. "Where do you want me to start?"

"I understand you received a letter with a razor blade?" Dorothy asked.

Troubled, Trisha provided a quick and dirty rundown of the injury. She handed over a sealed plastic bag that contained the envelope and the blade, complete with blood splatter.

"Thorough," Dorothy said.

"Almost too thorough," Newman added.

"I know enough about crime scenes to follow procedure," Trisha said.

"You've never followed rules or procedure in my experience," Newman said.

"Look, detective, you want to know what happened or you want to snipe at me?" she asked.

"Tough choice," he said. "More fun to do both."

She'd gotten off on the wrong foot with Newman years ago, on one of her first stories. She'd noticed his mistake. She could have gone to him directly, given him a chance to correct it. But she'd published it instead because he was an ass, an old-school NYPD cop who didn't like being challenged. Newman had never let her forget it.

Now, he stared at her with unveiled hostility. His barrel-chested body, six-foot height, and nasty stare tended to intimidate people. But she was used to him.

"Did you come for a statement or to harass me?" Trisha replied with a sigh.

"Statement," Dorothy said, elbowing her partner, gently. "What happened after you were cut?"

Trisha described the mess and the cab ride to the ER. "I'd have left the whole thing intact in the kitchen, but I figured this would hardly be a crime scene that would rate a visit. It's a minor injury, after all. What are you two doing here again?"

"Working a case," Dorothy answered. "Was this the first letter you've received?"

Trisha narrowed her eyes. "Sounds like you asked that question because you already know the answer."

"Until you answer my questions, I won't know anything," Dorothy said.

Trisha smelled a story, a bigger one than her simple cut. Dorothy, like all major crimes detectives, was overworked, and while Newman was an ass, he didn't waste his time.

"Easier to show you than tell you." Trisha handed over the brown paper bag stuffed with the other letters. "I tossed them together before going to the hospital. Evidence."

Dorothy opened the bag and raised an eyebrow at their crumpled condition. "You saved the earlier ones. Why?"

Trisha shrugged. "The Bible quotes struck me as odd. Usually, my hate mail runs the gamut of 'fuck you' to 'all women are cunts,' to death threats and bravado about kicking my ass."

"You knew you had something unusual and waited to call it in?" Dorothy asked.

"Because there was *nothing* to call in." She pointed at the mail. "Just letters and, like I said, I get hate mail a lot. I tried to bother the cops with it once, back in the day. Got brushed off."

"I bet." Newman narrowed his eyes.

A patient on crutches maneuvered past them. They were in a corner of the ER waiting room, but Trisha wondered if anyone was trying to eavesdrop. Paranoid. She was becoming paranoid.

Dorothy cleared her throat. "We'll send the letters to be dusted for fingerprints, but tell me your thoughts on them, Trisha, since you obviously have some."

Trisha brought her attention back to the detectives but decided to keep track of the man in the suit slumped and slurring over near the nurse's station.

"The letters are Bible passages concerning vengeance, but they're typed, not handwritten. From that, I infer the sender is worried about being caught by someone recognizing their handwriting. And, of course, they know their Bible, or they have one handy to consult. But they also have a grudge they consider personal against me."

"Can't imagine why," Newman said.

"The list of people with grudges against me is a phone book, for sure," Trisha agreed. "But what set the sender off doesn't have to be something I actually did. I've found I get slammed for stuff people think I did or might do."

Dorothy wrote that down in her notes. "Excellent distinction. Yes, it could well be someone with a one-way obsession."

"Ex-boyfriend?" Newman asked.

Trisha snorted. "Not one who'd quote the Bible."

"Ex-girlfriend?" Dorothy asked.

Trisha raised an eyebrow. Dorothy didn't miss much. She could refuse to answer in front of Newman but, hell, Trisha wasn't ashamed.

"There are some women but, again, nobody who'd quote the Bible at me and no relationship of any duration, anyway." She focused on Newman. "I'm very wham-bam-thank-you-ma'am."

Newman flushed. Good, she'd embarrassed him. Petty, but she'd take what little bit of fun she could at his expense.

"I was very short term with, um, people, until Grayson," Trisha added, glancing at Dorothy. "I assume he's not a suspect."

"No, not *him*," Newman drawled.

Now what did that mean?

Dorothy dropped the letters into her overstuffed purse. "Since I'd rather not open the letters and add more fingerprints to them before they're dusted, tell me about them. Do you remember where the Bible quotes were from?"

"The first letter said: 'Say to them that are of a fearful heart, Be strong, fear not: behold, your God will come with vengeance, even God with a recompence; he will come and save you.'" Well, God had certainly not come to save her. "Isiah, though I forget the passage number."

"You memorized that from a letter?" Newman frowned, as if she'd done something wrong. "That's handy."

Again, that weird undertone.

"Nah, I knew the passage already." She pulled out the Celtic cross she wore under her shirt. "Catholic upbringing, though obviously, the letter writer likes the King James version, not the new revised version that most Catholics use."

"Oh, that's bullshit, Trisha," Dorothy drawled. "I know the Bible, and I'd be hard-pressed to quote that passage from memory."

"All right, fine." Trisha held up a hand in surrender. "I went over the letters a few times, looking for clues. Even looked up the quotes."

"Knew it," Newman snapped.

"Knew what?" she asked.

"Enough, partner," Dorothy said. She'd written the quote in her notebook. All business, of course. Hell, Dorothy usually was. Look at how she'd worn one of her impeccable gray blazers to an ER visit on the weekend. "Let's go on to the second letter."

"'But, O Lord of hosts, that judgest righteously, that triest the reins and the heart, let me see thy vengeance on them: for unto thee have I revealed my cause.'" Trisha shook her head. "That passage calls for God to avenge in a more violent way, but then that's Deuteronomy 32, and the Old Testament is full of 'God will avenge' stuff."

"It certainly is." Dorothy turned to Newman. "Give us a minute. Go get the woman a soda, partner."

The big detective grumbled but rose.

"A Coke, Newman," Trisha said, smiling to bug him. "It's the real thing."

Newman ignored the jibe and strode to the soda machine in the corner.

"You like antagonizing him," Dorothy said. "Stop it."

"Life's full of little pleasures. And he's trying to antagonize *me*."

"It would be easier if you'd stay on his good side."

"What's the fun in that? Why?" Trisha asked.

"You trust me? Then take my advice on this one."

Newman returned and held out the Coke can at arm's length. Instead of drinking it, Trisha held the bottle against her forehead to cool the growing headache.

Dorothy grunted. Newman loomed over her. Trisha ignored him but wondered why it was so important to stay on his good side.

"The last letter, the booby-trapped one, contained a passage everyone knows: 'Vengeance is mine; I will repay, saith the Lord,'" Trisha said. "I saw that through the blood splatter. And I knew it all already."

"Romans," Dorothy muttered.

"Yeah, Romans 12:19. I hate it when people quote the short version because they miss the point. The full quote is 'Dearly beloved, avenge not yourselves, but rather give place unto wrath: for it is written, Vengeance is mine; I will repay, saith the Lord.' It's not about you getting revenge, it's about you leaving it up to God." At least, that's what she'd learned in Catechism.

"Maybe you should teach Sunday school," Dorothy said.

Trisha almost dropped the Coke as she choked out a laugh. "Yeah, me at catechism: do as I say and not as I do. That'll go over well." She finally opened the soda and chugged half of it. "Anyway, I'm an ass for opening the last with my finger instead of a letter opener."

"Not the only reason you're an ass," Newman said.

"Christ, Newman," Dorothy said. "You're not helping."

"Hey, it was too good an opening," he replied.

"Gotta give you that." Trisha finished the Coke, pleased as the cool liquid soothed her dry throat.

"You should have reported this after the second letter," Dorothy said. "You knew they were odd and you kept them. What bothered you specifically?"

She had a better glare than Newman. Hell, a better glare than any severe Catholic nun.

"The Bible stuff came from a fanatic. That bugged me, okay?"

"You're saying your instincts perceived a threat?" Dorothy asked.

"My instincts said something was off. So I kept 'em."

"So noted," Dorothy put away her notebook. "Anything else?"

"That's all I got. What about you? What are you doing here? What's the connection of these letters to Major Crimes cases?"

"Wouldn't you like to know?" Newman growled. "Just sit tight. We may need to talk to you soon."

"Now is good," Trisha said.

"None of your business. Yet." Newman shook his finger at her.

"Enough, partner." Dorothy brushed the finger aside. "I'll let you know what I find out, Trisha."

Trisha mirrored her. "Lieutenant, what do you know about this that I don't?"

Dorothy made a show of putting her coat on. "Do you believe *I* have good instincts?"

"You wouldn't be the cop you are without them," Trisha said.

"Then trust me," Dorothy said again. "When I'm certain what I'm dealing with, you'll be the first to know."

"Gee whiz, thanks, Lieutenant," Trisha snapped. "And it's not *you* that I don't trust." She pointed at Newman.

"Trust the truth," Dorothy said, loud enough for the other residents of the waiting room to finally stare at them.

"Meet me outside, Newman," Dorothy said.

A curt nod. "All right," Newman said.

After he left, Dorothy pulled Trisha aside.

"Look, there's a connection between your letter and another crime. It also included a hidden razor blade in a letter. It's possible your case is related, but it's a longshot. You know what police work is like."

Trisha took a deep breath. "Right. A matter of crossing off what's not related to leave what's relevant to the crime. Lots of tedious paperwork and reports."

"Exactly. In the meantime, do something for me."

Trisha zipped up her coat. "What? Be careful?"

"No, you'll never do that. But stay alert and stay on the straight and narrow. This is already a sensitive case."

"Maybe I'd be more alert if I knew what the other case you're working on is…" Trisha prodded.

"Can't comment," Dorothy said. "If it relates to your case, then we'll be in touch." Dorothy picked up her oversize purse. "Tell Edmund about this. He's got the resources to protect you, just in case."

I can protect myself, Trisha wanted to say, but given she was in the ER with stitches, she let it go.

As Dorothy left the ER, for the first time, fear replaced Trisha's anger. Whatever case Newman and Dorothy were working, it had to be serious. Perhaps even murder.

Just how afraid should she be?

CHAPTER TWO

TRISHA WISHED for a few extra inches as she craned her neck to see over the crowd gathered to greet the travelers who were home from Thanksgiving. She vowed never again to visit an airport on a holiday weekend. She wondered if it would have been better to wait for Grayson at his place, especially since her finger throbbed like it would burst through the bandage any second.

She spotted an opening in the crowd and slid to the front, using her sign to gain space and provide her a clear view of those deplaning.

The crowd parted and there was Grayson walking up the ramp. Those behind him fell back instead of trying to slip around. Subtle power, hidden but seeping out on the edges, that was Edmund Grayson all over. Even now, with passengers surging to find their loved ones, no one cut in front of him. His battleship gray hair, sun-kissed from his sojourn in Florida, provided the final, dignified touch.

He glanced up, focusing on something overhead. His eyes narrowed. Ah, he'd spotted the new surveillance cameras they'd installed at Newark Airport. Once a Fed, always a Fed, even though he was private security now.

Trisha fiddled with the sign she'd made, white with the word "TEDDY" written in black marker, and tried to catch his eye. She wanted to see the surprise on his face, to know whether he was annoyed or pleased.

Grayson spotted her. His eyes widened, he smiled, and her heart did a ridiculous pitter-patter.

She adjusted the chauffeur's cap and gripped the sign tighter, careful to keep the hand with the injured finger in her pocket. His face softened as he reached her, his mouth settling into a half-smile. Damn, he looked relaxed. Sailing agreed with him.

"Ready for a ride?" she said, her voice low.

He leaned over to speak directly in her ear. "Here?"

"Hell, yes." She tucked the sign under her arm, grabbed the lapels of his coat, and pulled him into a kiss. For a second, the throbbing in her finger vanished, the crowd receded, and it was just her and Grayson in a little bubble of warmth and desire that curled around her.

Someone muttered "get a room." Without breaking the kiss, Trisha flashed him the finger.

Grayson ran his thumb down her cheek as he broke the kiss. Part of her cursed that he could get to her so easily.

"Too many spectators for the full ride." She stepped closer and pressed her body against his. Even through their layers of clothing, she could feel the heat.

He raised an eyebrow. "Indeed."

She cleared her throat. "May I take your bag, sir?"

"Certainly."

She exchanged the sign for the duffel. He packed light. She could carry it without pulling the injured hand out of her pocket.

"Dare I ask if you have an actual limousine?" he asked.

"I pulled in some favors and had one ready so I could park in the taxi lane," she said over her shoulder as he followed, "and then I got to thinking about taxi licenses and how tight-assed and ill-humored airport security can be."

"Ah." A pause. "Does that mean you brought your bike?"

His voice was so dry, she couldn't tell if that was a tease or not. "Hah! No, the Indian's in storage for the winter. I stole your car for the evening."

"I suppose I'll overlook that."

Dry humor. *Good. The day is improving by leaps and bounds.* "Thanks. So how was the flight?"

"Delayed."

Plenty of irritation in that one word. They sidestepped a family hurrying by on the sidewalk to the underground lot, joined a crowd waiting for the elevator, and filtered to the back, keeping the people in front of them. She'd always done that. She'd never dated anyone else who did.

"I'm flying nonstop from now on. They should leave more time between flights," he said. "Insanity."

He would hate the illogic.

He slipped his arm around her waist. She finally settled. This would be fine. Now she just had to figure how to explain the injury and the damn letters in a way that wouldn't mess with their reunion.

The doors opened, and they piled out of the elevator. She led him through the parking garage to his Mercedes. He glanced around, still in guard mode. She set down the duffel, opened the trunk with the key, and tossed the duffel inside, congratulating herself on doing it with one hand.

"Are you testing your strength?" he asked, practically on top of her.

"What?" Startled, she slammed the trunk shut.

He set his hand over hers and covered her fingers. "You're being careful to keep the right hand hidden. What's wrong?"

Now she was in for the interrogation.

———

Her delay in answering signaled to Grayson that she didn't wish to talk about it. Finally, she shrugged. Nothing good, he thought, came from her shrugs.

"It's nothing serious, and the story can wait until later."

Grayson tucked her hair behind her ears, leaned over, and kissed her. Her lips were cold, her mouth warm and inviting, and he felt hotter than if he'd been in front of a bonfire. She grabbed the lapel of his coat as the kiss ended.

"This is new," she said.

"Kissing you?" He frowned. Sometimes dealing with Patricia was like holding a lit firecracker in his hands. There was no telling when it would go off. And wasn't that also part of the attraction?

"I mean the public displays of affection," she said.

"I missed you. Is that a complaint?"

She ran her hand under the lapel of his coat. These layers between them needed to go.

"Nope. Not even a little," he said.

"Good." Her eyes were bloodshot, and black circles had started to form under them, visible despite the make-up.

What had happened over Thanksgiving break? He should press her on that, but it had been more fun to kiss her. "Now tell me what's wrong with your hand."

She sighed, being overly dramatic, and displayed a heavily bandaged index finger. "I sliced my finger. There's a story with it, but nothing urgent."

He looked over the finger, fighting a surge of unnecessary panic. Patricia had been getting into scrapes long before they met. But the reluctance in which she presented the injury and the worry in her face declared it was more than a simple accident.

"I want to hear the whole story," he said.

"Yeah, I figured. Let's get home first. I have dinner ready. And you must be tired and hungry too."

She'd neatly sidestepped his request. "I'll drive."

"No! I drove here no problem. I'm good."

Argument now or later? He chose later. "All right." He opened the driver's side door for her.

She slid in and waved at the back. "Chauffeurs up front, clients in the back."

He took the front passenger seat anyway, not sure if he was being contrary, but he wanted to be close to her. "We don't have to be that specific in the role play."

"Okay, though maybe at some point, we'll talk about role play where we do get specific."

He felt heat rising in his face. That was no tease, that was a real invitation. Part of what made Patricia Connell so intriguing.

She backed his Mercedes out of the parking space, handling it with ease. "So how did the big Thanksgiving family get-together go?" she asked as they headed to the exit.

Now she wanted to distract him from any questions. He played along. "It was perfect weather for sailing, the company was mostly good, and I was thrilled to eat Gulf seafood again."

"The company was only 'mostly' good? Was Amanda a problem?"

She missed nothing.

"It's complicated." He adjusted his shirt sleeves that had ridden up under his coat. Every year, his family and two other families who'd been close in the service spent Thanksgiving break together. "Amanda and I got on decently, for once. Having solved the problem at the museum helped. No, the issue was Eleanor."

Patricia winced. "Ouch. I bet the poor kid saw her parents being nice to each other and got her hopes up about them getting back together."

"I wish I'd seen it that quickly." How had she guessed that when he hadn't? "Maybe you should have come. That would have put the idea to bed."

"And then she'd hate me forever. No thanks," she said.

"She wouldn't. She's a reasonable person."

Patricia snorted. "She's a teenage girl who loves her mom and dad. I'll be lucky to get silent indifference from her."

He set a hand on her leg. "She'll come around."

"Yeah." Patricia increased speed and changed lanes, cursing at the driver who'd wanted to block her. He smiled.

"Enough about me. What did you do at Thanksgiving? Were you working the whole time?"

She adjusted the car's heat before answering. "Research, mostly. For Thanksgiving, I stayed up the night before to see the Macy's Parade assembled in the Park and then served dinner at the shelter."

She hated admitting kindness. Strange, as she was one of the kindest people he'd ever met, though she'd laugh at that thought. "Nothing festive?"

"Well, I planned a serious bender Friday night, but I wasn't feeling the vibes at the punk club where I usually hang. It's gotten too nihilistic," she said. "Not the same scene anymore. Or I'm not the same. God, I'm getting old, maybe."

"I'm not sure if you're pulling my leg or not," he said.

"One hundred percent true. I had some head-banging to do, and this was frustrating." She laughed. "You asked." But she frowned as the traffic came to a dead stop. "Holidays. Gah."

He'd been exhausted when he stepped off the plane. Now he was wide awake and fully alive. That's what she did for him.

"Next year, you're coming with me."

"Don't threaten me, Grayson."

"You also might try using my first name."

"No way. Every time I hear 'Edmund' sound in my head, it's your ex saying it in that upper-crusty, snobby way of hers. I'll stick with Grayson or Teddy."

No way to argue with that.

She smiled at the Manhattan skyline as they wound down to the Lincoln Tunnel entrance. The Twin Towers loomed over the Hudson River just before they entered the maw of the tunnel. Patricia's quiet breathing was the only noise inside the car.

They passed the line separating New Jersey from New York, but the traffic slowed to a crawl, giving him far too much time to stew. His friends all told him they would never last, the dignified security expert and the rebellious crime reporter. They had an age difference too, of over a decade. His male friends urged him to enjoy the hell out of it while it lasted. His female friends, like Dorothy, silently tolerated his "whim."

He was determined to make it last. He *knew* her. And she knew him the same way.

She spotted an opening as they left the tunnel and jumped two lanes at once. Horns blared.

"Being with you is never boring," he said.

"Hah." She cut off two taxis and slammed the brakes as a pedestrian jaywalked right in front of them. The jaywalker trotted away without acknowledging the close call.

"Did you ever drive a taxi?" he asked.

"Not officially," she said.

"Ah."

She turned left at Central Park, pulled into his street on the Upper East Side, and descended into the private parking spaces underneath. The attendant waved her past with a nod. She parked between another Mercedes and a Ferrari.

Staying in character, she settled the chauffeur cap on her head and opened the door for him. He stepped out, watching her. She approached him, wary of an interrogation about the injury no doubt.

Handle with care to prevent explosion.

"Patricia." He reached up and stroked her cheek with his fingers.

She leaned into his touch-soft, feather-light caresses against her skin.

"Save that for inside."

"You bet."

CHAPTER THREE

TRISHA TOOK the lead to the garage's elevators, annoyingly nervous again about showing Grayson the damn tree. He reached for her hand inside the elevator. The touch steadied her. Lust, she could handle.

Once they reached the lobby, they went around the corner for the building's residence elevators. Kevin, the building's uniformed doorman, waved and smiled at her. She'd never have gotten the tree into the elevator if not for him.

"Thanks for the help," she called.

Kevin straightened his shoulders, making the creases in his colorful doorman's uniform disappear. "Anytime."

"What did Kevin help you with?" Grayson asked.

"Mmm…that's a surprise."

When they reached the elevator doors, she stabbed at the button with the thumb of her injured hand. At least the throbbing had died down.

"How many stitches?" Grayson asked.

"Six," she said. "Little ones."

"*Six?*"

"It's fine."

The elevator doors opened, and he took her hand again as they went inside. The gold-plated walls acted as mirrors, and she turned into him to keep him from noticing her nerves.

"I hope you didn't injure yourself as part of the surprise."

"Nope, and why are we talking about that when we're finally alone?"

She set her right hand, palm flat, against his chest and pushed him against the elevator wall. He swallowed, catching her gaze, intense.

She wrapped the bandaged hand around his neck, slid her other hand under his coat, rose to her tiptoes, and kissed him. He caught her mood, and the kiss turned hard and fierce.

This was so much better than worrying.

"I missed you," she said.

"You hide it so well."

She laughed as the doors opened, and they stumbled out of the elevator together. They went through the door of his home entwined.

Yes, sex now, talk later.

He slammed the wooden door shut behind him with his foot, and she heard the satisfying click of the lock. He dropped his duffel and let his winter coat slide off in the entranceway. Her fingers fumbled with his shirt buttons. Damn clumsy bandages.

He picked her up and took two steps toward the bedroom.

Whoa. She forgot sometimes how strong he was. And the bedroom, great, they'd avoid the tree and…

No. Get it done with.

"Wait." She put her fingers over his lips. "The other way. The living room. Where the surprise is."

"You intrigue me."

"Hell, I hope so."

His erection pressed against her butt as he carried her to the living room. Oh, yes, he was glad to see her. But the tree?

He stopped abruptly as the tree, sparkling with a string of Christmas lights, came into view.

He gaped. His mouth literally fell open.

"You did this? For me?"

The surprise pitched his voice higher than usual. Okay, so he was surprised but…pleased too?

"Don't sound so shocked." She slid out of his grasp.

He blinked, as if the tree might vanish between one second and the next.

"Dammit, Grayson, say something, even if you hate it!"

He finally focused on her.

"I love it."

"You do?" Her voice cracked.

"I do." He pulled her close. "It's perfect."

"Oh." A deep sigh escaped her. "Good."

He liked it!

He smiled. "Let me show you how much this means to me."

He knelt, pulling her down to the floor with him, the heat from touching near-burning her.

She fumbled with his belt buckle, he went after the buttons of her blouse, and then actions were more than enough to reveal how they felt.

———

"Welcome home, lover." Trisha kissed his cheek.

Grayson met her eyes. "That is the finest welcome I've ever received."

"Yeah, it didn't suck for me either."

He rolled off her to the side. Separated, her skin chilled. He stroked her breasts. She closed her eyes and made happy noises at the back of her throat. His fingertips trailed lower, to where the razor blade scars decorated her stomach. She fought a flinch. Not that he'd ever been turned off by them.

But the scars represented her past, one she doubted he'd ever accept: the killings, the time in juvie. Grayson kept dancing up to asking her the full story but had never quite had taken the leap, as if he was also worried about what the truth would do to them.

Better to live in the present, which was how she'd ended up gloriously fucked on a carpet in front of a Christmas tree.

His stomach rumbled.

She laughed. "I better get dinner."

"I won't say 'no.' What's on the menu?"

"Beef tenderloins and sweet potato strings. I have to sauté the beef, pop the strings in the oven, add dressing to the salad, and we're set."

"Sounds perfect."

She rose on her elbows and kissed the red mark on his shoulder from her teeth. Damn. "Sorry. I got a little carried away."

He traced a fingertip down the line of her jaw. "I enjoy it when you lose control."

During sex, yes.

She stood. He stared at her. "What?" She snapped.

"You look so beautiful."

She flushed and enclosed the Celtic-style cross she always wore that hung between her breasts. "I'll get dinner."

He laughed, softly, knowing he'd disconcerted her. "Let me drop my bag in the bedroom and I'll help you."

"Sure." She gathered up her clothes, followed him into the bedroom, and slipped on one of his robes while he changed into jeans, a short-sleeved button-down shirt, and tassel loafers. That was as informal as he ever got. Well, except for sailing, she supposed. She wondered what he'd look like in a Hawaiian shirt.

They cooked together. He opened the wine, too, and cooking became cooking and drinking together, with a few kisses thrown in for good measure. Once or twice, he patted something in his pocket. Had he brought her a surprise gift?

Maybe a seashell? That would be nice. She wondered what was next after this. No, live in the present. The past was fucked up and the future, well, you could never count on it.

CHAPTER FOUR

GRAYSON SIPPED the sauce from his wooden spoon. Perfect. The teriyaki flavor held the right amount of sweet, enough not to be cloying. Patricia claimed not to be a cook, but she'd done remarkably well with this dinner.

But more important was the effort to make tonight special.

While she set the table in the dining room, he shoved his hand in his pocket, rubbing his thumb nervously on the corner of the ring box. The purchase had been irresistible, given the design of the ring matched the Celtic cross she always wore.

Not a traditional engagement ring. Logic said that he should wait to ask *that* question. Logic, however, had very little to do with his relationship with Patricia.

He walked to the dining room to refill their wine glasses. She stood in the entranceway between the living and dining room, staring at the tree. The reflections from the tree lights danced through her hair, turning it into a virtual blaze.

If he had the skill, he would have painted her, to preserve this moment forever.

Wordlessly, she held out her empty glass. He refilled it.

"You picked a nice red."

"Just bought what Kevin recommended. I asked him after he helped me get the tree in the stand." She sipped and smiled at him. "You spoil me, Teddy."

"All evidence is that you're spoiling me, certainly tonight." His mind flashed to her scars and the new cut on her hand. "Besides, you're overdue for pampering."

"Maybe."

She lit the tall white candles on the dining room table while he served the food. They sat down and clicked classes in a toast.

"To surprises and fresh starts," he said.

"To excellent sex," she said.

They talked. Little things, like how he'd learned to sail as a child, and more about boats. She seemed to pay attention, though he wondered if he bored her. She mentioned the new leads in her freelance career and how she was waiting for an answer from the *New York Times Magazine* on her pitch about a long-form article on the juvenile justice system.

"Your article would be excellent," he said. "When do you expect to hear?"

"Who knows? They do these things on their own timetable. Probably best not to think too much about it right now."

They spoke of mutual friends, too, most of whom seemed settled in their lives. David came up. David worked for him at Gray Associates, his security firm. But David was also one of Patricia's close friends, which was part of how Grayson had met her.

"Yeah, even David isn't convinced we'll last," she finally admitted.

A challenge? "I'm David's boss. He only sees that side of me. Not the personal side."

She raised an eyebrow, perhaps conceding the point, and finished her plate. He waited until she'd eaten the last sweet potato string, waited until she'd drunk at least two more glasses of the wine, and waited until her shoulders finally relaxed.

"Patricia, let's talk about the hand injury."

"You've been more patient than I thought you would about that." She leaned back and drank the last of the wine in her glass. "So, here's the deal."

He listened while she detailed the threatening letters. His hands curled tight around the stem of his wineglass as the situation became clearer.

"So, a letter I got yesterday was booby-trapped with a razor blade," she continued.

"*What?*" He slapped the table.

"I'm *fine*. And that reaction is why I didn't tell you right away. I didn't want our reunion ruined." She tucked the hand to her chest. "Anyway, when I pried the letter open with my finger"—she made a cutting motion with her good hand over her finger—"slice-o-rama."

"Bloody hell."

"It's never good when your English accent comes out," she said.

He'd picked up the accent from his late mother, a war bride. And, yes, it came out when he was upset. He reached for her hand. She curled his fingers around his and told him about the ER visit and Dorothy and Newman's appearance.

"I gave them all the letters, including the one with the blade, but tracing them won't be easy. Fingerprints are useless if they went through the mail. Plus, if I were this guy, I'd have dropped the letters in a mailbox on the street and not gone into a post office where someone might see me." She shook her head and pulled her hand back. "Tell you what, if I get any more, I'm not opening them."

"For certain." The involvement of Dorothy and her partner indicated this was more serious than booby-trapped letters. "Why would major crimes detectives immediately respond to your call to a local precinct? How did they find out so fast?"

"My questions exactly. I asked her."

"And she said…?"

"She implied it involved a similar letter, but it would be a longshot if they're related to the crime she's investigating." Patricia tapped the table with fingertips, exposing her nerves. "Newman was downright snippy the whole time, but that's Newman for you. They evaded my questions, pure and simple."

"Yes." He rubbed his brow, hoping to make sense of this. Dorothy looked out for Patricia, more than she knew, but Patricia hadn't called her in on this case. Dorothy simply being thorough? But Newman's presence indicated something more substantial.

Patricia herself was more concerned than she admitted.

"You kept the earlier letters. You knew them by heart," he said.

"That's what I just said. Weren't you listening?"

"Don't take that tone. You know what I meant. You received those letters before I left. You never mentioned them to me. Why not?"

"I didn't think they were important."

"Wrong. You saved them. Something disturbed you about them. You should have told me."

"And watch you get all protective and worried? I *handled* it!"

He pointed at her finger. "All evidence to the contrary."

"Okay, okay. They bugged me, all right?"

His breath whistled through his teeth. "And you're lousy at asking for help."

"And I'm lousy at asking for help." She repeated with a grimace. "Guess I'll have to carry my switchblade with me at all times now."

He grunted instead of shouting that a knife would not work against a gun. He flattened his hand against the polished wood of the table.

"Stop glaring. I'm telling you now," Patricia said. "What's your professional assessment of all this?"

"This is someone who started with verses, and now they've resorted to a small violence against you. You're in danger. Maybe imminent danger."

"I'm already on that page. Hope he moves in on me fast, so we can get this over with."

"You need protection," he snapped. "You need a full-time bodyguard. And you need to move in with me until we catch this person."

"See, that kind of reaction is why I kept it to myself until now." Her neck stiffened, and her chin jutted out. "I'm not going to let whoever this is change my life."

"It's not a game."

"Damn right, it's not. It's my life, and I'll run it the way I want and fuck the stalker."

"I see," he drawled because yelling would serve nothing.

"Do you?" She stood up, walked into the living room, and stopped in front of the tree.

He followed. "You said give my professional assessment. That was it."

"I hardly think you ask all your clients to move in with you."

He blushed. "No, not *with* me. But I have safe houses for them. You can have one, if you'd rather."

She fiddled with the sash of the robe. "If Dorothy thought I should have protection, she'd have said so."

"I'm certain she told you to ask for my help. And have you considered how much *I'll* worry about you in the meantime?"

She pointed to him, then to herself. "Jesus, Grayson, if this was you, you wouldn't change things in your life either. You'd go after him. Or stay in the open so he'd come for you."

The only way Patricia dealt with fear was to tackle it head on. Maybe even pick a fight to cover that fear. Years ago, he'd have escalated this disagreement. Years ago, his insistence on being right had resulted in a divorce.

He rubbed the back of his neck and then stuffed his hands into his pockets, curling his fingers around the ring box. "I'd take appropriate precautions in your situation. But I recognize we might not agree on what's appropriate."

She closed her eyes, almost as if it hurt to look at him. "Okay. Understood." She whispered the last word. "Look, I did the right things so far. I reported it. One of the best cops working in the city is on it. I'll consider your appropriate precautions."

He stroked her face with his fingertips. "You don't have to do everything alone."

"Yes, I do!" She waved at the tree, animated now. "No, I suppose I don't." A deep sigh. "I make no sense."

"I read it as 'I've managed fine until now and don't push me.'"

She laughed, another mood shift, and the tension in his shoulders loosened. "You push me all the time, Teddy."

He frowned. "I don't understand."

"The tree, the dinner, the whole damned thing."

"I…had nothing to do with those things."

"You had everything to do with *everything*." She put a hand over her heart. "Know what scares me the most?"

"Snakes?" he ventured.

She touched his chest, right over his heart. "See what you do? Relax me with a word. That's what scares me. I'm way into you, and that's never ended well for me."

Everyone she loved had died. Her foster father. Her first husband. "I'd also given up on having something like this. Until I met you."

Two people, different worlds, in a bright, shiny new relationship. His reaction: joy at a second chance. Her reaction: terror. All right, he admitted, terror for him too. He'd had moments during the trip wondering whether she'd even be around when he returned.

He walked to the fireplace mantle and put a hand up to it to brace himself. "You've been entirely unexpected."

"I know I don't make this easy." She gestured again, accidentally opening the robe partway and revealing her breasts.

Focus.

"Do you doubt me?" she asked. "I'm sure someone told you I'm toying with you. I'm not."

"I don't doubt you in the least." But he suspected she doubted herself.

He stuffed his hand into his pocket again and fingered the ring box. He took a few steps to the tree and looked down at the boxes. The start of a new life? A chasm opened between past and future.

"You did this for me."

"For us." Patricia hugged him from behind, wrapping her arms around his chest, enclosing him. For the first time in days, he felt solid ground under his feet.

Some insane impulse made him slip the ring box out of his pocket. "I have something for you."

She froze, eyes wide.

His fingers trembled as he opened the box, revealing the ring, silver with etched Celtic cross designs and a center diamond bracketed on both sides by sapphires.

"Marry me, Patricia?" he blurted out.

CHAPTER FIVE

GRAYSON'S QUESTION was a punch of joy to Trisha's mid-section, doubling her over with love, hope, and happiness. Giddy, lightheaded, she could hardly see two feet in front of her.

But I can't—I'm not—I don't deserve this.

His question, the ring, similar in design to her cross, the intent way he regarded her, as if she was the most amazing thing in the world. The joy turned to acid in her stomach. She took a step backward, right into the edge of the couch. She stumbled and let herself slide to the floor instead of trying to regain her balance. Balance? That was shot, maybe for good.

He knelt in front of her. "That went better than I feared."

An invisible hand closed into a fist around her guts. "What did you fear?" she whispered.

"That you'd run out, screaming."

"I'm not much of a screamer, and it's too cold outside." Tears welled in her eyes, and her stomach twisted into a tight, constricted ball. "Teddy, we've known each other less than two months, we bicker, and our friends, not to mention your daughter, think this is some whim of mine or a mid-life crisis of yours."

"We've been together seven weeks, six days, and ten hours," he said.

She closed her eyes and smiled. *How can I give this up?* "Which would be my point. Why the rush?"

His mouth settled in a flat line. He blinked twice and narrowed his eyes. She'd never seen him this nervous before.

"Last time—" His voice trembled.

She hardly dared breathe, waiting for him to speak again. She twisted the sash of the robe around her fingers.

"The last time I had the chance to close the deal with a woman, I hesitated." He looked away at the tree.

"Knowing you, it was for a good reason. And even if it's true, you're overcompensating in the other direction, yes?"

He winced. "Perhaps." He cupped her face in his hand. "You haven't answered the question."

It hurt to breathe, as if her lungs were too big for her ribs. "Was that a question? Seemed like a command. Why aren't you pissed at me? You should be. You've got this beautiful ring and instead of answering, I argue with you. Where's that cold Grayson anger?"

Would he scream or something? She knew what to do with anger.

"I saw the look on your face before you remembered to be afraid." His thumb rubbed her cheekbone. "Pure joy."

She snatched his hand away from her cheek and entwined their fingers. She concentrated on taking long, deep breaths. "It's a helluva lot to think about."

"It's not a rational question," he said. "It's an emotional one."

"Says Mr. Logical."

He smiled and squeezed her hand. "I know when logic is useless."

Stop making me smile. Air returned to her lungs. She could breathe again. "Answer *my* question," she said. "Why would you want to marry me?"

"The usual reason." He pulled back his hand and straightened his shoulders. "I love you."

Fuck.

She closed her eyes and tilted her head back, wishing she could bury it inside the couch or, failing that, wishing she could fall through the floor, straight to Hell. She remembered the distorted bodies of her rapists after being riddled with bullets.

If she'd killed the men in self-defense, Grayson would understand it. One problem: she hadn't done it in self-defense. She'd killed them out of rage and hatred and some demon that she knew still lurked inside her. A demon that Teddy would probably deny existed. She couldn't stand to lose his respect.

He settled next to her. She let her head rest on his shoulder. She tasted bile at the back of her throat. How could he be so calm?

"I know the difference between love and infatuation," he said. "I'm not some young man whose head has been turned by a pretty face."

"I don't have a pretty face?" But the tease sounded weak even to her.

"You're beautiful," he said. "But it was too dark that day in the tunnels to see it. Not too dark for you to save my life, however."

"Do you fall in love with everyone who saves your life?"

"Since there's been only you, it appears so."

"Isn't there a word for that? Stockholm Syndrome or something?" She let her head sink deeper in his shoulder, his cotton T-shirt soft against her face.

"Stockholm Syndrome refers to the tendency of hostages to bond to their captors." He stroked her hair. "And it's not a good theory, anyway."

She shivered. "But am I the captive or the one with the gun?"

He took her hand and placed the ring in the middle of her palm. "You are definitely the one with the gun."

She closed her hand around the ring. The metal seemed hot, as if it might bore a hole in her palm. Damn him. He'd rushed this, jumped the gun, acted impulsive for once. And now her answer would either bond them or break them, and they both knew it.

What he didn't know is that she had to say "no." Marriages should be based on truth, and she'd kept part of herself a secret. She opened her hand and stared at the ring. It was perfect, damn him. Her palm was so sweaty that the ring almost slid to the floor.

"Teddy." Her stomach dissolved into one large quivering mass, doubling her over. "I lov—, I mean, I feel the same, what you said." Oh, that went well. Maybe they should wait to do this until she could say the damned word?

She wanted to explain why she had to turn him down. He had a right to know. But she couldn't.

She made eye contact with him, frozen in her indecision. He held her gaze for a long time, unblinking, trying to figure her out. Maybe when he did, he'd let her know.

He gathered her into his arms and pulled her into his lap. She went without protest and let her head settle against his chest. Her stomach quieted and her guts unclenched.

"Let's try this again." He kissed the top of her head. "Patricia, what do you want?"

This, this, this. "To be with you." He'd thrown his heart and soul at her feet. The least she could do was spit out some honesty.

He let out a deep breath and held her tighter. She put a hand on her scars. Teddy set his hand on top of hers. His thumb traced the line of the longest one, which went from between her breasts down all the way past her naval. She quivered, her nerves on fire.

"Is the past what's stopping you? Can I help with what haunts you?"

He thought the attack haunted her, not the aftermath. He saw her as a victim, not an aggressor. What would be the harm in letting him believe the lie? She *wanted* to be happy. She wanted him.

He leaned in to kiss her. With the first touch of his lips, she knew what she wanted and gained the courage to seize it, the past be damned. What did it matter?

Now mattered.

She kissed him back, falling, sinking into his warmth, wanting to keep falling forever. Her hand trembling, she pushed on his chin and broke the kiss. She licked her lips, tasting his breath with her tongue. They both looked down at the ring in her hand.

"We can put off the date for a long time, right? Until I'm used to it?" And maybe be calm enough to say out loud that she loved him because that would be good.

He nuzzled her neck. "How long is a long time?"

"Pushy, pushy," she said. "Months. In double digits. At the very least."

"Reasonable."

His hand shook as he slipped the ring onto her finger. The silver, warm from her body heat, felt impossibly heavy.

"By the way, I would have accepted any time frame less than 'when hell freezes over,'" he said.

She punched him in the shoulder. "Nice bluff."

"Just desperation."

He wrapped his arms around her. She stared, stunned, at the bare Christmas tree. When she'd learned to drive a motorcycle, the first leap had been equal parts exhilaration and panic. But his marriage proposal? Exponentially more of both emotions.

He stood and helped her up, help she needed because her legs were rubber. "Shall we decorate the tree?"

"Sure." She grabbed a plastic shopping bag with a department store logo.

He grimaced. "Not icicles."

She smiled. "Why not? Icicles are the best part. All pretty and shiny."

He frowned. "Messy."

"Festive and lovely." She ripped the plastic covering off the thin rectangular box, gathered some icicles in her hand, and displayed them to him. "See? All sparkly."

He stood in front of the tree and raised his arms to ward them off. "Poor tree."

"Then I'll have to"—she drew back her arm to throw—"decorate something else." The silver strands landed all over his hair and shoulders before he could dodge. He grabbed for her but she danced out of the way, laughing, and the joy from accepting his ring soared into her, giving the laughter a manic edge.

Changing tactics, he gathered the icicles from his shoulders and tossed them back at her. She ducked and he snatched her around the waist and wrestled her to the floor. They landed with a soft thud on the carpet. Still laughing, she took the remaining icicles out of the box and dumped them over his head. He spit a strand out of his mouth.

"Maybe you're right about the tree. The icicles look better on you anyway. They match your hair."

He pretended to glower, but a smile escaped. Damn, she loved to see him relax. Her mouth went dry. Loved him. Yes.

"You wanted to know why, love?" he said, looking at the ring on her finger. "This is why."

"Hey, serious time is over. This is playtime."

"That's exactly what I mean." He jerked at the sash of her robe, opening it. "I think," he said as he shook his head, and the icicles fell down over her breasts, tickling her, "these look better on you."

"I'm less prickly than the tree too."

"Are you sure?" He lowered his head to nuzzle her neck with his lips. "Let me check."

CHAPTER SIX

WHEN THEY FINALLY WENT TO bed, the ring's unfamiliar weight on Trisha's finger kept her awake long after Grayson succumbed to slumber. But he woke up early the next morning, in more ways than one, jump-starting her day sooner than she ever would have alone. After, they took turns staring at the ring when each thought the other wasn't looking.

"I'll call Dorothy first thing this morning to find out what's really going on," he said.

"Better you than me that gets their head bit off."

"She likes me better than you."

Trisha laughed. "True enough. But she might not tell you anything either."

He grasped her hand. "How's the finger feel today?"

She shrugged. "I'd forgotten it. I guess sex, rings, and Christmas trees are a helluva distraction. Should be okay for a regular Band-Aid now."

Already fully dressed, he sat next to her on the bed. "I love you."

She took a deep breath, staring at the ring, rather than him. "Give me some time to get used to this, okay?"

"Okay."

She wondered at what he hadn't said. Like, "Why won't you say you love me?" Or, being more practical, as he was, why didn't he ask about a possible link between the razor blade in the letter and her razor blade scars?

He'd likely dance away from both for a while, giving her space. One of the reasons she adored him. He had *patience.* Besides, chances were nearly nil they were connected. The people who'd attacked her were dead, after all. She'd killed them.

"You'll check in the minute you get home, as promised?"

"I will."

"If you don't, I'll be on your doorstep."

"Got it." Hell, calling him was easy enough and a reasonable request, especially since, being who he was, he'd worry about the worst-case scenario.

He frowned. "I still wish you'd move in with me until we catch this person."

She fiddled with his tie. "We may never catch this person or, even if we do, it could be a while. I'm not going to make major decisions in my life, like moving in with my guy, based on being afraid of an asshole."

She braced for more pushback.

He fingered the cufflinks of his dress shirt. "So, you are thinking about moving in with me."

"I could get used to your bathroom, for sure. And your cooking." She licked her lips. "Everything tastes good here." Including him.

But he refused to be pushed away from his point. "If the situation worsens, will you reconsider moving in on a temporary basis?"

"Yes, Teddy, if a new Son of Sam is after me, we'll have to figure something out, okay?"

"Good enough." He kissed her goodbye and left, leaving her alone in a bedroom that was only just smaller than her whole apartment. And that was without that awesome bathroom.

Weird that last night, when she'd said yes, she hadn't considered that she'd eventually move out of her apartment and leave that part of her life. Because, no way Grayson would move into her place in Hell's Kitchen. And she didn't want him there. That apartment was hers and Nicky's. And now she'd be leaving the place she and Nicky had built behind. Leaving him behind.

Sobered, she showered, dressed, and headed out, waving to the day doorman, and she left. She stopped at the Upper East Side street corner. Not her scene, not her neighborhood. But it fit Grayson.

Him, she could handle. But everything that came with him? She curled her hand into a fist, staring at the ring once more.

Annoyed with everything, including herself, she cut across Central Park for a walk. She'd come out on the West Side near the upper borders of Hell's Kitchen. Eventually.

The cold bit at her, despite the warm jacket.

Even though it was only just morning, the park already bustled with life. Joggers getting in a morning workout, street vendors with food that sent vents of steam into the sky, dog walkers, and the homeless, huddled into whatever shelter they could find.

She bought a bag of pretzels from a cart, took it over to a guy re-arranging his cardboard box, left it on the grass a few feet from him, and jogged away so he wouldn't be afraid or have to thank her. When she'd been homeless, she'd hated having to take charity.

Finally, as her feet touched 10th Avenue, she relaxed. Gentrification might be happening but the old neighborhood hung on, not ready to let go. The dingy, squat apartment buildings still stood, for the most part, and Hell's Kitchen's Irish bars remained open, stubborn and not ready to leave without a fight. Outsiders liked to call the Kitchen "Clinton" now. Outsiders could fuck themselves.

She finally halted at the nondescript, five-story apartment building that was her home. Despite the cold, the street window of the first-floor apartment was open. She caught the smell of onions and sausages.

She cupped her hands. "Kitchen fan not working again, Mrs. D.?"

A weathered face surrounded by tufts of gray hair and lined with character appeared in the window. Anne-Marie Donohue—aka Mrs. D. to the neighborhood—never changed. "Ya got that right, Red. Landlord's still being an ass about fixing things."

"The landlord wants to sell out, make a bundle, and damn the rest of us," Trisha said.

"Right again." Mrs. D. narrowed her eyes. "Been out all night as usual?"

"Yep," Trisha agreed.

A gleam shone in Mrs. D.'s eyes. "I remember those days."

"I bet you do." The old lady had probably been a hell-raiser. "Let me take a look at your fan. I had to fix my own last month."

"Sure. Come around."

Trisha bounded up the steps, Mrs. D. buzzed her in, saving the need for the key, and Trisha slipped inside the old lady's apartment.

As always, Trisha noted the shrine built for the Kennedy brothers, John, and Bobby. The Great Catholic hopes. The framed photos of them book-ended an ornate ceramic cross, while below sat a set of rosary beads and funeral cards surrounding a third photo: a young, smiling man dressed in an Army uniform. Mrs. D.'s son had been killed in the early days of Vietnam.

"I notice you don't have Reagan up there." Trisha jerked her head at the shrine as she slipped into the narrow kitchen.

Mrs. D. poured her sausage and onions onto a plate and waved at the smoke. "Reagan's not Catholic. And he's not dead yet."

"Can't argue with that." And he'd just gotten another term too. The asshole.

Trisha uncovered the fan above the stove, hoping the motor hadn't burned out. Luck was with her because loose wires had created a short. "Pliers?"

Mrs. D. dug around in the junk drawer in the kitchen. Nosy, as always, Trisha looked over the newspaper clippings on the refrigerator. One featured cheerleaders and a high school football team from 1954. Twenty-six years ago. Those kids could be grandparents now.

Below it was news of a fatal fire in 1956.

"These don't exactly go together," Trisha said.

"Oh, I was reminded of it when I pulled the cheerleader article out. The woman who died in the fire, she was a cousin of one of the cheerleaders my daughter knew." She shook her head. "That poor family. Only one body and the rest were unrecognizable ashes. They never found out who did it. Maybe something you could dig into, eh? Seems to me no one did much at the time."

"Not a bad idea," Trisha said, thinking that cold crimes were the worst. But maybe if it was tied to the checkered history of Hell's Kitchen, there might be possibilities for a long-form piece.

"Somebody should find out what happened to that poor family.

Anyway, here you go." Mrs. D. slapped rubber-handed pliers in Trisha's hand.

"Thanks." Trisha pointed with the pliers at another clipping, this time of a sports team. "Haven't seen that before."

"I was looking in my hope chest." She smiled. "It's my son, in high school. Good days." But her smile vanished and she frowned. "I didn't realize…."

"Didn't realize what?" The old woman was staring at her so oddly.

Mrs. D. shook her head. "Sorry, wool gathering."

"We all need a reminder of good days." Trisha crooked her head to see the wires better. She twisted them together to re-connect the wires while wondering what kind of grief the woman carried around inside. Everyone was dealing with something. Mrs. D. coped by stuffing newspaper articles inside what seemed a bottomless hope chest. There were worst methods.

"That should do it," Trisha said after a few twists with the pliers. "Here goes nothing." She punched the power on.

No sparks. The fan whirred. The smoke cleared.

"Well. That worked better than what I tried."

"You smack the thing again, Mrs. D.?"

"Might have." Mrs. D. shrugged as she sat down at the small dining table. Half was empty. The other half was full of papers, coupons, and pieces of mail.

"Thank you for fixing it. My grandson's coming over tomorrow." She pointed at the fan. "My girl's oldest. He'll get me a whole new fan. He knows a guy. At least now I can close the window."

Trisha shut and locked the window, saving the older woman the trouble. "You're welcome. Maybe you can do me a favor too?"

Mrs. D. raised an impressively bushy eyebrow. "What?"

The implied question: what are you getting me into?

Trisha explained the letters and displayed her injured finger. As she spoke, Mrs. D.'s posture straightened, and her gaze became sharper.

"You think someone might come after you in *our* building?"

"Maybe. But I figure he's a coward, so if he comes around, he won't confront me, not right away. If you could keep an eye for anyone who doesn't belong?"

A firm nod. "I'll let the ladies at the market and the hair salon know too. And my kids, their kids, and anyone they know."

"Thanks!" Meaning, half the neighborhood, given how connected Mrs. D. was to the Kitchen.

"Still, it could be someone from the neighborhood. You can never tell with *some* of the people here. Bad people come and go, like good people." She stared at Trisha with that odd expression again. "But the Kitchen survives. I'll watch out for you."

"Thanks," Trisha said. "It's appreciated."

Mrs. D. pointed her fork at Trisha's hand. "Beautiful ring. You have news to share, Trisha?"

"It is pretty." Oh. She'd forgotten people would notice the engagement ring. "And, yeah, it's, um, a thing."

"Let me look at the sapphire." Mrs. D. lifted Trisha's hand to peer at the setting. "Very good. And about time. You've spun your wheels for too long." She waved. "Now go rest. And eat something before you fade away."

Not much to say to that, so Trisha followed orders, musing as she closed the door that she should check in on the old woman more often. Hell's Kitchen did take care of its own.

But sometimes, it also ate them too.

CHAPTER SEVEN

TRISHA TOOK the creaky wooden stairs up to her fourth-floor apartment. As always, she reached up and fingered the tape she'd left at the top of the door.

Broken in half. Someone besides her had opened this door in the last two days. An intruder? How dare someone fucking break into her home.

Trisha pulled her switchblade out of the pocket of her jeans and flicked it open. She unlocked the door and pushed it open.

Someone tackled her, strong arms enclosing her waist and slamming her to the floor. Trisha stabbed at the intruder but missed, coming up with nothing but empty air.

The intruder grunted and rolled off her. She slashed at his leg as he regained his footing, ripping his jeans and drawing blood.

"Jesus Christ," he exclaimed and danced away. He snagged a book from her shelves and tossed it at her. She ducked, which gave him time to pull a gun.

She scrambled to her feet, knife out, breathing heavy, focused on staying alive. He wore a ski mask and stood about six feet tall with broad shoulders. Powerful guy. White skin peaked out between his jacket sleeve and his gloves.

He held up his free hand. "Take it easy."

"Fuck you." She held her ground. She could attack, but he had height and weight on her, not to mention the gun. The best bet might be for her to fling the knife at him and bullrush him while he was distracted. But that would mean giving up her only weapon.

He stared. She stared.

"I don't want to hurt you," he said.

"Bullshit. You broke into my home, tackled me, and pulled a gun on me." A little snub-nosed .22 caliber. But it'd do damage, all the same.

"You slashed me!" He inched toward the door. "I'm leaving. If you follow me, I'll stop on the first floor and shoot that old lady you seem to like."

"Fucker," she snapped.

"Probably." He kept the .22 aimed at her as he reached for the door-knob. "Nice cross, by the way. Good design. Maybe you'll pray for me?"

"Not a chance in hell."

"I'm probably beyond prayer anyway."

He opened the door, backed out, and slammed it shut behind him. She rushed to follow, pulled the door open, and caught the sound of footfalls running down the steps. She froze. Dammit, he was armed, and he'd broken into her home. He might be serious about shooting Mrs. D.

It would be idiotic to run after an armed intruder armed only with a knife.

She slumped over, hands on her knees, drawing deep breaths, hoping to banish the panic overwhelming her. Focus on the details, she thought. The .22 would have only a limited number of shots. Plus, he'd have to break into Mrs. D.'s place before getting to her. The woman had like five zillion locks on her front door. Not likely.

Why hadn't this guy shot her? He'd had a clear shot. And why had he commented on her cross?

Trisha tightened her fingers around the switchblade. A few drops of his blood lingered on the steel. Fucker. He'd left something she could trace, at least. Move, she thought. Call it in. No, check on Mrs. D. first, then call Dorothy.

Then she'd have to call Grayson and explain. He'd want her to move in with him. He might be right.

———

Trisha trudged back up the four flights of the building. Mrs. D. had noticed the masked man running down the front steps, but he hadn't stopped to harass her.

Trisha cursed. She could have followed him. Should have. Her foul mood worsened when she made the call to Dorothy's precinct and had to leave a message. "Lieutenant's out on a case," said the desk sergeant. Trisha left a terse message and slammed the receiver back into its base on the wall.

Grayson next. Damn, she did not want to hear, "I told you so." She fingered the switchblade and looked around her apartment. Nothing seemed disturbed save for a few newspapers on the coffee table. She should check her lockbox, hidden behind the Shakespeare volumes.

Then she thought of that story with Sherlock Holmes. "A Scandal in Bohemia." Where a break-in was meant to force someone to check their most precious possessions. Gah, she was paranoid. No one was watching her right now. At least, she hoped not.

A knock sounded at the door. She flinched and slipped out of sight behind her kitchen counter.

"Trish! You in there?" David called.

David. She slumped against the cabinets. Thank God.

She practically flung the door open for him. "Hey."

"Hey!" He grinned. "You didn't show at the Y. I tried to call. You didn't answer. Figured I'd check on you."

"Shit. I forgot." They had a standing date to work out together at the Y on Monday mornings. Even before the break-in, it'd slipped her mind with Grayson's proposal preoccupying her.

He glanced at the knife still in her hand. She set it on the coffee table and smoothed down her hair. Dammit, she'd jumped at shadows.

"Trish, what's wrong? Are you hurt? There's blood on the floor!"

"Not my blood. I'm glad you're here." She hugged him. She needed it. Every time Grayson hugged her, fear lurked at the corners, fear that she'd lose him. But not with David Valesquez. With him, she had no fear, only the steady ground of a long friendship.

"Yeah, I can see you're glad." He frowned as he looked her over. "What's wrong?"

"What's right is that you're here."

She looked David over. Tight-fitting jeans, Chuck Taylors, a Living Colour T-shirt under his jean jacket. A super great guy who'd been through some hard times connected to being forced out of the NYPD. But he'd recently reconnected with his high school sweetheart. Their wedding was in a few months.

"Humor me and tell me how your Thanksgiving went. I need to hear something happy."

"Okay." David, used to her shifting moods, shrugged and flopped on her couch. "Darlene was great, though we had to keep ducking conversations about how soon we'd be having kids after the wedding."

"You'll be a great dad." Trisha sat in her comfy chair and put her feet up on the table. "And I say that seriously."

"Yep," he agreed. "But Darlene's going to get her Masters first. Semester starts right after the wedding."

"Smart." She glanced at the ring on her finger.

David's eyes widened as he followed her gaze. "Well. I guess you had a helluva break too. Congratulations. I assume my boss?"

"Yeah, Grayson. We didn't set a date though."

David shook his head. "You don't seem thrilled. Is that what's wrong?"

"No. The ring, I mean, the thing with Grayson is, um, fine." She closed her eyes. "It's been a morning, though."

She explained the intruder, the fight, his weird comments, and her decision not to follow.

"Good decision not to follow," David said.

"I wish I had. Maybe then I'd have answers."

"Or a bullet in you."

Trisha shrugged. "Anyway, I called Dorothy Gilbert because it could be related to this whole other thing."

Then she had to explain the letters. Again. She stared at her boots the whole time, not wanting to meet David's eyes.

He leaned forward, his hands on his knees. "Damn, Trish! Why didn't you stay with Grayson? Why come back here?"

"Because it's my home!" She scowled and paced away. "And it was only letters."

"The last one resulted in six stitches." He pointed at her finger.

"Because I was stupid."

"Because there's an asshole we need to catch." David fiddled with the class ring that he always wore on his right hand. "Right, right. Sorry. I'm a little freaked. I wish I'd been here a half-hour sooner. No wonder you needed a hug."

She pointed to her knife and the blood drops near the door. "At least I got a little of him. But I can't figure out if he took anything."

Another knock sounded. They both flinched. Trisha playfully punched his shoulder. "Glad it's not only me doing it." She walked toward the door. "Who's there?"

"NYPD. Lt. Gilbert sent me," came the answer.

David cut in front of Trisha and checked the peephole. "Hold up your badge," he ordered.

"That seems overkill," Trisha said.

"Not under the circumstances. Gold badge. She doesn't look dangerous."

"Then let her in," Trisha said.

CHAPTER EIGHT

GRAYSON SETTLED into his chair at the Midtown offices of Gray Associates, facing a long list of items on his to-do list because of the holiday weekend.

He pushed worry for Trisha away. She was better suited to protecting herself than anyone he'd met. He would find this stalker. They would get married. Life would be good.

In the meantime, he needed to clear his calendar to be there for her. He sorted the checklist by priority, everything from clients needing to confirm details to potential jobs to organizing time off for staff for the upcoming holidays.

But first, he called Dorothy Gilbert. He had to bottle his frustration when leaving a message with her desk sergeant.

Grayson stared across his desk to the black leather coach in the corner, where he'd made love to Patricia, only weeks ago. Sometimes, when he closed his eyes, he could still hear her saying "You're so fucking sexy."

He studied the painting on the wall across from him, a ship being tossed about by waves in a stormy sea. His late mother's work, perhaps a representation of how she'd felt at times, buffeted here and there by his father's various postings as a Marine officer.

Today, he could see himself onboard the ship, with the sea of Patricia tossing him about, almost lost.

His office manager, Lois, opened his door, interrupting his foul mood. Lois carried a stack of papers close to her chest.

"Welcome back, boss. For your enjoyment, here's our latest health insurance offer, with all the attendant riders." She dropped the stack on his desk with a flourish.

"Lovely." He'd expected to handle rent and payroll when he'd partnered with Tony to found Gray Associates, their security firm. But businesses seemed to come with endless paperwork, even more than the FBI had required.

Lois leaned against his desk and crossed her arms. Her earrings, silver ornaments in honor of the upcoming holiday, swung back and forth. Her hair today was equal parts orange and brown. Tomorrow, it might be some flavor of neon. For the Christmas holidays, it'd be red and green.

He'd have never hired Lois on his own, but she was Tony's niece and, Grayson quickly discovered, the best office manager that he could have found: efficient, smart, and unflappable. Score one for Tony and a lesson for Grayson about preconceptions that he'd never forget.

"I've divided the pile into life insurance, workman's comp insurance, and health insurance, with the last sub-divided into medical, dental, and vision." Lois tapped the stack. "I've put my recommendations on the top, in a summary, though, you being you, you'll insist on reading everything."

He smiled. "And you being you, you'll argue if I disagree with your recommendations."

"I don't tell you how to conduct a security detail, you don't tell me how to deal with insurance companies."

He put up his hands in surrender. "Then let's not waste time." He picked up a pen and wrote "Approved, E. Grayson" on the bottom of her list. "There. Done."

"Not even an argument?" Lois cocked her head, studying him. "Are you sick? Dying?"

He brushed off her tease by shooing her away from his desk. "Preoccupied. I need to clear my schedule, as quickly as possible."

"I see." Lois tapped his "in" basket. "I'll triage your messages but there are some I know you'll want to return personally. That client who paid a bundle last Christmas is coming back to New York for the holiday. We need that business. And there are a few others, similarly urgent." She shuffled through the messages and made two stacks. "Tony or I can handle these others."

"Thank you, that's appreciated." He stared out his window at Midtown, at the streets Patricia walked. Alone.

"Boss, everything all right?"

"I'm trying to head off a problem."

"Gotta be related to the redhead." Lois smiled. "Trisha's good for you. You need some ridiculous things in your life."

Ridiculous. Is that how others saw him and Patricia? "Shall I dye my hair various colors like you as well?"

Lois laughed. "Nah, silver is your thing. But is something wrong between you and her?"

He finally smiled. "The opposite. But she has a…work issue that could become dangerous."

"Okay, be cryptic. But be careful too." Lois closed the door behind her.

Grayson set to work answering the messages. That was his arrangement with Tony. The ex-NSA agent crafted the alarm systems and hired the techs, while Grayson provided security details—bodyguards—and managed the clients. It was a setup that worked well, thanks to several early and prominent clients, along with the recent publicity surrounding the recovery of the lost paintings during the case where he had met Patricia.

Gray Associates provided Grayson with more money than he ever thought possible. Between that and the trust inherited from his mother, he lived well. But money didn't solve every problem. Such as Patricia. Unlike his ex-wife, she understood why he was drawn to such a dangerous career instead of being scared by it. But Patricia might not understand his next move. As he reached for the phone to call Tony, he knew this decision would come back to bite him in the ass.

But if it helped save her life, it'd be worth it.

———

Tony arrived shortly after being buzzed. Grayson gestured for his partner to close and lock the office door. Tony made a big show of doing just that, his way of asking a question without using words. Finally, he settled into the leather couch, stretching out his short legs.

"I need to use the firm's resources on a personal matter," Grayson said.

Tony leaned forward and rubbed his wispy beard. "The redhead? What's she gotten into now?"

Grayson rose from behind the desk and sat next to Tony, quietly outlining the stalker who'd sent the letters, and Dorothy's interest in the case.

Tony pulled out a notepad and wrote something in shorthand. He often did that to remember details. "Sounds like a serial stalker and sounds like they've escalated already, or Lt. Gilbert and her partner wouldn't be involved."

"My read exactly."

"We can't interfere with a police case, Edmund, but you must know that. You must also know I'd be happy to sign off on a security detail for Trisha. Hell, she saved our asses with the museum situation. We'd have no shortage of volunteers." He laced his hands together. "But you must have something else in mind to have me close the door."

"Yes." Many people underestimated Tony. Tech experts were supposed to resemble nerds with protractors. Tony more resembled a mobster from a *Godfather* movie, but there was no sharper mind for research and alarm systems. Not to mention his insight into people. He liked Patricia. He even approved of Grayson's relationship with her.

He might hate what Grayson would ask him next.

Grayson rose from the couch and studied the angry seascape hanging on the wall again. No answers there.

"I believe this stalker has something to do with Patricia's background." A pause. "When she was fourteen, she was a victim of a brutal gang attack. It left permanent scars on her torso from here to here." Grayson gestured to his chest.

"Not news. I saw the video, remember?"

Grayson flushed. He wanted to forget that Tony had watched that scene of Patricia and him after they'd inadvertently set off the conference room camera.

"You did delete the footage?"

"For the millionth time, of course, though if this case is related to her scarring, an image of them could have proved useful."

How much of their night had Tony watched? No. No good would come from asking that question.

"Spit it out, Edmund. It's the easiest way."

"Razor blades were used in the assault on her."

"Suggesting this stalker who sent the razor blade in the mail is referencing that past assault."

"Yes, though, as she herself pointed out last night, razor blades are a common enough weapon," Grayson said. "She's never given me details of her attack, and I haven't pushed, for obvious reasons."

"But you want them now," Tony said flatly. "The best place to get them would be from her."

"I know that!" But she'd refused to provide details. "She's reticent. I believe she fears me knowing exactly what happened." His chest constricted. This was violating her trust. And he was afraid of what he'd discover. "Tony, I don't think her…attackers…got away with it."

Tony rose. "For certain, she hardly seems the type to let something like that pass."

"Whatever happened back then, it's putting her life in danger. I want, no *need*, everything you can find on Patricia's past. Her time in the Catholic orphanage, the accident that killed Father Mike and led to her time in foster care, and anything related to an assault or gang attack in the year she was fourteen."

Tony whistled. "You want a deep dive to uncover anything and everything about her."

"It's the only way to keep her safe."

"It might also permanently blow up your relationship, since I assume you're doing this without her permission."

Grayson turned his back to Tony, thinking back to how angry Patricia had been after he'd done a simple background check on her. But she'd done something similar on him.

"I will tell her. As soon as I can."

Tony brandished the little notebook at him. "Soon should be immediately, and you'll want to make it sound like you're asking her permission or you might not have a girlfriend much longer."

"Fiancée," Grayson corrected. "As of last night."

Tony clapped him on the back. "Congratulations!" He set a hand on Grayson's shoulder. "All the more reason not to do this behind her back."

Grayson swallowed away the lump of worry. "I'd rather risk her wrath than her life."

"Have you thought this might do her another kind of injury?"

Grayson shoved his hands in his pockets and made no answer.

"Do you want to do this to protect her, or are you driven by a need to know what she won't tell you?"

"Careful, partner." Grayson nearly growled.

"I'd keep a hold on that temper, if I were you. With me and her."

"Will you do it?"

"I see the need, if only because I'm mercenary enough to know that if the two of you get married, I, as your business partner, need to know what background she's bringing in." Tony clapped him on the back again. "But my condition for cooperation is that you tell her. Within twenty-four hours. Or I'll tell her myself."

"I'll tell her," Grayson ground out.

"Better you than me." Tony laid his hand on the doorknob. "I'll get my research staff started. They'll keep it confidential and I'll try to keep her name out of it as best I can."

"How long for results?"

"Could be a few days to a few weeks." He paused. "It'll be faster if she provides more information to direct us."

Grayson put up his hands. "Enough. I heard you the first time."

"Let's hope your redhead hears you too."

Tony left, leaving Grayson's office door open. Grayson shoved his hands into his pockets. Bloody hell, Patricia might crucify him for this. But perhaps only for a while? She would see the need for the research, especially if she weren't the only one being threatened. Hell, the *only* reason she'd see the need would be to protect others.

"Lt. Gilbert's on line 2," Lois called through the intercom. "Oh, and the redhead called. Said she was checking in, as ordered."

"What line is Patricia on?"

"She hung up. Said David was with her and not to worry."

David? Good, he'd arrived, as hoped. That eased his mind, though sometimes it galled Grayson that she'd more easily accept help from David and not from him. Of course, David wouldn't go behind her back and dig into her past.

Grayson picked up Dorothy's line.

"How about noon at B. Dalton's on Fifth?" she asked.

"How about now at your precinct? I need a full update on this."

"Nope, I'm in a time crunch, I have to buy books for my younger son's birthday, and I'd like to do this away from the precinct, English. You know why."

Because people misinterpreted their longtime friendship as something else. The gossip affected him not at all. But it could be detrimental to Dorothy's career. He should have thought of that.

"I'll be there," he said.

————

Grayson found Dorothy in front of the science fiction shelves at the B. Dalton.

Her arms were crossed, her dark brown face in a frown.

"What did the books do wrong?" he asked.

She shrugged. "Michael's into science fiction and I'm trying to find people who look like him in these damn books. Not an easy job."

"What about the case?" he asked. "What do you know? More than you told Patricia, I'm certain."

"I always know more than I tell people, especially nosy reporters or private security people." Dorothy pulled a Samuel R. Delaney book off the shelves.

"What about close friends?"

"It depends on the circumstances. You need to know what I say you need to know." She pulled another book from the shelf, read the summary, and replaced it. "This case is a homicide, Edmund. I have a victim who also received letters that could be exact copies of the ones sent to Trisha Connell."

His heart sank. He *hated* being right. "Bloody hell. *When* did you know this?"

"Not for certain until this morning." She grabbed several other books, shifting him to the side. "Take it down a notch, English. I've just come from the coroner's office for official cause of death. You're getting this ASAP because you telling Trisha will save me time, and I figure you're the only person she might listen to about protecting herself."

"I'll lock Patricia in a room until we find this murderer," he growled.

"Good luck with *that*." Dorothy tapped the Delaney book against her palm.

"Yes, overkill, I suppose." He glanced over the shelves and idly wondered if Trisha liked science fiction. "But if you hope to avoid both of us harassing you for details, you could give them to me now."

"Fair." Dorothy slipped three books into her basket, including the Delaney. "The homicide victim is a criminal defense attorney. Cause of death is exsanguination. Weapon was a razor blade that sliced his throat. He was tortured for some hours prior to death." She said all that in a flat tone but Grayson knew it disturbed her.

"We were already working the case when I put out a call for crimes involving razor blades. That's how Trisha's report over Thanksgiving was forwarded to me so fast. But it was unclear that her incident was connected until we found similar letters in my homicide victim's work correspondence today. Same Biblical quotes."

Grayson allowed the fear to course through him, but only for a second. When he spoke, his voice was clipped but steady.

"Are there other commonalities or connections between Patricia and this other victim?"

Dorothy answered in the same tone, cop to cop.

"My victim was older, male, and lived in a different neighborhood. I haven't found a personal connection between him and Trisha. But one is possible, somewhere, perhaps through Trisha's work on the crime beat. She'd have run into lawyers there, particularly criminal defense attorneys."

"So it might trace back to one of her stories." He took a deep breath, evaluating, staying calm, fighting the urge to run to her apartment. David was with her.

"It's a theory I have to track, yes," Dorothy said. "Among others."

And what of Grayson's own concern that it could trace to her past? No, he owed it to Patricia to talk about that possibility with her first. He had to tell her about the background checks. Soon.

"What next?" he asked.

Dorothy went silent as she paid for the books and shoved the paperbacks into her oversize blue purse. Often, Grayson wondered what else she kept in there.

"What next?" he repeated once they stood outside.

"I have a meeting to update my team and my superiors, given my victim was a so-called pillar of the legal community, and Trisha's high profile too, at least since the museum case. Soon, we'll have press on this. I'm assuming she'll know how to handle that."

"Those are not enough details to get me started. To protect her, I need to know everything and anything about the case."

"I've told you what I can." Dorothy tapped the lapel of Grayson's coat. "You ask her to think of any connection, no matter how small. I'll have to interview her either today or tomorrow. Maybe after that, I can reveal more details."

Patricia would see this as a police interrogation. That would not go well.

"Does she need a lawyer?"

Dorothy hesitated. "That's her call."

"What does that mean? What's going on here?"

"Nothing will be going on if you and your people can watch over her and account for her movements, all right?"

Anger. Uncharacteristic of Dorothy.

"I'll advise her about the lawyer. We can do the interview at either my office or my home."

"She comes into the precinct." Dorothy glared at him. "I won't play favorites."

"Then she's definitely going to have a lawyer." Grayson trusted his friend. Given the NYPD's checkered background with high-profile cases, he didn't trust her department.

"I expect you to tip me off if she's holding something back. That would ensure she's safe."

Or it would ensure he betrayed Patricia. Why would Dorothy ask him to do that? "Why would she keep something back?"

"You would know the answer to that question better than me."

"Are you saying Patricia's *lying*?"

"I'm saying we're pursuing all angles, English. I want the truth, not evasion. That's the best way to prevent another murder." A pause. "Also, the best way to protect her."

The police radio at Dorothy's waist crackled. "Damn. Gotta go."

"I don't understand. Do you suspect her of something?"

Dorothy opened her car door. "I'm a detective working a case. I suspect everyone."

Dorothy slipped into the Chevy Nova that she'd parked in a restricted zone and drove away.

Grayson stood there for a few minutes. *I suspect everyone.*

What the bloody hell did that mean?

CHAPTER NINE

"DETECTIVE ESTELLE BRICKER," the plainclothes officer announced as Trisha let her inside her apartment.

"Dorothy busy?" Trisha asked.

"*Lt. Gilbert* has weightier crimes on her plate than a minor break-in."

Trisha smiled because she'd deliberately used Dorothy's first name to get a rise out of this detective and it'd worked. Dorothy was known for gathering dedicated, smart people into Major Crimes. But they also tended to be humorless, and Trisha could never resist tweaking them. And if Bricker was Newman's recruit instead and Trisha could annoy Newman by proxy? Even better.

"If it's related to the stalker who sent me booby-trapped letters, it's more than a minor crime," Trisha said. "Which is why I assume you're here and not a uniform simply taking a statement."

"And we're glad to have you here." David cut in and introduced himself. "Good you came so fast, Detective Bricker."

"Of course." Bricker took out a notebook and a pencil. But before she wrote anything, she knelt. "Are these bloodstains on the floor? Were you hurt, Ms. Connell? The message didn't indicate that."

"Not me. Him."

Trisha provided as dry a version of the incident as possible, matching Bricker's mood.

Bricker frowned as she glanced at the knife on the coffee table. "He made a remark about your cross?"

"Puzzled me too," Trisha admitted.

"I would think a thief would be more likely to notice the expensive ring on your finger instead."

Good point. Her estimation of Bricker went up. "You'd think."

"Mind if I look around your apartment?" Bricker asked.

"Sure. I haven't found anything disturbed or missing, though. Maybe he didn't have time to steal anything."

"Maybe. Still, you're right, this doesn't seem like a standard burglary. He could have demanded you to hand over the ring, for instance."

Bricker started in the kitchen, making special note of the model motorcycles in an open cabinet above the sink. She glanced at the bedroom area, which was semi-blocked from the rest of the place by an oversized bookcase. Quiet woman, Trisha thought. Uptight, shy, or simply efficient?

"The bed's made neatly," Bricker remarked. "It's more organized than the rest of your apartment."

Trisha raised an eyebrow and exchanged a glance with David.

"If you're wondering if I was home last night, no, I was not. Your Lt. Gilbert knows where I was."

Bricker hmphed and peered at the bookcases that lined the walls.

"You looking for a particular title, detective?" Trisha asked.

"I was looking for any areas where the dust had been disturbed," Bricker snapped. "It doesn't appear so."

Oh. Score another for the detective.

"Smart," Trisha said.

A slight nod of acknowledgment from Bricker. "Thank you. Are any of these books valuable?"

"Only to me."

Bricker pointed to Trisha's audio cabinet and the albums stored next to it. "The receiver, turntable, and speakers look expensive."

"Not top of the line but, yeah, pretty high end," Trisha acknowledged. "I wondered why they weren't disturbed. Easy cash when sold at a pawnshop."

Bricker made a note. "Perhaps you interrupted him just as he entered, as you said. How did you know someone was inside your apartment?"

"My tape." Trisha stood and opened the door, showing off her piece of Scotch tape.

"Clever," Bricker said, almost grudgingly.

"The lock's a piece of crap, like all the locks and doors in this place so…" Trisha shrugged. "When I'm home, I slide the bolt on top of the door from the inside."

"You're lucky the intruder didn't lock you out," Bricker said.

"He probably didn't want to be trapped. It's the fourth floor. No fire escape."

"Ah." Bricker finally put away her notebook. "I see marks on the lock but none that look new."

David, who'd been watching all this from the couch, finally stood. "I wish you'd have let me install better locks when I offered last year, Trish."

"It's not a strong enough door," Bricker jumped in before Trisha could answer. "Add a stronger lock, and someone would have busted the wood instead."

"Exactly," Trisha agreed. "And then I'd have to pay for a new door as well as replacing my stuff. I figured there's nothing worth much here except heavier stuff, and they'd have to drag it down four floors. There's easier pickings in the neighborhood than my place."

"Agreed," Bricker said.

Trisha jerked a finger at Bricker. "I think I like her, David."

"Thanks for the vote of confidence," Bricker said. "You said he was wearing gloves. In your opinion, Ms. Connell, is it worth dusting for prints?"

"Nope," Trisha said.

"Yes," David said. "The doorknob."

"C'mon, David, he wore gloves. You'll never get a good print, unless it's yours, since you were the last to come through."

"She's right," Bricker said.

Still, David walked over to the door, opened it, and peered at the outer doorknob. "I suppose that's true."

He closed the door and walked to the coffee table. Bricker stood over the switchblade, put on a glove, and picked it up by the handle. "This has your intruder's blood?"

"Yeah," Trisha said.

Bricker pulled out a paper evidence bag from an oversize purse that was almost identical to Dorothy's. "I'll have to take it in for evidence."

"No!" Trisha grabbed for her blade but Bricker snatched it away. "That was a gift."

"It's evidence." Bricker shoved the bag and the knife inside into her purse. "When we have a suspect, we can try to match the blood to this."

"I don't care," Trisha snapped her fingers. "Give it over."

"Hey, Trish, she's right on this too." David set a hand on her shoulder. "Besides, even if it's not related to your stalker, the police might be able to match the blood type to other break-ins and catch someone."

Bricker pointed at David. "What he says is true."

"Fuck," Trisha muttered under her breath. "At least give me a receipt."

Bricker pulled a pad from her seemingly bottomless purse and wrote a receipt. For a minute, the only sound in the apartment was the scribbling of her pen. Trisha fought her temper. Nicky had given her that knife.

Bricker offered the receipt. Trisha snatched it. "Just don't lose it."

"Of course not. I'll take excellent care of it."

Bricker's police radio went off. She stepped away from them, to the kitchen, and answered. When she came back, her face was grave.

"Ms. Connell, Lt. Gilbert just informed me that whoever sent you the letters is likely responsible for the murder of a prominent attorney, Theodore Brennan. Do you know him?"

Another murder. "Brennan? Sounds vaguely familiar. Defense attorney? I might have heard his name before." She picked up the Rolodex next to the typewriter on her kitchen table and scrolled through the Bs. "Nope, he's not in here. This makes no sense. That guy today could have killed me, if he wanted."

"Perhaps your break-in is unrelated to the letters. It's impossible to tell at this point," Bricker said. "But Lt. Gilbert says you need to take serious precautions. I will point out that your apartment is obviously not secure."

"I'd be more secure if I had my damned switchblade," Trisha said.

"We'll take the warning seriously," David said.

"Very good." Bricker adjusted the bag on her shoulder, holding it tight against her chest. Trisha wondered what else she'd find in there if she dumped it.

"Lt. Gilbert will be in touch," Bricker said as she slipped out the door.

"Damn," Trisha said. "I should *never* have called it in. I want my switchblade back. So much for going by the book. Fuck."

"I'll get you a new one," David said. "And, hell, Trish, a killer's after you, and you're worried about a knife?"

"It was a *gift*." Trisha paced the small apartment, needing to do something, anything. If she stayed still, she'd go mad. "Nicky had it made for me for our last Christmas. I better get it back or I'm storming the Midtown precinct for it."

She paced in a circle. David said nothing, used to this mood.

"Jesus, I hate this. I'm not safe in my home, I don't have my knife, and this asshole is still out there." She stopped. "I'm not hiding."

"I know," David said. "So what do you want to do?"

"We check in with Grayson, first, because I have to tell him all this. Crap." She grabbed her jacket and shoved it on. "Then we go to the *Herald* and see if I've ever covered a story that featured Brennan. There's got to be a connection between us."

"Agreed." He tossed her the gloves she'd left on a kitchen chair.

"Why are you looking so happy?"

"Because I know this mood. It means someone's about to get their ass kicked."

Trisha laughed, releasing the tension. "Damn straight."

CHAPTER TEN

TRISHA STRAIGHTENED her shoulders and stepped into the *Herald*'s newsroom, bracing herself.

For a moment, she let the noise of the city desk flow over her. The click of keyboards, the ringing of phones, the shuffling of papers. The miasma of cigarette smoke seeped out of the office from the far corner, where Annie, the senior staff photographer, had her den.

The desks were arranged in several squares in the long open center. She'd had the desk closest to the window that looked out on the East River. Oddly for such prime real estate, her old desk sat empty. Almost forlorn.

Damn, she'd poured almost half her life into this place. Now it was gone and even her home wasn't safe anymore. *Fuck.* She flexed her fingers, angry all over again. She needed the morgue files with her old clippings, but maybe this was a lousy idea on top of the break-in.

"Shit," she muttered to herself. At least David wouldn't see her nerves. He'd agreed to use the pay phone downstairs to report they'd arrived here safely.

The urge to escape flared.

"Trish!" Kimba Sue called from the far right corner.

Busted, Trisha thought. But she had little time to regret being spotted, as Kimba Sue rushed from her desk, her waist-length curly red hair flowing behind her.

"What a surprise! So glad to see you!"

Some in the newsroom halted their typing to check out the disturbance, others pretended to be engrossed in their work. Today's juicy story: The Prodigal Returns: How Long Before the Asshole Boss Kicks Her Out Again?

Trisha stuffed left hand into the pocket of her black leather jacket to hide the engagement ring. Even juicier gossip.

"Hey, how goes the new job, Kim?" Trisha drawled.

"Job's great, thank you." Kimba smiled and, as always, it lit up her face. The woman was a damned ray of sunshine and it still confused Trisha that she was such a great crime reporter.

Kimba leaned closer. "So what brings you here?" Her question was practically a whisper.

Trisha glanced at the newsroom. "Long story but mainly research. We have somewhere quiet to talk?"

"Absolutely." Kimba crooked her arm in Trisha's. "Joe's out for the week." She grinned, all mischief. "We'll use his office."

"Hah!"

With nearly every eye in the city desk newsroom on them, they walked into the office of City Editor Joe Wilson and shut the door.

Trisha collapsed on the familiar threadbare couch where she'd slept more than once while working on a story. She patted the cushions. Good times. "Pretty ballsy to steal Joe's office for a fired employee. Especially for a mellow California girl, Kimba Sue."

Kimba laughed and perched on the edge of the beat-up metal desk. "I owe you for the job and, besides, Joe will get a kick out of this once he hears anyway."

"Probably," Trisha agreed. "He's great, isn't he?"

"Everything you said. I still can't believe you recommended me to replace you."

Trisha set her dirty boots up on the battered coffee table. "You're the best. Other than me, anyway. And I still can't believe you wanted to leave your newspaper to work for Weinstein the asshole."

Weinstein was the publisher who'd fired Trisha for insubordination, over Joe's objections. Weinstein was a stuck-up, classist jerk.

Kimba wrinkled her nose. "It's a question of proximity. My city desk editor got far too handsy. Joe doesn't, plus he's a better editor. Weinstein might be a problem, eventually, but he's not around much and he's not handsy either."

Trisha nodded. Kimba had hinted that'd been the reason she needed a new job. "That's good. Glad for you."

"I know you are. You have a good heart, Trish."

Trisha scowled while Kimba laughed again. "So what do you need the morgue files for?"

Trisha leaned forward, her elbows on her knees. "I need to research anything on a lawyer named Theodore Brennan."

Kimba's eyes widened. "The homicide case Lt. Gilbert is working?"

"News travels fast."

"It just came over the scanner. Are you doing something freelance? Want to collaborate?"

"It's something personal." Damn, she had to explain her stalker yet again. Luckily, Kimba was a good listener. When Trisha finished with the break-in this morning, Kimba sat next to her and put an arm on her shoulder.

"Hell, he broke into your home! Are you okay?" Kimba was wide-eyed, worried.

"I'm pissed is what I am." She liked the anger. It kept fear away.

"Damn, Trisha, you haven't had the best time lately."

She thought of Grayson. "It's not been all bad."

Kimba enclosed the hand with the ring and touched the sapphires. "Yeah, I can see that. *Details*! I know the who. Tell me the when and how."

"I suppose you have a smart comment? Everyone else does."

"Other than it seems incredibly romantic, the dignified security guy and the incorrigible reporter, meeting over murder, saving each other's lives, falling in love within weeks, nope, no smart comments," Kimba said.

Trisha put her head in her hands. "Gah. When you put it like that."

Kimba patted her back. "There, there. It'll be all right. You'll just have to live happily ever after. You'll get used to it."

"Hah, hah." Trisha stood. "Anyway, can you get me access to the files?"

Kimba hugged her. Trisha let it happen. It was kind of nice. "Absolutely." Kimba flipped her mass of hair behind her shoulder. "By the way, you know this means I get to throw you a bachelorette party."

"God help me," Trisha said as they left. "Will it be pink?"

"Pink, ruffles, and frills." Kimba Sue grinned.

"Add booze. And music."

"Noted."

As they walked past the newsroom to the stairs. Tony Borelli, the court reporter, waved to her without looking up from his phone call.

"You figure they'll rat us out to upstairs?" Trisha asked.

"Not a chance. You're their folk hero." Kimba pushed open the door to the basement steps. "Why else do you think they left your desk empty? It's a big finger to upstairs."

That warmed Trisha's heart. "Remind me to send the city desk some booze. I love those guys."

"They know," Kimba said.

————

Trisha searched the morgue files alone, as Kimba needed to work, and David was consulting with Grayson, probably debating the merits of a safe house. The smell of the newsprint and musty paper triggered yet more memories of the hours she'd passed in this very room, finding a new angle on a story or information that would give her an edge.

And there had been the rare quiet days literally spent clipping and filing her articles. There was talk that now everything would be saved on computer files or something and that would end the morgue as she knew it. Would be nice to pull the stories up with a few strokes of a keyboard but, for now, it would be all paper clippings, unless she had to go further back, to microfiche.

Brennan's name triggered a memory but Trisha couldn't pin it down, still. She pulled open the "B" file cabinet but found nothing under him specifically. Looking under "A" for attorneys yielded the same result. She finally had to drag out all the folders on criminal cases.

Thankfully, she was spared reading her own copy, as most of these were Borelli's work. Finally, she spotted her byline with Brennan's name in the lead.

Trisha laid the clipping out flat on the big metal table that ran the length of the file room, ignoring the ink stains on her fingers.

Brennan. Big-time defense attorney. She vaguely remembered the case, a charismatic couple killed by their daughter's lover. She remembered the killer, all smirk and little regret. But Brennan hadn't represented him. He'd represented the daughter and done it well. She'd gotten off with probation. The big talk had been how culpable the girl had been. Trisha had spent half the night arguing with Borelli that a fifteen-year-old girl wasn't responsible for what her twenty-three-year-old "lover" had done.

Lover, hah. That had been statutory rape.

She kept reading.

Brennan, who said he'd seen many an underage offender in his work as a prosecutor in juvenile court, said his client was innocent and had been abused by the older man…

Trisha's finger froze under "juvenile court." Her hand curled into a fist. No, no, juvie could not be the connection between her and Brennan.

She splayed her hands over her stomach, conscious again of the old scars, and tried to remember that day she'd pled guilty in juvenile court to four counts of manslaughter for killing her rapists.

Could Brennan have been the prosecutor who'd agreed to the deal? All she remembered of the D.A. in her case was that he'd pushed to move it to adult court.

But if Brennan had been the prosecutor in her case, how could that be related to his murder? He'd tried to hold her accountable, wanted a tougher sentence, wanted harsher penalties. So if someone out there wanted revenge on her, they shouldn't go after Brennan.

"Trish."

She snapped to her feet. "Jesus, Kimba, warn a person."

"I knocked. You didn't answer. I wanted to see if you were ready or needed help. I'm free now."

"I'm done." A deep breath. "Okay." She picked up the clipping. "I only need to copy this."

Kimba held out another clipping. "I thought you might like this too. It's a long piece that Borelli did on Brennan a couple of years ago. He was using it to as background for the obituary going out today."

"Thanks."

"You're not okay, are you?" Kimba asked.

Trisha turned her back to Kimba, concentrating on using the Xerox machine. "No, probably not. Someone breaking into my apartment threw me more than I thought. I hate that some slime was touching *my* stuff. I feel like I need to dump bleach all over it or burn my clothes."

"Your wardrobe could use some updating, like adding colors other than black or dark blue," Kimba Sue teased. "But don't wreck your records! You promised to lend me that Ramones EP."

"The Ramones wore black or dark blue a lot."

Kimba laughed. "Point made. Anyway, your friend in the lobby is getting antsy waiting for you."

David. Great. He'd notice how off-balance she was, and all she wanted right now was to go on a bender. Exactly the thing she needed and exactly the thing she shouldn't do.

"Thanks, Kimba. You've gone above and beyond for me." Trisha shoved the original article back into the files and restrained herself from slamming the drawer closed. She stuffed the article copies into her backpack. "Let's go."

She followed Kimba back through the newsroom. Kimba's phone rang as they headed past her desk. "Gotta get this."

"Thanks. Go score some stories."

Kimba answered the phone. "Wait!" Kimba grabbed Trisha's forearm. "This might be connected to"—she glanced around the room. Half the eyes were on them—"your thing," she finished.

Trisha peered over Kimba's shoulder to check the number calling. A police precinct. A source?

Kimba shooed her to the side, obviously not liking someone breathing over her neck. The conversation didn't last long but Kimba wrote down notes in an illegible scribble. She hung up the phone gently and turned to Trisha.

"There's another murder, same method as Brennan, just discovered, but it's unclear when the killing took place." Kimba wrote a name down on a pad and showed it to Trisha. "Another attorney. A retired judge. Know him?"

Trisha clenched her hands tight behind her back, not sure if she wanted to recognize the name or not. Malachi Martin. Yes, it rang a vague bell. A bad one.

"Damn, Kimba, I live in Hell's Kitchen. I know too many Malachis," she said out loud. "I'm not sure I could sort this one out, even if he's a lawyer. I need more info than that."

"Looks like he specialized in juvenile court," Kimba offered. "And Brennan prosecuted juvenile cases, as you just discovered."

"It's a good lead," Trisha said. "What's the address on the police scanner?"

Kimba rattled off a home that placed it squarely in Little Italy.

"You're going there," Kimba said.

"Gotta talk to the neighbors, find out if it's the Malachi I'm thinking of." And if it was, someone else was in danger. Besides her, anyway.

"Keep me in the loop," Kimba replied.

"When I can," Trisha said the words slowly, wishing she had Grayson's gift of preternatural calm.

A gleam appeared in Kimba's eyes. "This is a big story."

Trisha had to laugh. "If you're not at the center of it. Then it's just fucking annoying."

"You are good copy, my friend." Kimba tapped Trisha's chest with the telephone receiver. "But take care of yourself. If I find anything, I'll let you know."

"Call me here." Trisha wrote down Grayson's number, which had an answering machine attached. Her ring flashed as she finished the note. Great. Now she'd announced the engagement to the whole newsroom.

"You'll keep me informed even if I can't tell you what's going on?" Trisha asked.

"Sure. I owe you. Or, if it's a big enough story, maybe you'll owe me one someday."

"Absolutely."

———

Trisha met David in the downstairs lobby, impressed that no one in the newsroom had teased her about the engagement ring.

I can move on. At least, she could put her old job behind her. Unfortunately, her past life looked to be coming for her. At her own damn home, no less.

"You've got a smudge there." David pointed at her nose.

Trisha rubbed the newsprint off with her sleeve. "Happens." She filled him in about what she'd found about Brennan, and the new homicide of Malachi Martin.

"That must be why Dorothy sent Bricker to investigate your break-in instead of coming herself." David shook his head. "What's this about, Trish? Did you get a clue in there?"

"I..." She shook her head. "Maybe a clue. I need to know more about Martin. Let's head to his neighborhood."

And if what she'd found what supported her hunch, her life was about to blow up.

So much for happy endings.

CHAPTER ELEVEN

LIKE HELL'S KITCHEN, progress was killing Little Italy. It once had taken up more than fifty blocks, but it kept shrinking, especially since the rents had begun to go up. And Chinatown, too, encroached on its borders.

The immigrants and their descendants were mostly gone to the suburbs. The remaining Italian stores and shops were run by those who hung on tight, like Mrs. D. in the Kitchen.

Trisha knew the area well enough to have eaten at Puglio's more than once. And, of course, there were the zillion pastry shops with the best cannoli in New York. She'd been to a rooftop rave on Mulberry Street, too, but that had been years ago. No doubt the hosts were gone by now as so many of the apartments were being converted to expensive condos.

David drove down Broome Street, where Martin had lived. A black and white was parked outside the address from the scanner. Trisha slouched low in the seat to hide from the media she recognized gathered outside. No news trucks, though. No one had made the connection to Brennan's murder yet, though Kimba Sue would be working her sources. She never showed up to a scene without being fully informed. A difference in philosophy. Trisha liked to dive in and shake the trees.

In some areas of Manhattan, Trisha would know the neighborhood gossips. But Little Italy was a law unto itself. Working the street would be easier if it weren't below freezing, as there would be more people outside.

Still…people had to eat, right?

"Let me out in front of Sal's," she said to David.

Local pizza place less than a block from Martin. Best place to start.

"No way. You shouldn't be walking around alone, Trish." David rolled past Sal's and turned the corner. "Anyone who's been stalking you would know you'd hit this crime scene."

Fuck. He was right. "Park, then."

"No spaces. Damn." His eyes narrowed. "You have got to be kidding me." He hit the brakes.

Across the street, Grayson had just parked his Mercedes in the only spot available.

Trisha opened the door. "Problem solved, David."

David rolled down his window as she crossed the street. "You are too damn much alike!"

Trisha flipped him the finger, zipped up her leather jacket against the cold, stuffed her hands in the pockets, and waited for Grayson on the sidewalk beside his car.

Grayson buttoned his gray tweed overcoat and curled a matching scarf around his neck.

"Stalking me, are you?" she asked.

"Fancy meeting you here." He stared after David's departing Camaro. "He's right, you know. We are alike."

Except one of us has manslaughter convictions on our record. "You have any luck with Dorothy this morning?" Weird, he seemed more closed off than earlier. But he was like this when working. And she was a case.

"Dorothy told me about Brennan's murder. Then she cut our meeting short to answer a call. I assume it was for this." He focused on her. "David filled me in about your break-in."

"Does that mean I get another lecture on moving in with you?"

"Call it a professional suggestion?" he ventured.

"I'll take it under advisement, sir." She slipped her arm around his.

"That's all I ask." He finally smiled. "I could come to your place."

Damn, she'd like him there. After today, she wanted to sleep curled up next to him in her own home. "Need to inspect my crime scene?"

He kissed her cheek. "Inspections can be fun." He looked around. "How would you investigate this crime?"

"Usually, as a reporter, I'm looking for quotes on the record about the victim, so I'd start by knocking on his neighbor's doors. What about you?"

"Find his garbage, sort through it."

"*You* would personally sort through the garbage and get this fancy coat all dirty?" She brushed of imaginary dirt from his scarf.

"It usually doesn't take much for a lead. Tossed bills, takeout containers, anything that provides a clue to where the person has been."

"Then we are simpatico since I have an idea about food." She led him, arm-in-arm, to the corner. "Sal's Pizza is right there. It's the closest Italian place. If we get lucky, Martin stopped in regularly, rather than having everything delivered."

"And what information are you hoping to discover, other than his favorite pizza topping?" Grayson asked.

"Don't knock favorite toppings! You can tell a lot about a person from them. For instance, the pineapple people. So wrong." She stuck a finger in her mouth and mimed gagging. "They have dine-in too. Servers notice things. Can you follow my lead?"

"Dare I ask what you'll do?"

"Nope. I won't know until I get there."

"I'd be easier to slip them a few twenties," he grumbled.

"Then you can't know if they're saying whatever you want for the cash." They stopped under Sal's long, green sign, hung right on the corner so it could be seen in all directions. "Peer inside, like you're checking the place out. Look disapproving."

"Why?"

"Trust me."

After a few seconds of Grayson staring into the window beyond the neon sign that read "espresso," Trisha opened the door. "C'mon! Stop standing in the cold. It smells great in here, Edmund."

She smiled at the pizza guy behind the counter. Shorter, a little round, and bald. Like so many pizza guys. "What's the best you got?" she said in her most pronounced New York accent.

"Depends on what you like." He jerked his head at Grayson. "His type is usually more entrée than pie."

"Do you have a dine-in section?" Grayson asked.

He looked as skeptical as Trisha hoped he would.

"Down the corridor," said pizza guy.

A quick walk down the brick-walled hallway led them to a similarly brick-walled dining room with stout hardwood tables. Several older men sat in a corner booth, talking in whispers, and sipping espresso. Other tables held single diners, one a young couple, another a younger mom with five kids. Good luck there, Trisha thought.

A family place. It'd been more than a decade since Joey Gallo had been gunned down over at Umberto's on Mulberry Street. Long enough for people to feel safe here.

Judging by the clothes of the diners and the jackets strewn over the seatbacks, this crowd was mostly residents with money. This dining room probably appealed to the ever-gentrifying neighborhood and residents with deep pockets who were more entrée than pizza. Grayson would fit in with that group, at least outwardly.

An older woman in a pretty pink dress seated them. Trisha tossed her coat over the back of the chair. Grayson allowed the woman to take his coat and scarf to hang up.

"This is lovely," Grayson said to a waiter in a shirt and tie who poured their water.

A nice condescending note in that compliment. Trisha approved. Grayson was playing along.

The dark-haired kid smiled, seemingly oblivious to the backhanded insult.

"Thanks! Originally this was just a pizza place, but the last couple of years, we've been doing dine-in. People seem to like it."

"I'm sure we will too," Trisha said. After the waiter left, she sipped her water. "Looks like we're having lunch, lover."

"Any suggestions?" Grayson refilled her water glass.

"Oh, you should ask them to recommend the house special. I'm going for the pepperoni." She studied the men in suits in the corner booth. "This is perfect. Exactly where a retired judge new to the neighborhood might eat."

"I had the same thought."

She could do some digging at the courthouse about Martin's cases. But this would be more fun and probably faster.

The young waiter returned to take orders. Grayson peppered him with questions about the specials, first the fish, then the veal, and several questions about the pasta.

"It's homemade, of course," their waiter said.

"Really, Edmund, enough with interrogating the poor kid. This is Little Italy. I told you, everything will be wonderful." She rolled her eyes at him and turned to the waiter "Bring us the antipasto to start, your house red, he gets the house special, and I'll take a small pepperoni pizza."

The waiter beamed at her as he wrote down the order. "Perfect, thank you."

"A little early for wine," Grayson muttered.

"Then I'll drink yours." Trisha beamed at the waiter. "Just for that and since he's paying, make it your best red, okay?"

The waiter glanced back to Grayson. Trisha laced her fingers through Grayson's hand, making sure the waiter got a nice look at the engagement ring.

"The best red. For me, babe?" she asked. "Just think of it as pre-celebrating for when we find the place we want to buy in Little Italy."

Grayson brought her hand to his lips and kissed it. "For you, the best."

The waiter actually blushed. "Very good, sir." And he hurried off.

"You played him well," Grayson said in a low voice.

"Ah, he's a kid. Eager to do a good job. And you look like a big spender. He's hoping for a good tip and repeat business now."

"He's hoping you smile at him again."

A busboy brought them out the antipasto. The waiter came back with the wine bottle. Grayson made a big show of tasting a small amount from the bottle, sipping it, smelling it, and finally pronouncing it "more than decent." He let the English accent creep into his voice as well.

"Oh, don't mind him, it's wonderful," Trisha said to the kid. "Do you have more of these? We might take one with us."

And she stared at Grayson with intent, enough to make the waiter blush again.

"I'll ask in the kitchen for you," the waiter promised. "Usually we keep a bottle or two in reserve for regular diners." He stared at an empty booth and frowned.

"What's wrong?" Trisha said, voice full of worry.

"Sorry, I should go," the kid said. "I shouldn't talk about something like this with customers. I'll be back in a moment with your food."

And he scurried away.

"Gonna take more charm," Trisha said.

"I could bribe him."

"Grayson, money is not the solution all the time."

"You'd be surprised how often it is." He sipped the wine. "This is very good. I may truly want that extra bottle."

"Did you grow up with money?" she asked.

"My mother had money, a trust fund, that she brought into the family. But we tended to live on my father's military salary. Still, if we needed something…there it was."

"I wish everyone had that backstop."

"So do I." But he eyed her as he said it, so she knew he meant he wanted to share his money with her. Trisha sipped the wine, having decided to enjoy their impromptu date. She asked Grayson more about where he'd been stationed growing up. His description of Hawaii was so entertaining that she began to think she might dare getting on a plane to see that volcano.

Stupid, she thought. There was no future with him once he found out.

Grayson's house special came, something called Chicken Murphy, loaded with green peppers, potatoes, onions, and tomatoes. It was like no other Chicken Murphy Trisha had ever seen.

"That's not *Irish* Chicken Murphy," she said to the kid.

"It's a special," he said. "The same customer who liked the red always ordered it. Mr. Malachi. He lived across the street." The kid glanced at the empty booth again.

"Sounds like a man of good taste," Grayson said.

"Sounds like a smart man to live so close to Sal's," Trisha said. "But you said 'lived.' Did he move? Is his place available?"

"Yeah, I guess." Now the kid seemed in real distress. He stuffed this order pad in a pocket.

Trish decided to ignore that distress. "What's the address? I'll get our real estate agent right on it!"

The kid stared at the floor. "He passed away. We just heard this morning."

"Oh, no, that's awful," Grayson said but he sounded mercenary. "I told you, Patricia, maybe Manhattan isn't safe."

She chugged the rest of the wine, as if she were angry. "One person dies and suddenly a whole neighborhood is dangerous?"

"But he was murdered," the kid whispered. "I heard one of our customers say mobsters but that's insulting. Mr. Malachi was a judge, a respected one. We loved him here."

"Sounds like a wonderful man," she said.

"He had a party here once. Just him, a defense attorney, and some of the people who'd passed through his courtroom. He said they'd made good when they grew up, like he hoped," the waiter said. "Not kids, people about your age, miss. They ate *a lot* of pizza."

Trisha bit into a piece of the pepperoni. Juicy. Hot. Perfect.

"I can see why! This slice is heaven," she said through a mouthful. "What did you say about his guests? My age?"

"Yeah, still pretty young." The waiter blushed, worried now he'd upset her by mentioning age. "I think they came through his juvenile court because he gave me a lecture once about staying on the safe and narrow. I didn't always have a good job." Red flushed his cheeks.

What had the kid done? Didn't matter.

"Looks like you took his advice to heart," Trisha said. "Good for you!"

"Thanks. Sorry, I got off the track. Sal says I do that."

"We appreciated the information, and, yes, I'm thankful it wasn't mobsters." Grayson slipped a twenty to the kid. "If we do buy in this neighborhood, I'll remember you."

"Thank you, sir." And he left with a smile on his face.

Trisha took a deep breath and a long swallow of wine to wash down the slice. Grayson eyed her but instead of asking questions, he dug into his lunch.

When the kid returned to present them with a second, unopened wine bottle, Grayson drew out another twenty and held it out. "Bring us some espresso, too, when you see we're finishing up."

"Sir, yes, sir."

"He'll remember you for sure now."

"I'll remember Sal's. This Chicken Murphy is wonderful."

Trisha let herself enjoy every last semi-greasy, wonderful bite of the pizza but, inside, her mind whirled. Juvenile court judge. Brennan had been a prosecutor. Martin a judge. And they both worked at juvenile court at the same time she'd pled guilty.

If it was about her case, that meant the next target would be her defense attorney. Trisha wished she could remember the woman's name. Some female hippie with jargon about love and forgiveness and all that crap. But Trisha knew where to get that name, at least.

All this was about her past catching up to her. But why go after everyone involved in her case?

"Something clicked for you just now, Patricia," Grayson said in a low voice. "What was it?"

Trisha shook her head. "Let's say I know all I need to know. Look, we have great food and wine. God knows when we'll have a quiet moment again. Let's take a few minutes for each other."

Again, that searching look from him again. He wanted to ask. He wasn't going to ask.

"Tell me about how you drive a sailboat," she asked.

"You don't drive one, you sail it," he said.

And, as she asked, he launched into an explanation that included words like "jib," "trimming," and "stern."

She let his smooth voice roll over her, absorbing it, making it part of her. In case she never heard it again.

After the espresso, the kid wrapped up the remains of the Chicken Murphy for Grayson. Trisha grabbed the bottle of red.

As they left the restaurant, they ran right into Detective Estelle Bricker.

"What the hell are you doing here, Connell?" Bricker demanded.

"Having lunch."

Trisha brandished the wine. "I highly recommend the pepperoni pizza, detective."

The cold turned the breath pouring out of Bricker's nose into something that resembled steam. "Two people are dead and you're eating pizza and getting drunk?"

"It's most excellent pizza," Trisha drawled.

"I'd also highly recommend the Chicken Murphy," Grayson added.

"What is *wrong* with you people? We have a murdered man in a house less than one hundred yards from this corner."

"Our having lunch isn't going to make him any less dead," Trisha said. If only.

"Easy, detective." Newman, Dorothy's partner, arrived, looking disapproving as always. "Connell's playing you to get you off-balance. They're here to dig around our crime scene."

"I thought it was Lt. Gilbert's crime scene?" Trisha stared at Newman, unblinking. "Find anything that will help you catch the killer before he attacks me?"

He pushed past them. "I'm not in the habit of sharing police details with you, Connell."

"You should, since it's her life in danger." Grayson whirled to face him.

Trisha slipped her arm in his.

They didn't need to be brawling with Newman right now. Teasing him had been a distraction and she'd grabbed at it without thinking. Time to go. Face the music, so to speak.

"Is Connell really in danger, though?" Bricker asked.

"What the hell is *that* supposed to mean?" Trisha took a step forward, forgetting her intention to avoid confrontation. "What do you know that I don't?"

"The question is what you know that we don't." Bricker pointed at her.

Grayson stepped in front of Trisha. "She's given her full cooperation to you, detectives."

"Has she *really* now?" Newman asked.

"She reported the initial crime, she gave a statement, and she called you today after the break-in at her apartment. Yet you nearly assault her in the street." Grayson stood toe to toe with Newman. "Why?"

Trisha tugged at Grayson's arm again. Still waters ran deep, which meant Grayson might just be capable of getting into an actual fight with Newman.

"C'mon, we've got another bottle of wine," she said.

He gave her a look, eyes narrowed, that could have melted steel, then his shoulders sagged, and he stepped away from Newman.

"Bye, detectives!" Trisha mock-saluted Newman. "Tell Lt. Gilbert she can find me at my apartment."

"You damn well better stay at your place until we can speak to you," Newman said.

They turned their backs on the detectives and finally headed to the car.

"Not like you to be the calm one in the fight," he said to her.

"Too cold, and we have wine," she teased.

"I needed to hit him," Grayson admitted.

"I know. Then you'd have beaten yourself up over it. C'mon. We have stuff to talk about."

It was going to be a long night.

CHAPTER TWELVE

GRAYSON INSISTED on going first into Patricia's apartment, clearing it before holstering his gun. One couldn't be too careful.

"It's safe," he said.

Patricia walked in and instantly noticed the tabletop Christmas tree he'd placed in her apartment earlier, before heading to Little Italy.

"Oh, wow." She tossed her jacket on the couch and stared his gift. "Damn, Teddy. You bought me a tree."

She'd said, "Teddy." Signaling a dropping of the tension? She'd donned that attitude she wore as armor during their ride crosstown. He'd assumed she'd tried to calm down after the confrontation with Newman and Bricker. But something else weighed her down.

"You gifted me with a tree. Turnabout is fair play," he said.

"It's great."

But her voice broke. She hugged herself tight as if lost in some terrible memory. A single tear on her face reflected the tree lights, making a mockery of the festive colors. On her left hand, the sapphire ring twinkled.

He stood next to her, their shoulders almost touching.

"Teddy, I mean, it's *really* great."

He enfolded her in his arms loosely, allowing her to pull away if needed. Instead, she rested her head on his shoulder.

She sniffled and wiped a tear away with her coat sleeve.

"Sorry." She cleared her throat. "I'm fine. Really."

"It's all right to be not fine." He lifted her chin with his fingertips so their eyes met. "Patricia? I know this must be a lousy day for you, especially with the break-in…"

"That's a part of it, but…."

Talk to me, he thought. Please finally talk to me.

Her eyes were red, but there were no more tears. "It's—it's the tree. I haven't done Christmas in a long time, not *here*." She approached the tree, reaching for, but not touching it the little tabletop shrub. "The last Christmas I had a tree, Nicky died. He was supposed to be coming home from the hospital, so I decorated our place to celebrate. He died that night."

Her outstretched hand shook.

"Nicky was the last person you bought a Christmas tree for until you bought one for me?"

"Yeah."

His heart grew three sizes at the wonder of the gift she'd given him. "He must have been something, your Nicky."

"He was the best." Her voice remained muted. "He was…we never had to explain anything to each other. We just *knew*. I adore you, Teddy, I do, but I miss him. Always will." She pulled a beer from her fridge and drank half in one long swallow.

"What was he like?" he said, voice thick, trying to dismiss his ridiculous jealousy of a dead man, one who'd known all her secrets. But then, he was keeping his own secrets too, wasn't he?

"I can show you a photo if you want?" she asked.

He answered with a quiet nod, worried anything he'd say would be wrong and pop this bubble of trust. She walked over to the bookshelves that lined the walls and reached behind several leather-bound Shakespeare volumes on the middle shelf. After feeling around for a moment, she pulled a battered metal lockbox from behind the books.

"Do you think that's what the intruder wanted?" he asked.

"It occurred to me but how would he even know it was here? I'm the only one who did. Well, until now." She shook her head. "I was coming back for this anyway so…"

She set the lockbox on the kitchen table, opened it, and started rooting around. What secrets were hidden in that box? He was seized by an irrational impulse to snatch it from her grasp and settled for looking over her shoulder. A stack of bound letters. A folded wedding certificate. A prayer card for Father Michael Connell, the priest she'd claimed as her father.

Something metal clattered inside as she pulled out a creased Polaroid. And, before he could see anything else, she closed the box.

He flicked on the overhead light as she offered the photo to him. It showed a teenage Trisha and a tall, young, Irish-looking man with dark brown hair. They were standing together, her arm around his waist, his arm cradling her shoulders in front of an outdoor basketball court. Nicky was grinning, looking down at her with delight in his eyes. Young Trisha had been caught in mid-laugh.

Dear God, please let me be able to make her laugh like that.

How old was she here? Eighteen?

"It's a wonderful photo, Patricia. It's obvious how much he cared about you."

"We took that the day after our wedding. Sky was the limit, or so we thought. But he was sick already." Trisha stared at the photo and finally set it on the bookshelf, image holding court on the immaculate shelf.

She opened the box again. No, don't ask, he told himself. Let her tell you.

"You're dying to ask what else is in there," she said.

"If the situation were reversed, you would snatch it out of my hands," he said.

"Hell, yes." She pushed the top open all the way. "It's not much. Bits and pieces of the past. Things I couldn't bear to part with. The things I need to save in case there's a fire." She moved aside and gestured for him to look.

He peered inside. A gold ring reflected the light. It rested on top of several yellowed newspaper articles, next to the prayer card.

"The ring is your wedding band?" he asked.

She held the box closer for his inspection.

"What are the articles about?" he asked.

"Father Mike's obituary. He died in a hit and run. Anyway, they never found who did it. I also saved a notice about my graduation from

Columbia. Summa Com something or other. I got good grades. That's what impressed the *Herald* enough to give me an interview. There's also my first published story in the *Herald*. Letters between me and Nicky from when… when…" Her voice broke again.

"You met Nicky after going into foster care?" he asked quietly.

"Yeah." She curled her hands around the Celtic cross she always wore around her neck. "You knew I was a foster kid."

"Yes."

"I wasn't trying to hide it. I'm just not big on talking about it." She played with the chain. "I had a fantasy as a kid that Father Mike might be my biological father and that keeping me in the orphanage was his way of taking care of me. Orphans do that, create fantasy parents. Still, he was all the father I had. That's why I took his name when I turned eighteen. Seemed right." She smiled. "Then I met Nicky. We became friends. We weren't always in the same foster home, but we kept in touch."

"That's what the letters were about?"

"Um, sorta." She ran both hands through her mussed hair, clearly distressed.

"How long were you and Nicky together?"

"We were friends first. I was ten, and Nicky was two years older when we met in foster care. Bookworms both. We were separated two years later when his mom got custody back. Idiot children's services." She flopped down onto her couch, pushing aside the newspapers that covered one of the blue tweed cushions. She rested her feet on a coffee table also full of papers and magazines.

"Nicky's mother was a drug addict. When she ran low on funds, she rented out Nicky for sex." Trisha curled her hand around the cross again. She stared at the blank screen of the television in her entertainment cabinet. "And yet, when his mom claimed to be clean, she got custody back, and the cycle started again. Maybe if she'd taken better care of him, he wouldn't have gotten sick."

Grayson sat next to her on the couch and put his arm around her.

"He was lucky to have found you."

"I'm the one who was lucky." She rested her elbows on her knees. "Nicky had a huge growth spurt at sixteen. He ran away from his mother, then came for me at my second, lousy foster home."

Grayson massaged her shoulders.

She leaned into him. "We ran away together, found an abandoned building in Alphabet City where we set up a home." Her voice strengthened and he could hear the grin in it. "We went through a whole box of condoms that first night. Damn, it was just so…it was…as if life meant something again." She closed her eyes, as if reliving that night in her memories.

"How long has he been gone?" Grayson tried to do the math of their ages in his head.

She moaned again and slumped forward. "Six years ago, next week."

"I'm so sorry."

"He had so much life ahead."

He'd been twenty-five. She'd been only *twenty-three* when he'd died. How old had she been when they'd first been together? Fourteen? Fifteen? Yet despite the early start, he'd rarely seen two people as in love as the people in that photo. Stop judging, he told himself, and start being grateful she had someone who loved her.

"Young. I never got a chance to be young, I think." She leaned back and burrowed her head against his chest. "I was nine when Father Mike died. One day everything was fine, next day, boom. Over. Like a freight train smashed into my life."

He hissed, remembering his own, more recent grief following his mother's death from a cancer that had ravaged her body. "That should never happen, especially to a child. I'm sorry."

She raised her head to look at him. "I thought, when Nicky died, it would be different. He was so sick, and he wasn't getting better and… It's supposed to be a relief, right?" She jerked upright and paced to the kitchen. "I was supposed to be happy he wasn't suffering. There's supposed to be closure. There is no closure." She slapped a hand on the refrigerator. "*Fuck closure.*"

He followed her. "Patricia, I didn't mean to make you relive tragedy."

"It's not your fault my life's been pretty screwed up." She rubbed her hands over her face again. "Or that the past is now coming back to bite me in the ass. I figure I owe you the story."

"What do you mean?"

An almost imperceptible change took over her as she pulled herself together. Her shoulders became straighter, her jaw tighter, and her eyes turned colder. The emotional armor encased her again but, still, she'd shared more than she ever had before.

"It's way past time. I should never have gotten distracted, dammit." She picked up the faded business card and handed it to him. "You need to find this woman. Fast."

"Why?"

She turned around one of the kitchen chairs and straddled it, staring at the tree again. "Why. A three-letter word. Seems so innocent. And it's the most tragic word in the dictionary."

He sat down in the other table chair. The air in the seat cushion fled with a whoosh.

"I would guess, then, that you're telling me that your stalker and the murders are related to your past."

She braced as if for an attack. "One prosecutor, Brennan. One judge, Martin. And that card contains the name of the defense attorney involved in the case."

He read the name. Heather Sather. "And you, the reporter who covered the case?"

"You know, I could kiss you for the chance to go with that lie." She buried her head in her hands.

"You can always kiss me."

"Hope springs eternal." She looked at him, all humor gone. "Anyway, one judge, one prosecutor, one defense attorney, and one client. Me." She jabbed a finger into her chest. "That's why you need to find her. If this killer knows who three of us are, they'll know who she is."

"Understood." He stood, his professional brain engaged, fighting to keep a lid on the personal reaction, fighting to hold back questions that would sound like accusations. "Can I use your phone? Tony can start a search for Sather right now."

"Do that. I wish I'd thought of it this morning. But I didn't make the connection until I saw Brennan had prosecuted some juvie cases."

"Then you discovered Martin was a juvenile court judge. That's why you said we had enough at lunch."

"Score the man a Triple Yahtzee."

"Anything else you remember?"

"She was a hippie, always wore these tie-dyed scarves with her business suits. And she was a lesbian. Out and proud. I liked that about her. The peace, love, and understanding stuff weren't my thing, though."

"That should be enough. The address is a huge asset, even if it's no longer valid."

"How long will it take to find her?"

"I can take anywhere from hours to a few weeks."

"Hope it's hours. Hope we find her before the killer does."

"That's why you wanted to come here right away. To give me this information."

"Yeah." Patricia stared at the tree while he made the call to his partner, finding Tony still at work. Tony said he'd make locating Elizabeth Sather his highest priority. He'd likely work all night, with a life dependent on it.

Tony ended with, "You should tell her right now what you started here, Edmund."

"I will."

Grayson held the receiver in his hand after the call was done. If he'd waited a few hours, he likely could have had Patricia's permission for the invasive search into her background. But now he had to confess what he'd done without asking. Without trusting her.

But she hadn't trusted details of her court case with him, even now. How could they have a future if they failed this test so badly?

"Patricia, I also have to call Dorothy with this information. The police may be able to find Sather faster."

She merely waved her fingers at him. "Figured."

He left a message at Dorothy's precinct and her home. He almost slammed the receiver down in frustration at not actually speaking with her.

"She does have a new homicide to investigate," Trisha pointed out. "I'm sure she'll check messages soon. Besides, I expect she wants to talk to me ASAP."

"No doubt." And Patricia would have a lawyer when that happened. He didn't like Newman's hostility.

Grayson sat down across from her again, wondering if it was better to confess his sin to pry her secrets out of her. Of course, that might make her angry.

No, better to get answers from her first.

Patricia unwrapped a chocolate ornament from the tree and promptly consumed it, licking the last vestiges of chocolate off her fingers. "Excellent," she pronounced, raising her face to him.

He felt an erection stir. He knew this mood. She wanted sex so she could lose herself in it. Lose them both in the moment. Usually, he welcomed it. Patricia communicated in actions so much more than words.

But…it seemed like so much had happened in a day.

"Patricia, what were you charged with in juvenile court?"

She flinched, as if he'd physically struck her. She stared past him. He waited, damped down his lust, damped down the need for the only act where she fully gave herself to him.

"Only this morning, I felt so happy. I want a day." She stroked the ring. "Can I have a full day to believe in happy endings? Please?"

His heart broke. He clutched her hand. She squeezed his hand back.

He spoke, his voice thick with lust and love. "Come home with me, love."

"Here."

"One night," he echoed her words. "Here. Together."

He pulled her to his lap and kissed her. She tasted of beer, chocolate, and tears, and he didn't care. The kiss lasted a long time. When it ended, she closed her eyes. He stood up and carried her over to the bed.

After they made love, desperate, almost violent in their mutual need, he remained awake for a long time, an ache centered in the middle of his heart.

One day to believe. Was that all they'd get?

CHAPTER THIRTEEN

THE NEXT MORNING, Trisha sat up in the bed, knees pulled up to her chin, careful not to disturb Teddy, gathering her courage. Someone would find Sather, hopefully alive, soon.

Past time for her confession. And she doubted reciting a bunch of "Hail Marys" would square things with God or, more importantly, Teddy.

He thought she was reluctant to talk about the rape. That part sucked, but admitting she'd gunned down the four men responsible for her attack not in self-defense but for revenge?

Teddy would never see her the same again.

Funny how when she knew she'd lose him, she could finally admit she loved him. At least they'd had yesterday. At least she'd had a day of hope.

She wanted to strangle this murderer for so many reasons. And wasn't that a problem too? She still wanted to murder someone?

She slipped out of bed, snagging an old, oversized Joe Namath jersey on the floor near her bed. A loud rap sounded on the door. Grayson snapped awake, alarmed, and reached for his gun and shoulder harness on the bookshelf above the headboard.

Trisha laughed. "Easy, James Bond. That's only Mrs. Donohue. Mrs. D. She lives downstairs, on the first floor. You remember her."

His hand moved away from the gun. "How can you tell it's her?" He looked at his clothes, which were neatly folded over her radiator near the window.

"Mrs. D. always raps on the door with her cane. It makes a distinct thud." Trisha slipped on a pair of sweatpants taken from a pile at the foot of her bed. "I better answer. Maybe she found out something about my stalker."

Grayson froze. "Patricia, I'm not dressed yet."

She smiled again because he looked so rumpled this morning, so unlike his dignified, public self.

The rap came on the door again. "Look, stay out of sight in the bed. She's not coming around the corner to look."

She padded in her bare feet to her door. The bookcase blocked off her bedroom area and would hide Teddy from anyone standing at the front door. His dignity was safe.

The rap sounded, louder this time. "Coming," she called, fumbling with her door locks. She opened the door with a flourish. "Good morning, Mrs. D."

"Good morning, Trisha." Mrs. D. inclined her aged head. A rectangular metal pan balanced precariously on top of her cane.

"What's that?" Trisha took a deep breath and put her hands on the pan to steady it. Food! Eggs? Bacon? Maybe sausage? Her stomach rumbled.

"A breakfast casserole, as a thank you for fixing my fan. After yesterday's excitement, I thought you needed to eat too." She leaned in close, so close that her white hair brushed Trisha's ear. "Mr. Mercedes can have some, too, even if he is being rude hiding from me."

"He's kinda naked at the moment," Trisha whispered back, lifting the casserole.

"I wouldn't mind." Mrs. D. laughed.

"It's a pretty good view, I admit." Trisha walked the few steps to her kitchen and set the casserole down next to the tree. Heavy for someone that old to be carrying up four flights. And she'd probably cooked it herself too.

"Everything okay?" she asked the older woman. "I left you a message yesterday."

"I got it. Someone broke into your place. Glad I missed it." She clutched the top of her cane with both hands. "Used to be people left this building alone."

"Yeah. Sit down and have some coffee? The pot's almost ready."

Mrs. D. waved away that offer. "No, no, I won't intrude. But stop by later. I've been going through my hope chest and found more information about that fire you asked about yesterday. I think it's connected to another crime. It's a mystery that's always bothered me, and, well, I'm glad someone will look into it, finally."

Trisha hadn't exactly asked, but sometimes Mrs. D. would not let things go.

"Is it related to the intruder or the stalker?" Grayson joined them, wearing his suit pants and an unbuttoned dress shirt over his T-shirt. His feet were bare.

"Good morning." Mrs. D. winked at him, flirting. "I don't believe it's related to the intruder, but who knows?"

Trisha knew she'd have to talk to the woman today or be visited by yet more casseroles. "I should be by sometime today. You going to be in, Mrs. D.?"

"Later, I will. This morning, I see my grandson."

Mrs. D. gave Grayson a long, lingering assessment. "You come visit too, Mercedes."

Mrs. D. shut the door behind her.

"Why does she call me 'Mercedes?'" Grayson asked.

"Your car. And a shorthand for you having money."

"Ah." He lifted the cover of the casserole. "This smells good."

"It is. I've had it before." She pulled out plates for them. Yes, have breakfast and coffee, like a normal couple. Forget she was a killer and she had to tell him.

"What's this arson she talked about?" Grayson asked as he poured coffee for them.

"Oh, an old Hell's Kitchen mystery. No one's ever dug into it. She's right, it could make a good story. She's got an eye for them. Problem is, she has a zillion clippings in that hope chest and it's hard to sort through them. Still, she's given me a few leads that turned into stories."

"How likely is it to be relevant to the current case?"

Current case. How he tiptoed around the discussion they needed to have. Trisha shoved a forkful in her mouth. "Not likely. This is from 1958. I wasn't even born, I think."

The phone rang. She let Grayson answer. Dorothy. Of course. But then it seemed she put him on hold. Trisha could wait. Soon enough, she'd be doing way too much talking.

She wondered what the killer was doing right now? Reading the Bible for justification of their murders?

"He that covereth his sins shall not prosper: but whoso confesseth and forsaketh them shall have mercy," Trisha muttered to herself.

Grayson studied her. "I'm on hold for Dorothy. What's that quote from?"

"The Bible. Proverbs." She shrugged. The killer missed most of the point of the Good Book. But then, most people did.

Grayson held up a finger as Dorothy finally returned to the call.

"She wants a meeting."

"I bet," Trisha said. "Where? When?"

"Now. She said they've located Sather, wants to talk to you after she visits her first."

Trisha snapped out of her chair. "Give me the phone."

She settled the receiver against her ear and put her back to Grayson. "You can't talk to Sather without me," she said to Dorothy.

"Why not?"

Dorothy was snippy today.

"Because she won't tell you anything about the background relevant to these murders without me there."

A pause. "Go on."

"I have to be there to waive attorney-client privilege."

Trisha thought Dorothy muttered a curse word. "Didn't know it'd be that upsetting to you, Lieutenant. You always said I was trouble."

"Not this much. I assume she was an attorney representing you in a felony?"

"You'd be correct."

Another long pause. "How are you involved, Connell? What are you hiding?"

"Someone wants revenge for what I did back then. But they should have come after me first. The others didn't deserve it."

Dorothy paused for long enough for Trisha to think she'd hung up. "Look, Connell, it's been suggested you could be involved in these murders."

"I just said I was."

"As the *perpetrator*."

Trisha dropped the phone, snagged it again in mid-air. "What? Are you fucking serious? Where's this coming from? *Newman*." Is that what he'd meant yesterday? To hint she was guilty of murder?

"It doesn't matter where it comes from. Let's just say it's not good you didn't give me this information up front."

"I didn't even know the name of the victims until yesterday! Jesus Christ, Lieutenant, I'm not the only one being closed-mouthed."

"You can't discuss a crime with a person of interest."

"You can't expect me to read your mind that I'm a suspect!"

Grayson loomed in the background to overhear the conversation.

"Granted," Dorothy finally said. "But after we finish with Sather, you're coming to the precinct with me to clear things up."

Trisha almost laughed, this was so ridiculous. "Should I bring a lawyer?"

"That's up to you. But I hope you've got an alibi for Thanksgiving night, and the Saturday after it."

"This is from Newman, isn't it? He needs to get his head out of his ass." Of all the things she'd expected, being accused of these murders had not been on the list. Of course, she was guilty of murder. Just not of Brennan's and Martin's deaths.

Grayson held out his hand for the phone. She waved him off. "Just give me Sather's address. I'll meet you there."

"I'm counting on it," Dorothy said.

This time, Trisha handed over the phone to Grayson. "You get the address. I'm done talking."

Grayson cleared his throat and spoke to Dorothy, writing down the address on a pad Trisha kept next to the phone. He asked her for more information but obviously didn't get it because he slammed the receiver onto its base.

Trisha paced. Her fingers twitched for a cigarette. Last night, the worse she envisioned was Grayson hearing about past killings. Hahahaha. Joke was on her, wasn't it?

Well, if she was formally accused of murder, she'd have a good excuse to smoke and drink. A silver lining.

Grayson held out the address for her to read.

"It's in the Village. Finding parking on those side streets will be a bitch," she said.

"I managed Little Italy. I'll manage this." He cleared his throat. "Patricia, what did Dorothy say that upset you?"

"I'm considered a suspect in the murders." She opened her fridge and slammed it shut again because it only contained beer when she needed Jolt.

"That's absurd," he said.

"Not so absurd when she hears what Sather says about my juvenile case." She shrugged into clothes, shoved her feet into her motorcycle boots, and snagged her black leather motorcycle jacket off the chair near her bed.

"Tell me what you've been keeping a secret," he said.

She set her jaw. He'd been patient. More patient than she would have been in his place. She would have started digging into his background already without permission.

She squared her shoulders and faced him. "No easy way to say this."

He stilled, bracing himself. Closing down his emotions. He could do that, think before acting or speaking. One of the reasons she liked him.

"My juvie conviction was for four counts of manslaughter."

"The ones who hurt you," he whispered.

She jammed her hands into her pockets and noticed that her floor needed sweeping. Grayson's home would not have dust. It'd be immaculate. Eh, what was a little dust when one was accused of murder?

"Yeah. *Them.* What the record doesn't say is that it should have been murder counts. I'd had a chance to escape, free and clear. What I did, I did for revenge because I thought they deserved it."

"Do you still think they deserve it?"

A quiet question. No good way to answer it.

"Yeah." She could barely squeak out that answer. "I'd probably do it again," she added. Let him know exactly who she was.

Blood roared through her head. Her face flushed, probably beet red by now. She swayed, almost dizzy, bracing herself for his reaction.

A hand settled softly on her shoulder. "Do you remember their names?"

"That's what you want to ask right now?" She paced away, still afraid to look at him.

"The relatives and friends of those killed would be logical suspects in this case." Grayson's words were dry, almost dust. "Better suspects than you."

"Yeah," she agreed. "Except I blocked out their names, just like I blocked out my defense attorney's name. I'm sure Sather probably has the file with those details." She closed her eyes. "All I remember is their faces."

She swayed again and slapped her hand against the wall for balance. The memories swarmed in her mind. She took deep breaths and thought only of air coming in and going out. Too much stuff to do. Talk to Sather. Prevent another murder. Avoid being arrested. Catch a killer that she'd probably created. Handle the break-up with Grayson.

His hand came down softly on her shoulder again. "Patricia," came a whisper.

"Yeah?"

"We have to go meet Dorothy now."

———

Patricia had all the body language of a prisoner being led down the corridor to a cell that would slam shut and never open. She sat slumped in the passenger seat of the Mercedes, in one of her rare silent moods, twisting the engagement ring around and around her finger.

Grayson concentrated on dealing with traffic, but his mind swarmed with so many questions. He wanted an explanation. He wanted the full tale. He wanted to scream and rage at her. He did none of those things. None would be helpful.

Because he still loved her. But did he love her enough to get past her deception? Ah, but he'd been deceiving her as well, setting Tony loose behind her back.

But keeping research from her wasn't the same as keeping four counts of manslaughter secret. It was part of her, an act that shaped her. He *deserved* to know.

"Would you ever have told me?" He finally snapped.

"No."

A firm answer. An honest one.

He gripped the steering wheel tighter, trying to reconcile the woman he knew, the one who'd helped him defuse a bomb, the one who took care of the old lady on the first floor, the one who remained unswervingly loyal to her friends, like David.

He'd done the math when he'd first seen the scars, and she'd let slip when the attack had taken place. She'd been fourteen.

Fourteen. And well able to kill.

She thought this would break them up. That was evident in her silence and her refusal to look him in the eye. It angered him further that she might be right. This was a huge part of who she was.

You don't know me.

He wondered if she knew herself.

"You think I did this?"

"Excuse me?"

"The murders of Brennan and Martin. You figure I'm good for it?"

"Bloody hell, no."

His car phone rang. He answered, turning the Mercedes with one hand. "Grayson."

"Found Sather. In the Village."

"Tony." Grayson almost smiled at the familiar voice. "You're about thirty minutes behind Dorothy Gilbert."

"Damn." Tony whistled. "I hate being second. In any case, do you want background on her?"

"Absolutely."

Grayson put the phone on speaker.

"Sather started in the public defender's offense. She served ten years before joining a big New York City criminal firm."

"Better paycheck," Patricia muttered.

"Ah, but it didn't stick. She quit two years later and co-founded a new firm with her, um, lover, Barbara Taylor. Changed her name to Taylor as well. And good morning to you too, Trisha."

Patricia straightened, pulling herself back to the world. She almost smiled. "Hi, Tony. When did they set up shop in the Village?"

"1975. They made a specialty of representing gay rights cases and pro bono work. Today, they're actively gaining support for the communities hit hardest by AIDS."

"A soft heart," Trisha said. "That's what I told her back then. But she had an iron will too."

Sather would've needed one, to deal with a teenage Patricia, Grayson thought.

"She still does, as far as I can tell," Tony answered. "One last note, she and Taylor have been out of town for the past week, on business in San Francisco. Plane just touched down last night about nine."

"Good work, Tony. Thank you," Grayson said.

"Just stay safe, both of you. And invite me to the wedding, okay?"

Grayson hung up without replying. If Tony had been tempted to tell Patricia about his other research, he'd hid it well.

Patricia slumped in her seat again.

"How did he know?" She seemed to be asking the question to herself.

He almost flinched. "What do you mean?"

She pointed at the ring. Oh, that. He had a guilty conscience. "I shared the good news with Tony yesterday."

"Oh." She seemed to shrink further into his passenger seat. He almost regretted the snap. "Guess you'll have to tell him there won't be a wedding now."

"What makes you say that?" he snapped.

"Oh, c'mon, Grayson. I've killed, and now I'm a murder suspect."

"You are not a real suspect. Dorothy is just ticking off boxes. Newman is out of line."

"It sounds horrifically possible. Disgraced journalist with a violent past starts a string of murders, stages an attack on herself to toss off suspicion and gain sympathy. Story practically writes itself. People have been railroaded for less. Look up George Whitmore."

"Any case against you is bullshit," he ground out. "And you know it."

"I know what I did and didn't do. You sure you do?"

"I didn't until this morning."

She crossed her arms over her chest and stared out her window. "Fair enough."

Nothing that flitted through his mind felt like the right thing to say. But his anger remained, leashed. He'd no idea how long he'd keep it under control.

"Look," she added after a few seconds. "You might want to start looking for a parking space, now that we're close."

It galled him that she was right—everything about her did right now—but finding parking in the streets of the warren known as Greenwich Village or, simply, the Village was truly a bitch, as she said. He circled the area three times. Finally, he parked illegally in a residential space. He tossed an old FBI parking pass on the dashboard.

"Rule breaker." She tapped the window over the sign.

He glared. "You almost seem to be enjoying this."

"I'm just being a wise-ass, as usual. You used to like it."

"Not today."

They got out of the car. She slumped against the passenger door.

"Look, I'm sorry about everything. I forgot to say that earlier."

"I—" Words fought with each other inside his head. "I'm sorry too."

"What are you sorry for?" She narrowed her eyes, scenting something.

"I suspected your stalker's motives traced back to your past attack."

"You said that. You turned out to be right. You get to say, 'I told you so.' Happy now?"

He shoved his hands into his pockets. "Yesterday, I had my firm start an investigation into your past. Full court press. To help save your life."

She stepped away from the car and paced in a tight circle. The silence was more chilling than an outburst.

"Nothing has been uncovered yet," he added. "Tony was pulled from it to find Sather."

"You…" she sputtered. "*You never trusted me.*"

"If you'd trusted *me*, we wouldn't be having this conversation."

"Bullshit." She smacked the hood of his car. "If I'd told you about my record, you never would have looked twice at me, you damn cop."

"That's not true."

"You trying to convince me or yourself?" She stomped around the car. "Fuck. I guess it doesn't matter now."

"It all matters," he said quietly.

"No, it matters we find the killer. That's it." She set off down the street, hands shoved in her jacket pockets. He kept pace as they walked past the Village's run-down brownstones and turned left at the cross-street. Sather's—rather Taylor's—residence was easy to find, given Dorothy was standing outside beside a black-and-white she'd double-parked.

"New ride?" Grayson asked her. She usually drove an unmarked Chevy Nova.

"If someone is stalking this woman, I want them to know the police are here," Dorothy said.

"Tony says she just returned from a trip to San Francisco," Grayson said. "Also, that she's had a name change." He related the rest of the new information to her.

"Good to know. Thanks for sharing." Dorothy glanced between the two of them, pursed her lips, but said nothing.

"If your attorney doesn't have your file, I'm going to court to legally open your closed juvenile record, Trisha," Dorothy said.

"I figured that was a given."

"It was on my list," Dorothy admitted.

Patricia twirled the engagement ring around her finger. "At least *you're* just doing your job." She glared at him.

"I take it someone else should have asked?" Dorothy said, also eyeing him.

Patricia headed up the steps before he could answer. "Let's get this over with."

Dorothy followed, Grayson behind her, his mind struggling to break free, to rage, to demand answers, to howl at anyone, anything, but especially Patricia.

And he wondered: if she'd never told him, if he'd never started a background search on her, if he'd been happy moving forward, would that have been the right choice to remain in ignorance the rest of his days?

CHAPTER FOURTEEN

DOROTHY RANG THE DOORBELL. A tired voice called for identification and Dorothy's terse reply was "NYPD. Homicide."

"Shit," was the answer. "Coming."

They waited in tense silence with Trisha concentrating on the colorful leaded glass embedded in the door. Dizziness threatened again. She casually leaned against the door, fighting the urge to puke. Instead, she concentrated on the anger. Grayson was investigating her behind her back. Not just him. *His whole firm.* He'd opened her life to them all.

So much for trusting her. Of course, she had been concealing things too. *I had a right to my secrets. He should have fucking asked.*

The door opened and they were ushered in.

Sather hadn't changed much. Oh, her hair had gone gray, and she'd grown it to waist-length (she and Kimba Sue should definitely compare notes), but the sharp eyes, the high cheekbones, and the black, square-rimmed glasses remained the same. She wore some sort of hippie-style long flowing dress and fluffy pink slippers.

Whimsy. Humor. No wonder Trisha, as a cynical teenager, had been hostile to her.

Dorothy introduced herself, Grayson, and finally, Trisha. As Sather—no, Taylor—shook her hand, recognition dawned in the lawyer's eyes.

The attorney smiled and it changed her face from slightly disinterested to warm. "Trisha," was all she said.

"Surprised you remember me."

"Some people are hard to forget." The attorney waved them inside. "I'm assuming this is not about one of my cases involving gay activists? We didn't lose another one to violence, did we?"

"No, it's about a past case," Dorothy said.

Taylor made eye contact with Trisha. "All right. Follow me to my home office."

She led them down a narrow hallway crammed with coats, shoes, and books and turned into an irregular-sized room at the back of the brownstone. The bay windows overlooked an alley, and slats of sunshine striped the comfy reading chair underneath them. Beat-up metal file cabinets occupied the other side of the room. A cozy couch with two chairs dominated the center, with a glass coffee table in the middle.

Workable but not fussy. That, too, fit what little Trisha remembered about her.

"Come, sit down, and tell me what you all want at this early hour." A gray cat jumped onto Taylor's lap as she chose what must be her favorite chair and settled in.

Trisha sat on the couch, as did Dorothy. Grayson remained standing, staring out the window, wrapped up in that isolation he'd donned since she'd told him the full truth.

Fuck his formal investigation.

Dorothy, all business, took out her notebook and started with the two murders. Taylor's face paled. She stroked the gray cat, who responded with a purr that echoed through the room. It almost made Trisha want a cat.

She needed to calm down. She should view this as a story, something to report objectively. Newman's theory about her as the killer was melodramatic but workable. Her as the main suspect would be a good story. Easy enough to fake stalking letters mailed to herself. Easy enough to slice her finger and make up a story. And the murder victims were two people she should hate, while the defense attorney who helped her was unharmed.

A decent frame, if completely circumstantial. A trial would wreck her life. She'd never work again even if found innocent and no guarantee she would be. The NYPD still was good at frames, despite the Knapp Commission.

Was someone setting her up? That didn't seem Newman's style, but you could never tell with some cops. She'd pissed off more than Newman in her time. But had she angered someone enough to resort to murder?

Trisha tuned back into the conversation just as Dorothy explained the letters to Taylor. Trisha held up her bandaged finger after Dorothy finished, though that injury felt like ages ago now.

"So, they've gone after me, the judge, and the prosecutor. That just leaves you from the case as a target," Trisha said.

Trisha watched Dorothy as she said that. No reaction. Quite a poker face.

Taylor, though, whistled through her teeth. "This is terrifying. But I haven't received any letters or, at least, that I'm aware of, though now I will be on full alert. They could be waiting for me at my office. Mail has piled up there. What should I do?"

"Help us catch the murderer," Dorothy said. "First, put aside any letters at your office that don't have a return address, or you don't recognize. There may not be any as our killer might have been thrown off by your name change and is yet unaware of how to locate you."

The cat cuddled closer. The attorney scratched its ears. Hugged it. "Yes, of course, I can do all that."

"Second, our working theory is a friend or relative of one of the victims of Trisha's juvenile case is out for revenge. I need any and all files you have."

One of your working theories, Trisha thought. Could Newman be a relative? That would be a motive. But Newman had met her years ago. Why wait so long to go after her?

"All juvenile cases are confidential," Taylor snapped so quickly that it had to be a reflex.

Trisha jerked her head at Dorothy. "You can speak freely in front of the Lieutenant and Grayson. I waive all attorney-client privilege."

That won her Taylor's full attention. The attorney leaned forward. Trisha closed her hand around the cross and fought the urge to run.

"Are you certain, Trisha? Once your case details are in a police report, it all may become public, and that will have consequences. And I do not like confidential case details being public. They could easily be used against you, even later. By all accounts, you've created a fine life for yourself. You've moved past this"

"'The past is never dead. It's not even past,'" Trisha answered.

"Faulkner?" Grayson chimed in.

"Faulkner," she confirmed. "Don't sound so surprised. Didn't you discover I have a minor in English lit in your '*research*?'"

Grayson had the grace to look away.

Taylor cleared her throat. "Be that as it may, the present is your journalism career, Trisha, especially the saving of the museum two months ago. And though you're not with the *Herald* anymore, I read the article about the history of the steps in the Bronx. You're a talented writer with insight. You have a future. Your case being public means any enemy has ammunition."

"Just how long have you been following my career, counselor?"

Taylor smiled. "I like to know how my clients are doing, even if they don't want to keep in touch. I was thrilled to spot your byline. What happened to your young man, the one who looked out for you so carefully?"

"He died. Sickness."

"I'm so sorry, honey."

Trisha grunted. Her face flushed. She'd never known what to do with this woman's concern. "I still waive privilege. We have to stop a killer."

"All right, though it's against my advice as your attorney. I've learned not to trust the NYPD. No offense, Lieutenant."

"None taken," Dorothy said.

Taylor rose, setting the cat aside. It meowed in protest. "Easy, Straggler, we'll get you breakfast soon."

She opened a file cabinet drawer marked Jane Doe and pulled out a thick folder. Trisha rose and began to pace. Grayson stared at the thick file folder like a cat burglar after a diamond.

Taylor set the file down in front of Dorothy with a thud. "This is my personal file, with my handwritten notes in the margins. You've my permission to read it and take notes, but it doesn't leave this house."

"Can we make copies?" Grayson asked.

So, the Sphinx speaks, Trisha thought.

"No copies. I'm not at all sure *you* should even read it. You're not the police," Taylor said. "Indeed, Mr. Grayson, why are you here? What's your role in this?"

Trisha sucked in a breath and twisted the engagement ring around her finger.

"I'm responsible for Patricia's safety," Grayson replied after a pause.

Unexpectedly, the attorney laughed. "Well, that probably keeps you busy."

"As you say." Grayson looked Trisha's way again. She met his gaze.

She knew this was the quiet before the thunderstorm. She'd seen Grayson angry once. A quiet, chilling rage. That was *fine*. Her rage was white-hot enough for both of them.

The cat meowed. "I'll be back in a bit, after I feed my impatient cat and have some breakfast," Taylor said. "Does anyone want coffee?"

"No." Trisha thought she'd probably puke up anything right now, especially since Mrs. D.'s casserole sat like a lump in her stomach. Dorothy and Grayson also politely declined the offer. As soon as Taylor left, Dorothy and Grayson both put hands on the file.

"Now, now, don't fight over a little thing like my criminal record," Trisha drawled.

Dorothy swept Grayson's fingers off the file. "I need the names of the four men killed post-haste, to call them in and set Bricker and Newman to work on their backgrounds. Family, friends, associates."

"Newman is Bricker's mentor?" Trisha asked.

"Yes," Dorothy answered.

"Figures. You sure you want them on my case?" No wonder she'd backed up Newman yesterday.

"I'd need a better reason than annoyance with you to pull them off," Dorothy said.

While she flipped through the file, Grayson and Trisha sat in uneasy silence opposite each other, with Trisha this time in the comfy chair. Dorothy finally finished scribbling in her notebook and pulled out a black-and-white photo from the file. She sucked a breath in through her teeth and displayed the photo to Trisha. "This is what they did?"

Trisha peered at her long-ago self. The scars had looked so much uglier back then. "Want to see the real-life scars? I can show you." She tugged at her shirt.

"Not right now." Dorothy rubbed the bridge of her nose. "Dammit. This doesn't help your case, Trisha."

"I get that." Trisha leaned forward, elbows on her knees. "When you've been convicted of killing someone, it ups the odds you do it again. But I didn't kill Brennan and Martin."

Dorothy tapped the photo. "I'm talking about something else. This murderer is carving your pattern of scars into the current victims."

"*WHAT?*" Trisha covered her stomach with her hands.

"The cuts on the current victims match your own scars. Same pattern," Dorothy said in her cop voice.

The world tilted. Trisha sucked in a breath. "I don't…how is that even fucking possible? They're just a random pattern. They weren't trying to create any patterns, they…" An image of the blade descending filled her vision. Trisha shook it off. "They only wanted to hurt me."

"And someone wanted to reenact your attack on these two men," Grayson said in a quiet voice. "Out of some twisted vengeance."

"Fuck." Trisha stood. She pushed her palms into her eyes, failing to wipe away the memories. "Shit, shit, shit. How could they know about my scars?"

"They've seen them, obviously." Dorothy rubbed the bridge of her nose again.

"Oh." Trisha let that sink in. "And who's more familiar with the scars than me, right? So I just moved up your suspect list, is that it?"

"You're not the killer," Grayson interjected, his words laced with the trace of the English accent that peaked through when he chose his words carefully, the accent that'd won him the nickname from Dorothy.

"I will need to bring you in for questioning." Dorothy slipped the photo in her overly large purse, despite the fact that Taylor had said to take nothing. "You should have told me about the scars when we interviewed you initially, Trisha. This looks bad."

"I didn't know you were investigating a murder. Christ, Lieutenant, I asked you directly twice why you were so interested in my stalker."

"And you didn't think the commonality of the razor blade injuries was worth mentioning?" Dorothy asked.

"Don't answer that." Grayson cut in front of Trisha. "Perhaps we should ask Ms. Taylor if she has an opening for a new client."

"If that's what Trisha wants," Dorothy said.

"What I want is to catch this damned killer," Trisha snapped. "And, if I did this, why would I lead you to evidence that incriminates me? Why would I set this all up?"

"A good question," Dorothy responded. "Guilt?"

Trisha just laughed. Grayson scowled, angry either at her failing to take this seriously or at Dorothy or the whole situation. Probably all of it.

"Dorothy, this theory stretches credulity," Grayson said. "You're smarter than that."

"As an investigator, I need to pursue all avenues until I can eliminate them."

"Take a bloody step back and you'll see it's far more likely someone is out for revenge against Patricia. You know the why now, which will lead us all to the who. Pursue *that* lead."

"Enough, Edmund. You've made your point. Trisha, you're within your rights to have an attorney present when you come to the precinct for questioning." Dorothy rose, patting her purse. "I'm calling the names in from the radio in my car. Don't go anywhere."

Trisha rose to pace again. "Dorothy's just doing her job," she said to Grayson. Dorothy, at least, wouldn't railroad her. But maybe it wouldn't be Dorothy's call, even if she outranked Newman.

"It's an idiotic theory," Grayson said. "Do you have an alibi? That would make this go away faster."

Oh, so now he was on her side?

"I don't know, Grayson, you're the one investigating my life. Didn't Tony or someone come up with a timeline of where I was over Thanksgiving weekend yet? I'm sure there's an alibi in there, right?"

He stuffed his hands into his pockets. "You're angry with *me* and not Dorothy?"

"You went behind my back. She's doing her job."

"You could have trusted me with your past, then I wouldn't be forced to dig into it."

"Oh, and the fact I murdered four people doesn't affect your opinion of me in the least?"

"Manslaughter, not murder." A pause. "You want an answer. I don't have one." He fiddled with his cufflinks and his words were clipped. "I'm not like you. I don't always know how I feel about something right away."

"Yeah, well, I know *I'm* pissed, all right?" Trisha twisted the ring around her finger. "Who knows, maybe I am a split personality, like there's a good me, but also a bad me, sabotaging my life. Maybe I'm like a psychotic killer in one of Stephen King's stories."

"You're lashing out because you're angry with me. But don't joke about that."

"Fine. Then answer a question: do you regret asking me to marry you?"

He opened the file without looking at her. "I haven't requested the ring back, have I?"

Ouch.

She slumped in the chair, wishing she could go anywhere but here. Hell, Nicky had never condemned her for what happened. Nicky would have killed her rapists himself if she hadn't. He'd argued against confessing. But when she'd been insistent about paying for what she'd done, he'd dragged her to the public defender's office, not the cops. No wonder her defense attorney remembered Nicky. At least someone still did.

She closed her eyes. Bottom line: she and Grayson lacked the trust she and Nicky had in each other. She should give Grayson's ring back right this second. But she could not make that gesture.

Only the flipping of paper broke the silence as Grayson read the file. His breathing remained steady and even.

A deep sigh, finally.

"Patricia, do you know why these men targeted you?" he asked.

"My captors didn't say, and I didn't ask. I was too busy surviving," she snapped.

"Patricia." Soft, cajoling. "Your attorney's notes seem to indicate these men had records, yet there's nothing criminal at the level of what they did to you. There had to be a reason."

She opened her eyes and pushed aside the memory of their laughter during the assault. "Look, I've tried *not* to remember. Hell, I didn't even remember my attorney's name and I sure didn't remember who the judge and prosecutor were. What I could remember at the time is in that damned file." She wondered if Dorothy would believe that.

He finally looked at her, not through her, as he had all morning. "I'm sorry you have to relive this."

"I told you before, I don't need saving, Grayson. I never did. I can face this. I *did* face it. I did my time. It should be done, for *you* as well as me."

"'The past is never dead. It's not even past.'"

Ouch. "I guess not, especially to you. 'My yesterdays walk with me. They keep step, they are gray faces that peer over my shoulder.'"

"Is that Faulkner again?" he asked.

"Nah, William Golding. The guy who wrote *Lord of the Flies*." She shook her head, started pacing again. "I'm never going to escape all this."

"I'm sorry," he said in a quiet voice. He ran a hand through his mussed hair. "I'm surprised your attorney didn't have your sentence reduced or waived to time served because of extenuating circumstances."

"I'd hoped to do that, but the district attorney initially insisted on trying my client as an adult." Taylor swept in and rejoined the conversation. "He jumped on the fact she had needle marks in her arm to label her an unreliable junkie, rather than someone forcibly drugged. Claimed she was lying about what happened. I did get the case shifted to juvenile court, and the charge reduced to manslaughter, but it wasn't easy, especially with an uncooperative client." She shook her head. "I told you then, and I will tell you now, you didn't need to be punished, Trisha."

"Someone obviously disagrees with you," Trisha pointed out, holding up the bandaged finger. "But maybe you were right. If there had been no case, there would be no trail for this killer to follow, and two people would still be alive." And she wouldn't be a suspect in two more murders.

"As a journalist, you should know the truth matters," Grayson said.

"That depends on whose truth you're talking about," Trisha replied.

She'd missed over three years with Nicky stuck in juvie, though he'd visited regularly. On the other hand, being inside had allowed her to wrestle with her guilt.

"You're not responsible for the actions of this murderer," Grayson said. "If not focused on you, he would have found other outlets for his rage."

"An eye for an eye. Blood for blood. Righteous vengeance. The killer's letters are full of the need for me to pay." Trisha stared out the window, almost in imitation of Grayson's pose. "I set this in motion. You know, I thought I regretted killing them." She looked at Grayson as she said it. "I sinned. I should be punished. But, in the end, I felt guilty about not feeling guilty."

Grayson's face never changed expression.

She clenched her hands into fists. "And now someone figures I should get what I deserve. Two people are dead, and I've brought this to your door, Ms. Taylor."

"I think it's perfectly natural to be glad those who tortured you are dead," she said. "If you liked hurting people, Trisha, you wouldn't have become who you are today."

Trisha flushed. "And who am I?"

"An award-winning reporter who gives voice to the voiceless," Taylor said.

"The job feeds me." Trisha waved away the compliment. "The other stuff is just a result of what I need."

Grayson stood. "Is that what you believe?"

"I've never lied to myself about why I do what I do."

He shook his head.

Dorothy returned and surveyed them. "All right, therapy hour is over, people. I need to get into the precinct, but I also need to talk to you, Trisha. Ride with me."

"Sure." Cool, dispassionate Dorothy working a case was preferable to more of Grayson. He needed space. *She* needed space.

"Do you want an attorney?" Taylor asked. "I seem to be available this morning."

"No, it'll just delay things," Trisha said. "Sooner they move past me as the killer, sooner they can move on to other leads."

"Or the sooner they decide to make you the scapegoat so they can move forward." Taylor scowled. "She's trusting you, Lieutenant."

Dorothy grunted.

"Thanks, counselor. If it looks bad, I'll clam up and call for you." Trisha knew she should never talk without a lawyer. But, dammit, she was so tired of being in this room. "Let's go," she said to Dorothy.

"I'll meet you at the precinct," Grayson said.

Dorothy set a hand on the small of Trisha's back, as if not trusting her to come willingly. "Once we're done, you can take her with you."

"If he wants," Trisha mock-saluted Grayson. "Lemme know what you find in my past. Maybe I'm a long-lost Kennedy or something. Wouldn't that be fun?"

CHAPTER FIFTEEN

GRAYSON WAITED until they both left to turn to the attorney. The less he focused on the revelations about Trisha, the more he could think logically.

"Ma'am, Lt. Gilbert is providing a car outside to watch your home but, with your permission, I'll assign a security detail to you."

"I won't say 'no,' especially since I don't trust the NYPD to protect me. I called my office to look over the mail that's waiting for me, in case I have received these letters. Sadly, they're used to looking it over for possible threats." Taylor tilted her head. "You were a Fed, weren't you?"

"What makes you say that?"

"You're the type, though if you're with Trisha Connell, well, that makes you more interesting than the usual Fed. I take it from the tension in the room today that you just found out your girlfriend's past?"

"The exact details, yes." He nodded, curt, and looked at his watch. "If I can use your phone, I'll call my people over here so they can introduce themselves and explain the procedures that will keep you safe."

She actually tsk-tsked him. "You can use the phone in a moment. Let's talk."

"Let's not."

She smiled. "You clearly have questions. We'll have coffee and I will answer the best I can." She knelt down and picked up the cat. "You know you want to."

He focused on her colorful scarf and did not reply.

"I'll take your silence as assent. I'll get the coffee."

Taylor returned shortly, before he could again pick up the file sitting so enticingly on the coffee table. Now that she'd dressed and composed herself, he could see the steel of the lawyer underneath the Mother Earth persona.

"Ask away since my client has waived all privileges," she said.

"My first priority is to keep her safe."

"There's safe physically, and there's safe emotionally." She reached down and dropped a treat for the cat, clearly waiting for Grayson to continue.

"If she's angry at me for wanting to protect her, I cannot help that."

"Oh, she's angry at you for more than that."

He loosened his tie. "As an investigator, my first question in a case is usually why. In Patricia's…situation…the question is why she was a particular target those years ago. The answers may help solve the recent murders."

"Patricia's situation being that she was raped, tortured, drugged, and reacted out of rage. She was not in a sane state of mind when she did what she did."

"Yes." His hands clenched at the thought of what she'd suffered. She'd only been fourteen. *I don't need pity*. That's what she'd said when he'd first seen the scars.

He finally tapped the file. "This indicates the four men belonged to a gang. They'd dealt drugs at a minor level, they'd done some enforcement work. But nothing with prostitution or sex crimes. Violent men off the leash, yes, but even at fourteen, I can't imagine Trisha being an easy target. These types prey after the most vulnerable. She was not, especially since she was with her Nicky most of the time."

"True." Taylor narrowed her eyes. "Even by the time she came to me, sullen and half crazed, vulnerable wasn't a word I'd use for her."

"By her own account, they followed her specifically from a bus station, one frequented by students. She'd wanted to blend in with them as a…"

"As part of a crowd to shoplift food," Taylor supplied.

"Just so." The system failed Patricia and Nicky. Left them on their own. "So out of all these girls, why pick her?"

"She'd be least likely to be missed?"

"If they followed her, they had to know Nicky was waiting at the street corner. He, by all accounts, was a formidable person." He shook his head. "My experience tells me this was planned, and she was a specific target."

"I see." Taylor sipped the coffee. "The case is nearly fourteen years old, Mr. Grayson. What do you expect the reasons to tell you at this point?"

"The current murderer wants to punish her. It's personal. So was Patricia's attack. It's all tied together." He caught her gaze. "I was a good investigator, counselor. I know my job. Their motivation mattered."

She looked at him over the top of her mug. "I imagine Lt. Gilbert may be thinking the same. Do you believe she views Trisha as a suspect in these recent killings?"

"I believe she's doing her job but, on her own, she'd have put Patricia at the bottom of her list. But her partner, Newman, and his protégé, Bricker, may be another matter. There are departmental forces that she's navigating."

"Police politics are dirty politics. Trisha *will* need a lawyer."

"Yes, you. I can take care of your fees."

Taylor adjusted her glasses. "All right, consider this a first consultation, conditional on her approval."

"Is there anything you remember from what Patricia said to you back then? Even fragments of a conversation would be helpful," he asked.

She set her coffee mug, with the Act Up! logo prominently displayed, next to the file, and opened it, flipping through past the mug shut and copies of the police files to some handwritten notes.

"I tried to read those but couldn't," he said.

"I'm the only one who can make out my scribbles." She flipped another page. "Here. 'Client says her captors claimed they had to keep her alive. Said the heroin was to keep her sedated until the handover.'" She took off her glasses. "At the time, I took that to mean they wanted to traffic her."

"But it could mean they were acting on someone's orders."

"But why? Who would go to this trouble for a fourteen-year-old orphan street kid?" Taylor tapped the file with her glasses. "It makes no sense."

"Not yet, no." Grayson picked up another note. "This is the address where it took place?"

"Yes. Her Nicky had been scouring Hell's Kitchen looking for her. Found her wandering in the alley nearby. But if you're thinking it will hold clues even after all this time, that building is gone now, destroyed in the construction of the new Javits Center."

"I see." He frowned. "That's it?"

"That's it." Taylor closed the file. "And might I recommend, Mr. Grayson, that when you ask your girlfriend these questions, you show a little more tact."

"Do you think me so cruel?"

"I think you're a Fed. Thus, you like control, and you hate when things are out of your control." She shook her head. "I watched her watch you. What you think matters to her, though God knows why. But no life can be controlled." She rose, walking to her window. "All we can do is hang onto each other." She turned to him. "That's what I've learned, anyway."

"I appreciate the advice." He readjusted his tie. "I'll call Ginny Lawrence in my office and put you on the phone with her. She'll make all the security arrangements with you."

"That's appreciated."

"And please send the bill for this consultation to me," he said.

"It's conditional. She'll have to agree."

"She will." He offered her his hand and they shook on it.

CHAPTER SIXTEEN

"CAN we run by my place before the precinct, Lieutenant? Not sure where I'm sleeping tonight, and I need to pack a bag."

Trisha braced herself for the answer, expecting a lecture or a refusal.

"Sure. If nothing else, you can have the couch in my office at the precinct."

Trisha winced. "Surrounded by cops who want to charge me in two homicides? Yikes."

Dorothy shrugged. "Then you better make up with Edmund."

"Not up to me."

"Maybe not," she conceded. "So, we'll move on. Let's assume for now you're not the killer. That means anyone who has seen the scars closely enough to duplicate them is also on my suspect list. Anyone ever take a photo during one of those wham-bam-thank-you-ma'am sessions you mentioned a few days ago?"

"Dammit, Lieutenant, I'd have given you that information in that interview if you'd told me about Brennan's injuries."

"That does not answer my question."

"Fine." Trisha frowned, thinking of the intruder. "Could someone have planted a camera at my place somehow?"

"Good question but I'm not sure a hidden camera would provide enough resolution to see the scars clearly. Edmund's partner Tony would know for certain. Seems like he should go over your place ASAP. Under police supervision." A pause. "Back to someone who might memorize the scars, then?"

Trisha snorted. "Nicky's dead and Grayson's not a suspect. Those are my repeat customers." She pursed her lips. "But there are existing photos in my sealed juvenile file."

"Occurred to me. Looking into it, though access to sealed juvenile files is tricky." A pause. "There's one faintly horrible possibility that I'm considering, assuming you are not guilty."

"Spill."

Dorothy slammed on the brakes as someone cut in front of her. She flicked on the lights and the police siren cut the air. Cars began pulling to the side. Not all, but enough.

"Police files," Dorothy finally said. "A detective must have been assigned to the case of those four homicides. He'd have notes. Your name and photos of your injuries might be in there."

"Not my name. I didn't go by 'Connell' back then. Legally, it was 'Smith.' I didn't change it until I was eighteen."

"That's useful information," Dorothy said. "All right, I hoped Taylor's files would include mention of a detective or someone from the NYPD assigned to the case, but the only names listed in her file were the prosecutors. You remember any cops who interviewed you back then?"

"Shit. I never thought of that. Someone with the case file of the murders. That seems horribly possible." Trisha closed her eyes, trying to remember, but nothing. "All I remember is suits, not cops. Investigators from the D.A.'s office. Even Taylor wore a suit back then, though she had a tie-dye scarf."

"Think harder."

"There's a cop bar in the Kitchen. I go by sometimes for background on Midtown cops and to hear about the old days." She frowned. "Or I did. It's been a while. We could stop there and ask around."

"After your interview."

Trisha threw up her hands. "Sure. After you grill me and waste time."

She watched the city zip by as Dorothy sped up. Christmas decorations were proudly displayed in storefronts and residential buildings as they zoomed up Midtown. They passed the tree at Rockefeller Center, majestically holding court to a mass of tourists.

"Did you approach the cops working Hell's Kitchen right now?" Trisha asked after some silence.

"Of course I did," Dorothy snapped. "I reached out to the 10th precinct when I went out to the car earlier."

"What happened?"

"They blew me off."

"Cops. You never know what you're gonna get."

The lieutenant should know. She'd gotten enough pushback over the years from the old guard who didn't like women or Blacks or both. This fucking city.

The falling snow clung to the sidewalks, keeping its white color at the edges. New York City in December was colder, noisier, more crowded, and yet somehow more peaceful than other times of the year. The energy of the city, deadened during the summer heat and refined during the fall, had been civilized by the onset of winter.

For some.

"Between the lines, you're saying maybe a cop did these new killings," Trisha said.

"It's not an avenue I want to pursue, any more than you as a suspect, but I have to look." Dorothy shut off her lights. "If this detective who had your case exists, and if he kept files in violation of procedure, then, yes, it could be him or a different cop who's doing the same background research we're about to do."

Fuck, if this was a cop, things were about to get uglier.

"Or it could be a former cop or a trained investigator who knows what steps to take," Dorothy added. "That fits a helluva lot of people in your circle, Trisha, from reporters to lawyers to cops. That includes people at Edmund's firm too."

"Shit. We're supposed to be narrowing down the suspect list." Fuck, Grayson would probably even want to investigate poor Kimba Sue.

"We are. It'll just take time."

"Just get me off the suspect list, fast."

"It'd help if you had an alibi."

Dorothy pulled an illegal left turn around 50th Street and headed downtown through the 40s.

"What time on Thanksgiving did the murder happen?" Trisha asked.

"I've got an eight-hour possibility in the middle of the day. Where were you?"

"I hit the soup kitchen about…nine a.m.?" Trisha frowned. "Stayed through lunch. Is a priest a good enough alibi?"

"Probably," Dorothy said. "It helps. What about the rest of the day?"

"Went out. CBGBs plus another place near them. Then Max Hudson's. People would have seen me. They won't talk to cops there, though."

"And they're hardly reliable witnesses. Did you stop at a convenience store? Bank teller machine?"

"I'm thinking!" Trisha said.

"Think harder."

"I probably don't have to," she said. "Grayson's investigating me. They've probably already developed a timeline on my day. Put his people to use." Bitterness crept in.

"And if one of *them* is setting you up?"

"Shit, and I thought I was paranoid."

The car started to skid. Dorothy turned into it, and they regained traction.

"It's going to be a long day," Dorothy said.

"It's already been a long day." What was it, forty-eight hours since she and Grayson had gotten engaged, and then everything had fallen apart? She was a suspect, her friends all suspects, her secrets exposed, and now old man Winter was sending a blizzard.

Trisha drew out the cross and closed her hand around it.

"Appealing to a higher power?" Dorothy asked.

"More Father Mike than God."

Cigarettes. She needed that emergency pack of cigarettes in her apartment. Right now.

Dorothy found a spot across the street from Trisha's building. Trisha followed Dorothy's lead and got out of the car. She noticed Mrs. D.'s window cracked with a light on against the gloom of the storm, though it was only late afternoon. "Want to talk to Mrs. D. with me? You'll love her."

"Does she have relevant information?"

"I didn't think it was relevant at the time but can't hurt to check." Trisha looked to the window again. At least the old lady wouldn't be smoked out anymore by her faulty fan.

A bright light flashed inside the apartment and, a second later, the window exploded.

CHAPTER SEVENTEEN

GLASS SHATTERED VIOLENTLY OUTWARD. The shards hit the sidewalk, sounding like an obscene version of Christmas chimes. A gust of heat blew out. Trisha covered her head. When she looked up again, flames were shooting out of Mrs. D.'s first-floor window.

Sound came roaring back to Trisha's ears.

"Police priority, emergency," Dorothy spoke into the police radio, adding some codes. "I have an explosion and fire at…."

Miraculously, Trisha's feet obeyed her. She ran toward the fire. Dorothy grabbed her arm.

"Stay here on the street. Tell the fire captain what happened." Dorothy shoved her radio in her pocket and rushed toward the inferno.

Trisha ignored the instructions and caught up to her. That was Mrs. D. up there! No way would she stay back. She and Dorothy hit the steps of the front stoop together. Smoke alarms blared, pushing aside all other sound. They paused in the first-floor hallway. Someone stumbled out of the apartment at the far end of the hallway, gesturing wildly.

"Help! My father!"

Dorothy rushed to them. Trisha ran in the opposite direction, to Mrs. D.'s door. She slipped and bashed her knee, cursed, but didn't slow. Smoke billowed into through the hallway. Trisha coughed as she inhaled. Her eyes watered. She put her shoulder to Mrs. D.'s door and tried to open it.

Nothing.

Trisha pounded on the door. No answer. Fuck, fuck. But if the door was as rickety as hers, there was a chance. She stepped back and kicked just below the doorjamb. The reverb spiked pain up past her knee. But wood splintered. She kicked again. And again. On the fourth kick, she screamed. The wood gave way. The door flew open.

Trisha stood in the middle of a dense, choking fog. Sweat flowed down from her forehead. The heat dissipated the last chill of outdoors.

Smoke alarms screamed incessantly

"Mrs. D.!"

Trisha unbuttoned her coat and tossed it over her head and around her nose and mouth for protection. She felt along the living room wall. Her fingers flicked past something and it fell. A crash. Glass splintered on the floor.

She'd knocked part of the Kennedy shrine over. Now she could orient herself. She took a deep breath from inside the recesses of her coat and yelled. "MRS. D!"

"Here!" The faint voice came from just ahead, but flames covered the ceiling, and smoke veiled the apartment.

"CALL OUT!" Trisha yelled.

"Here," came a fainter reply.

Trisha stumbled toward Mrs. D.'s voice. The heat penetrated her makeshift headgear. She swallowed the last of the moisture in her mouth.

A hand on her ankle. She flinched and knelt. Mrs. D.'s face formed a solid shape below. She'd been lying on the floor.

"Trisha." Mrs. D. coughed. Trisha put an arm around her waist. Mrs. D. coughed again.

She pulled Mrs. D. to her feet. "Hold on!"

Mrs. D. wrapped her arms around Trisha's chest and buried her head against the cotton T-shirt.

Trisha threw her coat over Mrs. D.'s shoulders. "Hide your face."

Trisha looked for the way she had come, but all was gray. Flames were working their way across the floor. They had to walk back through hell to safety.

Mrs. D. tightened against her and they stumbled as one toward the wall. Trisha felt it, knocked something else from the shrine, but at least she knew she'd gone in the right direction.

The heat became a living being, swirling around Trisha, burying itself into her jeans, her shirt, and under her skin. The leather of her sneakers seemed to melt around her feet.

There seemed to be an audible pop in her ears, a quick surge of pain in her lungs, and then the flames were past. She slammed into something solid. What?

"The wall." Mrs. D. croaked. "Door to the right."

Trisha shuffled them right and felt blindly for the opening. She encountered empty space and, off balance, fell, taking Mrs. D. with her to the floor. But air was clearer near the floor. Trisha grabbed a relatively clean breath.

Trisha tugged at Mrs. D., but the old lady didn't move, even when shaken. *Shit.*

Trisha swallowed. Her eyes stung. Tears formed but were instantly evaporated by the heat. A figurative cobra coiled around her, smothering her. Knowing it was smoke inhalation helped not at all. They had to get out of here. She grabbed Mrs. D. at the waist and the shoulder and lifted her in a fireman's carry.

The extra weight overbalanced her, driving Trisha momentarily to her knees, but she forced herself upright again.

One step and she nearly fell again. She took one hand off Mrs. D. and felt along the hallway wall, hoping she'd gone in the right direction. She closed her eyes and concentrated on each step. Her shoulders ached with the effort. Sweat drenched her neck, her vision blurred. Nothing mattered anymore but the next step, the next movement. Her hand was slick with sweat.

One…two…three…four…yes, five! Her brain detached from her body. She had a vivid image of the Little Engine That Could moving up the hill, going, "I think I can, I think I can."

Ten…fifteen…twenty… twenty-five…she stumbled and almost toppled over the railing that signaled the steps of the entranceway to the building.

Mrs. D. was completely limp. Trisha tried not to think about that. She returned to counting, this time the ten steps to the glass-front security door.

Thirty… thirty-two…she hit the landing, overbalanced, and landed on one knee again. Her eyes would have streamed tears if they had any moisture. Spots appeared in front of her, and the Little Engine disappeared.

She teetered and fell. Mrs. D. slid from her back. The old woman hit the floor with a muffled thump. Trisha curled her hands under Mrs. D.'s shirt collar and pulled. Nothing happened.

Oh, God, they weren't going to make it. She screamed, but she wasn't sure if any sound came out.

Hands grabbed her. Someone lifted her up so abruptly that she felt sick to her stomach. She lost hold of Mrs. D.

"No!"

"We've got her. We've got all of you." The firefighter's mask muted his voice, turned him into a monstrous form. He shoved a mask over her face.

Air. Oh, God, glorious clean air.

The entrance into the outside world came as a sudden and unpleasant shock. Snowflakes swirled around her while emergency lights cut through the storm's gloom.

The firefighter forced her to sit on the bumper of an ambulance. One of the waiting EMTs exchanged the firefighter's oxygen for a medical mask. She gulped in the air greedily once more. The world began to reappear. At first, the red and blue lights of the emergency vehicles were all she could see through the swirl of white from the growing snowstorm.

Indistinct shapes formed into fire trucks and ambulances. Firefighters were running into the building with hoses. A crowd gathered behind a police line. Around it all came the snow, whipped sideways by the wind.

She heard someone call the time on the police radio.

Only five minutes had passed.

CHAPTER EIGHTEEN

TRISHA SHIVERED. Sensation returned. She sat, unmoving, the mask on her face, breathing in, breathing out. People shifted around her, but their actions made no sense. Someone tossed a blanket over her shoulders.

Dorothy pulled the blanket tight. "I'm sorry. I meant to be right behind you, but I had to help someone in a wheelchair out. Then the firefighters wouldn't let me go back."

Grime streaked Dorothy's face. Her eyes were bloodshot, and her dark hair hung limply from her head. Trisha wondered if she looked that bad or worse. She hugged the blanket to herself and put down the oxygen mask.

"S'okay." Her voice was clear, surprising her. "How's Mrs. D.?"

"In transit. No word yet."

"Shit, shit, they were supposed to come after me! *Me!*" Trisha tossed off the blanket, took a step toward the building, and collapsed to her knees. The bruises from her earlier efforts ached, but it was nothing compared to the pain in the rest of her body. She couldn't see again, her ears were roaring, and her stomach seemed tied up in so many knots that it became one solid lump. She doubled over and threw up on the street. The agony in her stomach worsened.

Hands tried to pull her upright. She fought them. "Leave me alone!"

"You need to go to the hospital for smoke inhalation." Dorothy moved into her vision again. She reached her hand out for comfort.

Trisha stood unsteadily on her feet. "I'm goddamned fine. I'm not the one who's…." she choked on the words.

"You're the one who needs to stay still for just a few minutes." Dorothy pushed Trisha down onto the bumper of a police car again. Snowflakes danced around them.

"I need to report to the fire chief. You have to stay here until I get back because then we have work to do."

"Still going to interrogate the suspect, Lieutenant?" Trisha growled.

"Still going to get every piece of information I can from that stubborn head of yours." Dorothy said in a low voice. "Don't you want to nail the bastard?"

Trisha closed her eyes. She wanted to say that she was done. She'd tried and failed. Things got worse, with her life, with Grayson, with people around her. But she'd be damned if she'd go down without taking someone with her.

"Nail the bastard," she whispered.

"Good. Stay right here. I'll be back as quickly as I can." Dorothy looked around. "You! Check her vitals," she called to a paramedic.

The man stepped forward. Dorothy patted Trisha's shoulder. "Look, your Mrs. D. was breathing when the ambulance left. Have faith."

No faith. Only exhaustion and rage. Trisha twisted the engagement ring around and around her finger as the paramedic checked her pulse and blood pressure.

"You could use more oxygen, I bet," he said. "You need transport."

"In a minute." She supposed she couldn't catch the bastard if she passed out or ended up in the hospital. But still, she couldn't move, hypnotized by how the ring's sapphires reflected the emergency lights of the cars and fire trucks.

"Hear you ran into the building," the paramedic said.

Funny, his hair was the same color red as hers, though his face was hazy through her smoke-blurred eyes.

"Took guts. You did good."

"No." She shook her head and thought of Mrs. D.'s kids and grandchildren, having the police show up at their door, or getting that call to come to the hospital. "There's no good here."

"Hey, you!" someone yelled.

The paramedic flinched. "Oops. Gotta go. Nice ring, by the way."

Trisha blinked and stood as the paramedic rushed around the edge of a fire truck. Damn, that phrase sounded familiar.

Nice cross, by the way.

Her intruder!

She stood, unsteady, and grabbed the ambulance for balance. Her breath came in sharp jabs, painful in and out, as the cold, wet air was sucked into her lungs. She wanted to yell, but her throat only croaked out a word. A hand slipped around her shoulder from behind. "Got you."

A jab into her neck. Trisha grabbed for it. Her ring slid off and bounced away on the street. Her knees gave out, and darkness descended.

———

Grayson felt as if his bones were shaking out of his skin. Everything at the scene outside Patricia's apartment blurred together: the sirens, the spraying of the hoses, the yelling of emergency personnel, all framed by the snow coming down faster and faster each second.

He wove his way past the squad cars and danced over the hoses littering the street, searching in vain for any sign of Patricia. Finally, he spotted Dorothy speaking to the Fire Chief. Beside Dorothy stood her over-large partner, Detective Newman, and a slim, younger woman. Detective Bricker, he guessed.

"Let me know when you have the all-clear for me to go into that first-floor apartment," Grayson heard Dorothy say as he drew closer.

"It'll be a few hours," the chief answered. "And thank you. Lieutenant. You did a good job getting the first-floor residents out for us."

"I was on-scene, but thanks, Chief."

The chief turned away to speak to one of his firefighters. Dorothy finally spotted Grayson and braced her shoulders. Bad news, Grayson thought.

"Where is she?" he hissed out as soon as Dorothy was close enough.

"Left her on the bumper of the ambulance back there, a little worse for wear but essentially unharmed, Edmund."

The world finally cleared, and he could think again.

"What happened?" he asked.

"We came here to talk to her Mrs. D." Dorothy shook her head. "Trisha ran into the damned building after the explosion. Pulled the old lady out."

Mrs. D. The woman who'd called this morning with some possible information. Grayson pointed at the soot on Dorothy's face. "You went inside too."

"Yeah, I've been telling her to get checked," Newman growled. "You should know better, partner."

"Enough." Dorothy waved away the concern. "You and Detective Bricker start talking to witnesses. See if anyone heard or saw something before the explosion in that old woman's apartment." A pause. "Or even after. I was not in a position to notice at that point."

"Of course, Lieutenant." Bricker pulled out her notebook.

Newman frowned. "Connell should've stuck with you in that building or not gone in at all," he said.

"I left her, not the other way around. Let it go, Newman. Now is not the time."

He left, taking Bricker with him.

"What was that about?" Grayson said.

"He's just pissed his pet theory about your girl being behind all of this looks less likely. If that grief about Mrs. D. was fake, Trisha needs an Oscar."

Grayson moved to follow Newman, his anger ready to be unleashed. Dorothy grabbed his wrist. "Leave off. Not worth it."

Fine. "You think this was arson?"

"Working theory. Strange coincidence that the fire started in the apartment of a woman known to have information about the history of the Kitchen that could be related to my case."

"Where is she?"

Dorothy knew he meant Patricia. "Over here."

Grayson followed past the emergency vehicles to an ambulance. Dorothy frowned. "This is where I left her."

Fear crept into Grayson's belly again.

"Could she have been taken to the hospital?"

"No, I tracked anyone who was transported. Dammit." Dorothy slammed the side of the ambulance, a measure of her frustration. "Why the hell wouldn't she do what I said, *just once*?"

Dread seized Grayson's insides. "What was her mood?"

"What the hell do you think?" Dorothy looked around. "Upset. Traumatized. But pissed. My guess is she set out on her own. Look, here's David coming over. Maybe he knows."

Dorothy waved. David ran to them, clad in an unzipped jacket despite the near-blizzard conditions, and a Giants watch cap that was shoved haphazardly over his hair.

"Shit, shit. Tony called me. Said I was needed here ASAP." David pointed at the building. "Where's Trish? Is she okay?"

"We were hoping she was with you," Dorothy said through gritted teeth. "I left her right here. She promised to wait. I believed her."

David narrowed his eyes. "Why would she run from this?"

Because if Patricia thought the police would lock her up, she might run to pursue her own leads, Grayson thought. "If she had a notion of who did it, if she'd seen something, she might have run off on her own."

David winced. "That sounds horribly likely. But I think she'd have called me for help."

"Not if she was worried about your safety. What about inside?" Grayson cleared his throat. "Could she have snuck into the building once the fire was out without waiting for it to be cleared?"

"Sounds like Trish," David agreed.

"I'll ask the firefighters if they saw her," Dorothy pushed past them.

"I don't like this." Grayson brushed the snow off his shoulder, a useless gesture since it was immediately replaced by more white flecks. He filled David in about Patricia being considered a suspect in Brennan and Martin's murders.

"No. Just hell no."

"Obviously," Grayson said.

"But some cops will take any route to a conviction. I should know." David took a deep breath and zipped his coat against the cold. "I mean, it's why they ran me out. I was sick of them creating suspects." He walked around a parked police car. "If she took off, she might have left a note where we'd find it. She keeps a notebook and a pencil on her at all times."

A note could've easily been blown away or hidden by snow, but Grayson had no better suggestions.

A frantic search of the car's windshield yielded nothing save soaked gloves and numb fingers. David cursed and pulled off his watch cap. Out of desperation, Grayson peered at the sidewalk and street around the car, on the off chance a note had blown away.

He spotted something shiny where the gutters met the street. He knelt, knees weak, and his gloved hand trembled as he fished the engagement ring he'd given Patricia out of the snow.

He set it in the flat of his palm, looking at the blank space where it'd sat among the snow. Not been here long, Grayson thought idly. Snow hadn't accumulated that much. Maybe fifteen, twenty minutes?

She'd tossed it away.

She'd tossed him away.

"Grayson what—" David stopped in his tracks and stared at the ring.

Grayson stood and curled his fist around it. "Found it right there," he ground out and pointed at the spot now being covered by snow again.

"She would *never* throw that away," David said. "Don't you even think that."

"Out of rage, she might." Grayson took a deep breath and inhaled the cold of the night. "She was beyond angry at me. For good reason. I started research into her background without telling her."

"Then she'd have thrown the damn ring in your face, not run," David answered. "And you know it."

Grayson shoved his hand in his pocket and dropped the ring inside. "Perhaps you're right. But that makes it worse."

"How does that make anything worse? What the hell, Grayson?"

"Because if Patricia didn't throw the ring away herself, it means someone threw it away for her."

"Someone's got her." David covered his face for a moment. "Shit, shit."

"Bullshit." Newman appeared out of the snow's gloom. "She ran. She set all of this up and now she's running from it." He waved his hand at the still smoking building.

Fury engulfed Grayson.

"Fuck you, Newman!" David yelled. "She's out there, hurt or worse. She needs an APB out for her. Now."

"An APB, yeah, because she's the lead suspect." Newman pointed a bony finger at them. "She's finally lost it, going after the people who put her in jail, mailing letters to herself to throw suspicion off. When we—"

Grayson's fist smashed into Newman's face, a punch powered by rage and fear.

Newman staggered. "Motherfucker!" He swung back, wildly.

Grayson danced left, ducked, and slammed his fist into Newman's gut. The taller detective doubled over with another curse, dropping his guard. Grayson threw a right cross. Newman ducked the blow and struck back, but Grayson blocked the fist with his forearm. Pain sliced up Grayson's arm, all the way to the shoulder.

"ENOUGH!" Dorothy jumped between, facing Newman. "You stand down. Now."

Brave of her, Grayson thought. Newman was twice her size.

The knuckles on Grayson's left hand throbbed. He fought through the haze of rage still enveloping him, fought to control the driving need to strike again and wipe Newman and his words from existence.

David put a hand on his shoulder. "Easy, boss."

Grayson brushed the support away.

"Who started this?" Dorothy ground out.

Bricker appeared at her side. "I saw from the fire truck, Lieutenant. Mr. Grayson threw the first punch."

"Only because your mentor decided that Trish is a murderer instead of the victim!" David yelled.

"Arrest him for assaulting a police officer." Newman straightened. "I obviously have witnesses."

"No." Dorothy cut her hand in front of her face. "I'm guessing you threw that idiotic theory at him. Right when a victim we're supposed to be protecting, a woman he loves, is missing? Where the hell is your brain?" Her words were contained fury. "*Detective,* you go back to the precinct and work that list of names, even if it takes all night. We've got a victim, presumed taken, who might live if we can find her in time."

"She's run off," Newman said.

Dorothy gave him a look that could have frozen flames. "That's an *order*, Detective."

"Yes, ma'am." Newman gave her a sarcastic salute and stomped off.

Grayson wanted to punch him all over again. But then Dorothy would arrest him.

"Gone right under my damn nose. I hate this case." Dorothy turned to Bricker. "You, with me. We're going to work the scene. Together."

"Yes, ma'am." Bricker nodded, eyes wide, no sarcasm.

"Now. As for you, Edmund."

Dorothy finally pointed at him. Grayson felt his rage ebbing, but that made it worse because his terror took hold.

"Get the hell out of here. Go to your firm. Work the case with the information you have. I'll be in touch."

She turned and left Grayson standing in the snow with David. The younger man tugged on his arm. "Tony will call in nearly the whole of Gray Associates to help. We'll find her."

David's voice was high and desperate. Belatedly, Grayson remembered how much Patricia meant to him as well.

"Yes," Grayson agreed but found little hope in his heart. Patricia was in the hands of a killer.

He'd failed her. Failed to protect her, failed to believe in her, failed to save her life.

CHAPTER NINETEEN

IT WAS SO cold that Trisha expected her fingers to snap in half. She hardly felt the metal of the handcuffs against her wrists. She pulled at her arms, but they stubbornly remained over her head. She tried to stand but something hard dug into her ankles too.

Vaguely, awareness came. Handcuffs were looped around her wrists and the small bars of a metal headboard. Another set of cuffs around her ankles, looped around the footboard.

Like before.

Panic threatened, but instead of screaming, she floated. She blinked. Gray above. Gray all around.

But no Gray-son…

She almost giggled, or would have, if not for the gag she finally noticed around her mouth. Terror bloomed, only for it to melt away again, replaced by a warm splash of euphoria.

Motherfucking son of a bitch.

She was high.

Smack, most likely.

But how…she hadn't, had she? Indistinct memories flitted in and out. Overwhelming heat, smoke, glass shattering, Dorothy Gilbert yelling, flashing blue and red lights…

She tried to conjure Grayson. Gray pinstriped suit. Impeccably shined wingtips. No, there he was again, in an FBI T-shirt, hair-mussed, smiling at her…

Teddy.

Cold. She shivered, caught in a memory of him glaring at her. Freezing her out.

So hard to focus. Like last time.

Last time. But, no, last time she'd been naked. She had clothes this time. Only a T-shirt, jeans, and socks, all smelling of smoke and still half-soaked from the snow.

But, still, clothes. Not naked. Not raped this time.

Yet.

She swallowed hard, grabbing at the memory of last time, how she'd surfed the high, honed in on her anger, held it, cherished it, let it grow until it fed all her thoughts, until one of her captors had come close enough to loosen a cuff, close enough for her to act.

Trisha jerked at the wrist cuffs over and over, felt liquid ooze down her arms. The agony sliced through the haze, enough for her to remember the sheer terror of being grabbed from behind and feeling the needle go in.

She hyperventilated, terror taking hold, at being assaulted, at being helpless, at not even being able to scream. So much easier to fall into the abyss, fly away from all of it, escape…

Something shiny caught her eye. There, hanging on the door, a large, elaborate crucifix. The Jesus figure on it seemed to be staring at her. Mocking her.

Her stalker had promised divine punishment. So far, he was delivering. Trisha pushed her chin into her chest, seeking her own cross; Father Mike's cross. Father Mike, who believed in God. But he was dead, and she was getting close.

Her hands shook, her teeth chattered uncontrollably. But when she shifted her shoulders, she felt the chain. Yes. She still had the necklace.

Not dead yet.

She closed her eyes, kept the image of Father Mike in her head. Too long, it'd been too long to remember clearly. Only an indistinct image appeared of a dark-haired priest. Hell, she couldn't even remember what his voice sounded like.

If only she could fly away from here…go somewhere warm. Safe…But was flying safe? A long ago image, a Christmas, a roof, slick snow, a scolding…

A male laugh echoed in her head. Who…wait…

A long, long laugh. Father Mike wiped tears from his blue eyes. "Santa doesn't appear if you look for him, kid. The magic doesn't work if you see him. And you won't get presents if you fall and break your neck. Swear you won't be climbing to the roof again."

But I didn't fall, she'd protested at the time.

"Will you swear to be careful?"

What do you mean by careful?

He'd laughed again. Another memory flitted in. A church, a body ready for burial, a cross in his hands. A substitution, her catechism cross for his Celtic one, so he'd still have God with him, but she'd have part of Father Mike. Shoving the Celtic cross in her pocket as the casket closed. *Mine, mine, mine. My last gift from Father Mike.*

She blinked, focused on the feel of the cross against her chest, chilled like the rest of her.

I'm in trouble.

Give up now? Sleep the good one? Jump off the roof and fly?

Was that being careful? Time to let go?

Suicide is a mortal sin, Patricia Mary Connell.

Father Mike? What the hell?

She snapped her head back and bashed it into the hard, blocky mattress. Spots appeared in her eyes. So did light. No, Father Mike was dead. It was the heroin causing hallucinations. Or maybe she was crazy. Maybe this is where she belonged. Where she'd always belonged.

I taught you better, Patricia.

You went away, Father Mike. I was nine years old, and you went away and died, and I didn't have a home anymore. They said God needed you more. Well, fuck you and your God.

The voice didn't respond for a while. Fucking hallucination, going away when she needed to argue with it. Just when she was fading, it came again.

Patricia, you saved his life on the day you met. You saved a lot of lives in the museum that day.

His life? Teddy? Father Mike meant Teddy. She dug her fingers into her palms, felt the dried blood from her earlier struggles.

Teddy.

She'd lost his ring.

A voice echoed through her mind: *I haven't asked for it back, have I?*

Damned arrogant asshole. Fuck him, if he didn't understand.

A weird light glinted on the ceiling, or maybe that was her eyesight going.

Won't break my neck. Gonna fly out of here.

CHAPTER TWENTY

GRAYSON AND DAVID'S short walk from the car to his office building chased away any warmth. It also dispelled the last remaining vestiges of Grayson's optimism. Patricia was out there, somewhere, alone.

Sleet and snow blew sideways. Grayson flipped up the collar of his coat. Beside him, David speed up to open the glass doors of the building's entrance and rescue them from the storm.

They needed more leads, or they'd never find her in time. Tony apparently had some. Neither he nor David spoke in the elevator up to the floor where Gray Associates resided.

The Gray Associates offices were brilliant with light, a contrast to the rest of the floor. Lois, present at the front desk, buzzed them in. "Large conference room. There's coffee."

Grayson shrugged off the drenched overcoat. Lois reached out and took it, holding it at arm's length.

"You need a change. You both do," she said.

"On it," David said, as he tossed his wet jacket over a chair in the lobby.

Grayson felt the wet and cold in his bones. "I'll change in my office and meet you there."

Snow coated his pants. His socks and shoes sloshed with melting sleet as he walked.

Once in his office, Grayson stripped to his underwear. He stuffed the pants in the garbage in disgust rather than trying to salvage the pair. He covered his numb feet in warm socks and changed into the jeans Patricia had given him. "Can't ride with me on the bike in tailored suit pants," she'd said.

The bike. Her Indian. What he wouldn't give to wrap his arms around her as she drove them out of New York City to that state park in northern New Jersey.

A New York Yankees sweatshirt went over his T-shirt, another vestige of Patricia, one she'd bought him at a Yankee game they'd attended. So little time spent with her relative to the rest of his life but such a big impact.

If only he'd talked to her today, stayed with her, not frozen her out. He could have have—

No. He brutally cut off the train of thought. Not helpful. Dorothy had watched over her as best as possible. He needed to turn this rage and guilt at the enemy or he'd not be able to think at all.

He made his coffee, hoping the routine would add some measure of calm, and headed to the conference room.

He found nearly half his firm gathered around the table, not just Tony's research team. Tony and David stood in a corner, heads together. Grayson checked his watch. Almost seven p.m. Over an hour since capture.

"What are you all doing here?" Grayson blurted out.

"Helping a friend," Tony said. "Two friends."

Lois arrived, carrying pizza boxes. "These should hold you all for a while."

David grabbed a slice. Grayson wished he had the stomach for it because he definitely needed fuel. But he doubted he could keep anything down. Instead, he stood next to Tony and asked about the three piles of documents in the middle of the conference table.

"First pile." Tony tapped it. "Fourteen years ago, trying to track news stories about the original incident."

Grayson realized that half his firm now knew about Patricia's attack, if not all the details. Would she forgive him for that? Hell, he'd be glad if she were alive to rage at him for it.

"Second pile?" Grayson asked.

"Anything on Father Mike Connell, who ran the orphanage where she was raised. Someone dropped her at that particular place for a reason." Tony tapped the third pile. "The most important one. The names of the people who attacked Trisha Connell that you gave us today. It's the most urgent research. But we have enough staff to dig into all three."

"Which we should because we don't know yet what might be relevant." Grayson took a deep breath and faced the room. Tony's "nerds" were grouped together. Veterans of law enforcement made another group, as did those who'd been in the service. The only senior staff missing was Ginny Lawrence, who was running point on the Taylor security detail. But these were the best of the best.

Not too long ago, in this very room, Grayson had offered to hire Patricia away from her newspaper. He knew his people had some blind spots that Trisha, with her unusual background, could fill. She'd turned him down flat, not wanting to mix work and pleasure. Even though she would have made more money that she'd had in her life.

"Fill us in with what you know, Edmund," Tony prodded.

Grayson shoved his hands into his pockets, and related the events of the fire, Patricia's disappearance, the discovery of the ring, and the fruitless search tonight.

"You're certain she was taken?"

"I wish I weren't," muttered Grayson.

"She'd never have tossed that ring in a gutter," David said, looking at Grayson. "She might have run off, but she'd have made sure it got back to him."

Tony sighed and stroked his bear. "Time limit?"

Grayson's knees went weak. He sat, almost abruptly, and cleared his throat. "I don't know. The other two victims were killed in their homes. Not immediately, they were…"

His voice caught. He buried his head in his hands, praying for the strength to collect himself. He had to function. He had to find her. He felt a strong hand on his shoulder. He straightened and looked up at David.

"How long a time lapse, Edmund?" Tony asked quietly. "How long were the other victims kept alive?"

"Perhaps as long as eight hours, according to Lt. Gilbert," David answered as Grayson's words refused to come.

"What does Ginny report about Taylor's movements? Can we cross her off our list?" David asked.

"Yes," Grayson said. His main motivation in setting a security detail on the defense attorney had been to protect her. But it also allowed eyes on someone else connected to the case.

"Our attorney and her partner have been at their home all day," Tony reported. "I also have confirmation of them being in San Francisco all last week. They're well alibied."

Grayson swallowed coffee and found his voice. "Moving on then." He tapped the stack of research on Patricia's assailants. "What do we have to work with?"

"Death certificates listing next of kin. Two of them were brothers. The other two were cousins. Address possibilities pulled from the old registered voter records. Crossed out some of those due to them being razed to build the new convention center."

"Close family ties cuts down the number of people to follow up with." Grayson leaned on the table to glance at the top article. "What else would gain us leads?"

"Ideally, we need obituaries to give us relatives and family history, but a whole day's research of newspaper articles at the libraries resulted in nothing." Tony shook his head. "The more recent stuff, especially the local papers that don't exist anymore, aren't on microfiche."

"Boots on the ground. We need to knock on doors, as many as we can in the next few hours," Grayson said.

"But we have to know which doors, Edmund," Tony answered.

"I already have officers on the ground." Dorothy swept into the room, with Officer Bricker at her heels. "Time is short, ladies and gentlemen, let's not duplicate efforts."

Grayson took a deep breath. Dorothy's presence warmed his heart, as did her concern.

"We've already accounted for the immediate family of the brothers," Dorothy continued. "Their sisters moved to Chicago. Mother is dead. Father's been in prison since they were born. Prison logs show no family visits in the last two years."

"Fast work." Grayson flattened his hands on the shiny surface of the conference table. He could almost see reflections of the night he and

Patricia had made love on this table. The night he knew he wanted to marry her. "But we need a *lead*," he ground out.

"The morgue files," David unexpectedly said. "That's where the more recent newspaper articles will be."

Tony frowned. "What the hell are—"

"The *Herald*'s records. Clippings of their own articles and articles from other papers they keep as resources." Grayson stood. "Can we get in there tonight, David?"

"Kimba Sue will let me in, or if she won't, someone will. Trisha's name's still good there with the reporters, at least. You want more boots on the ground, well, that whole staff will help."

Dorothy waved at the door. "Go. If I team up my officers and your people, Edmund, to knock on doors, we can cut down the time even more."

Tony waved at the group of former police officers, local and federal. "You're under her orders. Remember, you're police support, not *police*."

Dorothy let them go past her and Bricker, telling them to check in with Newman at their Midtown precinct.

His old friend came to stand next to him. Grayson thought Dorothy would have some words of reassurance for him, but instead she just patted his shoulder.

"I need to leave Bricker here with a radio so we can coordinate efforts properly," Dorothy said.

"That's fine," Grayson said but he caught an undertone in the words. Dorothy likely wanted to keep Bricker separate from her mentor, Newman, tonight.

"Lieutenant." Bricker stood in front of the conference room door, blocking it. "I want to be out helping."

"You are helping," Dorothy snapped.

"But I feel responsible! I must have missed something from the burglary yesterday, and I was on board the theory with Connell as a suspect. I need to make up for that. I have to—"

"Be where I deem you are most needed," Dorothy said. "You've been awake eighteen hours straight, you need to be off the streets, and I need you here."

"Respectfully, ma'am, all that applies to you as well," Bricker shot back.

Dorothy crossed her arms over her chest. "That was an order, detective. You're stationed here until I say otherwise. Got it?"

"Fine." Bricker backed down. "Yes, ma'am."

Dorothy's voice softened as she turned to Grayson and tapped his chest. "Nice sweatshirt," she said. "You ready to go back out in this?"

"Yes." Hope stirred once more. "Where?"

"Back to Mrs. D.'s apartment. Trisha said the old woman had a lead, and I just got the all-clear from the fire department to go inside." She rubbed her eyes, trying to banish sleep, he suspected.

"And I need someone I can trust at my back," she said in a lower voice.

Implying she no longer trusted Newman or his protégé.

"Good idea," he said.

Patricia had thought the information Mrs. D. claimed to have wouldn't be a dead end. But given Mrs. D. had been a target, it damned well probably had been relevant.

"Let's go," he said.

As they left his office, once they were out of earshot, he voiced his concern. "You left Bricker there to watch over *my* people."

"Yes. and vice-versa. I was saying to Trisha before the explosion that everyone around her is a suspect right now. That includes your people."

"And yours?" he snapped. "Like Newman?"

She punched the elevator button. "Newman's already alibied. Checked myself. In the office during the two murders. I've got him tactfully asking around about other cops who've had run-ins with your girl. They'll talk to him because they know about his attitude toward Trisha. Fastest way. Plus, it keeps him the hell away from me right now. He should know better."

"Thank you." He closed his hand around her forearm. "We have to find her."

"I know," Dorothy answered.

CHAPTER TWENTY-ONE

THE NIGHTMARE CAME AGAIN.

Trisha became lost in it, blood on her hands, in her hair, running down her face. The dead accused her, pointing at her, faces destroyed from bullets and years of decay. She backed away into a corner. They kept coming.

The fire started and she fought to escape, stumbling into an alley. She was naked. The dead tore at her. The scars on her torso streamed red, and they lapped it up.

"Blood for blood," they chanted. Their faces, originally the men she'd killed, morphed into Mrs. Donohue, Dorothy, David, and finally, Teddy.

Teddy!

She wanted, needed to close her eyes and sleep, wrapped secure in his arms.

But only frozen clothes and cold metal lay against her skin. She became lost in endless shivers, exhausting what energy she had, and keeping her awake.

Something moved in front of her eyes. She followed the shadows and was transported into Grayson's living room to stand next to the tree they'd decorated.

Teddy stood silent next to her, naked except for a pair of blue-striped cotton boxers. Her engagement ring sat in the middle of the coffee table.

"I took it under false pretenses. M-m-marriage should be based on trust," she said.

"You threw it away!" He accused, looming over her.

"No! I lost it!"

"You never wanted it!" He grabbed the ring and tossed into the roaring fire. She dove after it, singing her hands. The ring ate through her palm, creating a round hole, as if a nail had been driven through it.

Stigmata.

But Jesus had been without sin.

An image flitted before her, the ghostly outline of the paramedic with the familiar voice and the familiar face but, in another blink of the eye, he disappeared.

Teddy's eyes were bright, his hair mussed, and his face flushed. "You ran. You were always going to run."

"And what the fuck has staying ever got me? Everyone I care about dies!"

"So you'd rather die instead?"

"No!"

And the scene ended, sending her back to that other room where she'd been handcuffed years ago. A man came toward the bed, smiling, belt undone. She feigned being unconscious while he unlocked the cuffs, hands and feet. *Time for my ride, bitch,* the specter of the past said.

I want to live!

She smashed her fist into him, breaking his nose. Blood spurted, he fell back and vanished into nothingness. She scrambled to her feet, her legs almost refusing to move, full of pins and needles as the blood came rushing back.

She could find no shoes yet wept as she pulled her beloved leather jacket on. *They'll pay, like you did. All of them.*

She grabbed a gun lying in the hallway. Metal. Heavy. She felt the cold steel against her palm, the handgun now slick with the blood of the man she'd just killed.

She could run.

No running.

Voices floated down the hall. Men joking, laughing. The sound of spoons clinking against bowls. She stalked toward them, turned the corner, saw them eating cereal, and opened fire.

She fired and fired and fired until the gun was out of ammunition. Bodies sprawled on the floor. The walls resembled an obscene, bloody, Jackson Pollack painting.

They deserved it. She shivered and, once more, the world changed and she lay on the mattress, cuffed, freezing.

Her mind cleared and she found herself back to the gray walls, the bed, the cuffs, the oversize cross hanging on the door. She looked down. No blood on her torso. No injuries at all.

Yet.

For a long time, she took deep breaths, in and out, only thinking of breathing, only wanting to think of air in through her nose and out.

For some reason, her captor hadn't finished the job. Hadn't even come back yet to give her another dose of the smack. Hell, coming down from the high probably caused the shivers and hallucinations.

Step one, get this fucking gag off.

Juvie had been boring as hell. She'd practiced anything to pass the time, including using her tongue to tie little stems together. It'd been a while but, well, she'd kept in practice with some tongue exercises. (Teddy had appreciated that….)

She relaxed her jaw and pushed against the gag. The acrid taste nearly triggered vomit. Not good. She swallowed and started again. Push, move jaw, ignore taste, repeat for what seemed like forever. It wasn't until her eye teeth met that she redoubled the efforts, ending in her spitting out the hated cloth.

She opened wide and sucked in air. Not fresh, a tinge of oil, somehow, and musty. Was she in a basement? She debated yelling but with walls these thick, they'd do her no good. Instead, step two, get out of the cuffs.

Sure, they'd look for her. But if they didn't find her? She'd do this herself. Whatever the reason for leaving her alone, her captor would regret it.

CHAPTER TWENTY-TWO

THE SLEET and snow had cleared the smell of charred wood and stone from the street in front of Trisha's apartment building. Only once he was inside the hallway did the fire's aftermath assault Grayson's nose.

"Did the hospital say when Mrs. Donohue would be out of danger?" he asked.

"Still touch and go. She's older, a smoker, and the lungs had a nasty shock from the smoke inhalation," Dorothy answered.

Bloody hell. If the woman died, Patricia would blame herself. He should have been with her. But, no, he'd been too eager to stay behind and talk to Patricia's defense attorney, too intent on learning the "full story," and too obsessed and angry with Patricia keeping secrets.

He and Dorothy turned left, through the smashed open door of Mrs. D.'s first-floor apartment. The furniture sagged from the weight of water that had frozen into a sheen on top of it.

"Did they decide where it was set?" Grayson asked.

"According to the fire department, the arsonist opened the gas stove and lit a match far enough from it to ensure an explosion." Dorothy pointed to the char along the floor. "Old lady was originally asleep in there."

Grayson noted the door to the bedroom. He knelt and picked up a stray red hair. "Patricia found her here."

She'd rushed through the smoke and heat right into the fire, without hesitation. And Newman had accused her of arson. Grayson balled his hand into a fist again.

Dorothy whistled through her teeth. "They knocked over stuff on that shrine on the way out. Surprised they even found the door through the heavy smoke. There's a hope chest in the bedroom. I'll check there for anything relevant. You search whatever's left of the kitchen."

Grayson shined his flashlight into the narrow kitchen. Oven and sink on one side, refrigerator on the other. Broken dishes in the sink. No door on the stove. The refrigerator seemed intact, complete with magnets of local stores and bars. He spotted a few waterlogged newspaper articles on the floor. Probably, they'd been on the fridge by the magnets. He knelt but quickly judged them too fragile to attempt to pick up. They'd only disintegrate in his hands.

Internally cursing, he turned his attention to the tiny two-person table. Yesterday's waterlogged New York Post sat on top. He peeled the tabloid away, exposing a collection of yellowed newspaper articles held together by a paper clip.

He swore because the first article had a dateline of December 1970, near the date of Patricia's assault, but the rest was unreadable. If it could be dried but…it would take time.

Underneath were two articles from 1956: the arson Patricia had mentioned in April, and another page full of miscellaneous neighborhood news, including birth announcements. Mrs. D. had clipped these three together.

Why? He resisted the urge to tear them up. Not helpful. Instead, he opened several cabinets until he found a usable plate and painstakingly transferred the paper-clipped bundle to it.

"Find anything?" Dorothy called.

"The only article that seems relevant is ruined," he said, his words clipped and terse. Waste of time, he thought. She could be out there, dead, being tortured, without hope, lost….

Dorothy returned with several folders in her hands. "Mrs. Donohue had a good filing system, year by year. But these folders from 1956 and 1970 were on top and out of order."

"And you believe she was looking through them?"

"My best guess."

He held up the plate with his precious clippings. "1956. Same year as the one folder, while the ruined one is 1970. This must be what she meant when she called today…yesterday." He shook his head. "Bloody hell, it's going to take too much time to make sense of it!" He almost smashed the plate against the wall.

"We're not the only ones working on this." Dorothy pinched the bridge of her nose. "I'm sorry, English."

"I know." Nothing else to say, nothing to do but keep moving, until he found her or….

"Let me check in on progress at your office before we do anything else."

They headed back to Dorothy's car. The snow had finally stopped falling, leaving a white frozen sheen over the entire neighborhood. Dorothy started the black and white and kicked the heater up. She was patched through to Bricker, who had nothing new to report.

Grayson resisted putting his hand through the window.

"Back to my office to decipher the articles?" he asked.

"Maybe. Debating my next stop." Her personal radio squawked. It was a diminished-sounding Newman reporting in.

"I'm still getting the runaround at the 1-0, L.T.," said Newman's voice.

The 10th precinct, the one that covered Hell's Kitchen. "Of course you are. Going to try a different tactic."

"Going to piss them off?" Newman asked.

"Oh, I hope so."

"Luck." A pause. "Maybe I was off earlier."

"You were more than off. You were *wrong*." Dorothy signed off.

"What made you convinced Newman's theory about Patricia was bunk?" Grayson asked.

"It was always too complicated but eliminating her meant I could get Newman and some others to concentrate on the real work. I thought I had time to do that. Miscalculation." Dorothy shook her head. "Plus, if Trisha had led me to the apartment building to witness the fire, the smart thing was to stay outside, especially as I ordered her not to go in. She could have died."

Might still die, Grayson thought.

"A better question is why *you* overreacted to Newman, English." Dorothy pulled into the street. "Trisha herself understood the need to cross the theory off. She laughed at it. And while some people might get railroaded, you have enough influence and money to hire a lawyer who would make certain that does not happen to her. So what got you all hot and bothered at a few insults?"

"No comment. Where are we going?"

"The cop bar in Hell's Kitchen. We need someone who remembers the homicides resulting from Trisha's initial attack, preferably one who's drunk and feeling talkative." A pause. "Trisha mentioned it earlier as a cop hangout where she picked up tips. It might be quicker than poking around the local precinct."

"It might at that." Patricia's sources were varied but tended to be reliable.

The short ride forced Grayson to ponder Dorothy's question about the fight. Certainly, Newman had pissed him off. But had Grayson been striking out at Newman or Patricia?

––––––––

Hours had to have passed since she'd been taken but, for some reason, Trisha was still alone. She had time, she hoped, to break free, to create a fighting chance.

Her one idea for escape depended on how much flexibility she had left.

Trisha curled into a tight ball, grabbing at the necklace with her chin, hoping to peel the metal away from the sweat that had stuck it to her skin. If she could grab the chain with her teeth, she could work around to the cross itself.

Get the cross in her teeth, transfer it to her fingers, use it as a shim on cuffs, pop them open.

Home free, right?

Except it all depended on whether she could get the cross in her mouth, transfer it to her fingers, and then have enough leverage to jam it into the teeth of the ratchets of the cuff. Going to hurt like hell, too, because the cuffs were already ratcheted tight and using a shim meant she'd have to push them tighter.

And, any second, her captor could come waltzing in.

She closed her eyes, falling into a rhythm, each twitch bringing the chain closer. The gag, now around her neck, wasn't helping. After a few minutes, or a few hours, or even a few days, Trisha felt the chain against her nose. She rolled onto her side to slacken the chain. The cross fell against the white sheet, so close, but not close enough.

Don't blow it.

She curled into herself, cramped muscles protesting, pulling her arms and legs closer, into as much in a fetal position as the restraints would allow.

Between her chin and her neck, her twitching again seemed endless until the moment her teeth closed around the cross.

Thank you, Father Mike.

Her neck spasmed. Her wrists and ankles throbbed with pain. Sweat beaded on her forehead. Exhaustion crept in. A cramp exploded in her legs.

She pulled her arms lower in the cuffs. Agony stabbed into her wrists from the sharp metal. Worse that her blood-coasted fingers couldn't reach the cross.

C'mon.

If Father Mike wanted to make another miraculous appearance, now was the time. There must be some Biblical advice about not giving up. Trisha's mind wandered back to catechism and mornings spent studying the Bible.

I have seen something else under the sun: The race is not to the swift or the battle to the strong, nor does food come to the wise or wealth to the brilliant or favor to the learned; but time and chance happen to them all.

Ecclesiastes, maybe? She repeated the last part over and over in her mind. *Time and chance happen to them all…time and chance happen to them all…time and chance happen to them all…*

There! She had the cross between her thumb and index finger. She shifted her hands and neck, to give her at least a partial view of what she was doing. That relieved one cramp and created another.

Stick the long end of the cross into the ratchets, hope it wasn't too wide to go in, hope it was long enough to go in, hope the cross didn't break, and hope that her captor didn't show in the meantime.

She jammed the cuffs tighter to allow the cross inside the gears and let out a scream as the hard metal sliced into her.

The bottom of the cross slid into the opening, almost without effort. Trisha willed her numb, shaking fingers to work, steadied her breathing, and pushed down against the ratchets.

A click, the ratchets gave, and the handcuffs fell away from one hand.

Tears flowed, for relief, for the return of hope, for the exhaustion of the effort. Quickly, she used the makeshift shim on the other cuff and her hands were free.

Trisha closed her eyes and sat up.

Dizziness swarmed her.

No, no, no sleep now.

She tried to use her T-shirt to wipe the blood off her fingers and the cross. She swayed and saw stars. She lowered her head to her knees. Breathe, breathe, breathe. The world stabilized once more.

Only halfway there.

She scooted up on her butt and examined the cuffs on her ankle. They'd been looped around the metal of the footboard. The cuffs had been jammed so tight around her jeans that she couldn't push them back down to her ankle, meaning she couldn't ratchet the cuffs tighter and get to the gears with the shim.

She'd have to literally pry apart the cuffs and hope the cross proved stronger. And even if that worked, it'd drive the metal deeper into her leg.

Fine. Worrying about pain was only wasting time.

————

Grayson stepped through the basement entrance, over the threshold, and into a bar that seemed stuck in time.

Only one man sat at the wooden bar pockmarked with age and wear. He stared at them with one eye open, one shut, while flicking ashes into a nearly full ashtray.

Somewhere in the back, the sound of a pool cue hitting a ball echoed.

The high-backed booths blocked sight but Grayson heard the shuffling of feet from within them. A black-and-white television over the bar flickered with sports images. For all he could tell, it might be the '57 Yankees.

The smell of beer and smoke permeated it all, creating a colorless world, save for the splash of green on the jacket of the bartender.

Grayson brushed the snow off his coat as the bartender drew a draft from behind the bar. He placed the brew in front of a balding older man who continued to stare at them, the only patron to take visible notice of his and Dorothy's entrance.

"Seems more like a mob than a cop bar," Grayson said in a quiet aside to Dorothy.

"There were times years ago when it was hard to tell the difference," she whispered back. "Maybe it still is."

The ties between the West Side Gang, notorious and feared in Hell's Kitchen, and the neighborhood police who looked the other way were numerous and well-known, if regrettable.

Dorothy strode past Grayson and put her gold detective's badge on the bar. The bartender allowed himself to notice her.

"I'm looking for someone who worked the Kitchen in the 1970s," Dorothy said.

The bartender poured another draft and sipped it himself, smearing foam on his graying mustache.

"What kind of cop are you?" he asked.

"The kind that's asking for the help of fellow cops. Or don't we honor that here?"

Grayson stood just behind Dorothy, with a view of the front door, his hand hovering near the gun at his waist. He wondered if these cops were Patricia's sources. The bar seemed just like the kind of place she'd frequent. She probably beat the regulars at pool, drank too much, and stayed till closing time. But she would drink whiskey, not beer.

A tall, thin man strode in from the back, carrying a pool cue. He wore an old New York Giants Y.A. Tittle jersey, and a cigarette hung from his mouth. Unlike everyone else in the bar, he was not white. Hispanic, Grayson guessed.

"We honor legit questions, but we hate being told by the new generation what we did wrong in the old days," the patron said. "What kind of answers do you want?"

Dorothy pocketed her identification. "The ones that can save a life. Are you the kind of cop that helps or does nothing but reminisce about the good old days?"

The bartender snorted. The pool player leaned against his cue. Grayson kept his hand near his weapon.

"Name, rank, precinct?" the old cop asked.

"Lt. Dorothy Gilbert, Midtown," she said. "Working an arson."

"This connected to the fire that sent old lady Donohue to the hospital?" he asked. "Heard that was deliberately set."

"You heard right. And, yes."

He eyed them, unmoving. Grayson counted to ten, then he'd had enough.

He stepped past Dorothy and wrenched the cue away from the older man. The player grabbed the bar for balance.

"We don't have time for you to wave your bloody dick around," Grayson said.

"So, it's like that?" The man shook his head and slapped the counter. "Draw me a big draft, Charlie." He jerked his head to the booth. "There. Sit."

The old cop slid to the far end of the booth. Dorothy sat opposite him. Grayson sat next to him, on the outside of the booth, keeping an eye on the door and the bartender.

"Name, rank, precinct," Dorothy said.

"James Santiago. Retired as a sergeant, Hell's Kitchen. What's this about? What's so urgent that brings you and a Fed here?"

"Not a Fed any longer," Grayson said. The old man had made him quick enough.

"Makes it even stranger that you're both here."

Dorothy shook her head. "Time's short. Explanations later. I need to know if you remember anything about the murder of four young men in the area where the new convention center is being built. 1970. Shot to death. Drugs, namely heroin, discovered with them—"

"I remember. Little bitty redheaded girl did it." Santiago leaned back in the booth. "We were baffled and then she turned herself in. Easiest case we closed that year."

"What's not in the official report?" Grayson growled.

The detective sipped his beer and glared at Grayson. "It's pretty bare bones. Most of us were out on the other call that night."

Another call?

"Details," Dorothy said. "C'mon, sergeant, we don't have time."

"I never knew arson investigations had a time limit," he said.

Dorothy tapped her fingers on the table. "Fine. Related to the arson, I've got a missing woman in the custody of a killer. Every second counts."

He pointed at them with two fingers. "Should have led with that." He chugged several swallows and put the glass down deliberately, as if afraid he'd spill it.

"Okay, okay, that was a helluva night. Of course, most of them were in the 1970s. An officer found the scene of the quadruple homicide, but we couldn't assign a detective because our whole team was at the scene of another multiple murder about a block away. Someone had done a number on the West Side Gang." He rubbed his bald head. "Seven dead, total, at a chop shop. Four men shot, two stabbed in the throat." A deep breath. "Another pinned against the wall by an old Chevy. Almost cut in half. Bled out on the way to the hospital. Unconscious when we found him." He shook his head and closed his eyes.

"So all your resources went to that case," Grayson said. Leaving Patricia's assault barely investigated, including the reasons behind it. He might never find answers to why she'd been grabbed off the street that day.

"Look, I'm not saying the quadrupole murder was minor, but we stopped working it once we had the confession. I later heard that girl got juvie time because the D.A. had a stick up his butt. Hell, the kid should have gotten a medal instead. Damn assholes carved her up."

Grayson kept his hand flat on the table, let the icy rage freeze him. This old man was not the enemy. The enemy was out there.

"You ever suspect a connection between the two crimes?" Dorothy asked.

"Banner week in the Kitchen, for damn sure, but..." the sergeant drained the beer. He set the empty glass down with a thud.

"The only connection is that the four killed by the girl were loosely affiliated with the West Side Gang. But then, nearly everyone living in the Kitchen at that point was loosely connected, okay?"

"Not okay," Grayson said. Two sets of murdered gang members on the same night. Too much coincidence for his taste.

"Look, the homicides by the girl were solved." Santiago stabbed a finger into the pitted wood of the table. "No sign of any other motive than the dead assholes deserved it. The other…the chop shop murders definitely was infighting in the West Side Gang. That's when it was the biggest bully in town, before the Italians came in."

"Did the girl who killed her captors have any loose affiliation with the West Side?" Dorothy asked.

A pause. "Don't know. Never thought of that."

"Never thought much," Grayson corrected.

"Look, you fucking Fed, we had no witnesses to the chop shop murders, and those who did know what happened weren't talking. We worked it, we worked the case hard, but we could never pin the original murder on anyone, never mind connect it to the other. You tell me, what's a rape and torture got to do with gang infighting?"

"We'll never know now, will we?" He wondered how hard they'd worked it. Given the time and the rampant corruption in the NYPD then, it was possible cops were involved in the massacre, too, and covered it up.

"You said you wanted information, I gave you information," the cop growled. "But if you'd rather pick a fight, I'm game."

"I've never heard of the chop shop massacre, and I worked Midtown not too many years later," Dorothy cut in. "What happened that it was just dropped and forgotten?"

Santiago glared at Grayson for a minute before answering.

"I told you, it wasn't forgotten, it was just a dead end. Then the brass happened. We had a crime wave in the middle of the Christmas shopping season. Bunch of uniforms were reassigned as protection over near Herald Square. We were told not to talk about the chop shop massacre. Bad publicity for the city. Our precinct captain hushed it up as much as possible, no press statements, no major newspaper coverage, though it made it into a neighborhood paper. No follow-ups, though."

Could this be Mrs. Donohue's unreadable clipping? "Cops talk to each other," Grayson said. "You must have theories."

"I put my failures away."

Or had been told to put them away.

"And you figured the gang ate their own without your help," Dorothy said. "Problem solved?"

"Ain't none of us Superman to take the West Side on. We protected the neighborhood people who needed it and stayed out of their way," the cop shot back. "We did what we could. Why are you asking about it again? It's water under the bridge."

Dorothy shot a look at Grayson. Obviously, she didn't trust his temper.

"Look, any of the chop shop vics related to those killed by your itty-bitty redhead?" Dorothy asked.

"Everyone Irish is related to everyone else Irish in Hell's Kitchen." Santiago rubbed his scraggly beard. "Though I seem to remember one of the younger men in the quadruple homicide had an uncle that was one of the chop shop victims. But that uncle had, like, ten nephews. That wasn't unusual enough for us to connect the crimes. Don't know about the rest. No similar names though, if I remember right."

"You never *bothered* to look for the connection," Grayson said through clenched teeth. "You just let the killers get away." Someone who might be hurting Patricia even now.

Santiago poked a long, dirty finger into Grayson's chest. "Fuck you, whoever you are."

Grayson grabbed the sergeant's wrist and twisted. A huff of pain echoed from the man. Out of the corner of his eye, Grayson saw the bartender reach for something underneath the bar.

"Let go, English," Dorothy ordered. "Now."

Grayson let go. Not helpful. He knew that. Santiago swore at him.

"It's his girl who's missing, Sergeant. Your itty-bitty redhead, all grown up," Dorothy said. "Someone's come back after her, someone possibly connected with your chop shop massacre."

"Shit." Santiago slumped in the booth. "But that don't mean it's my fault."

"I need your case files, now, on the chop shop murders and any other homicides that you think might be connected. Someone who thinks justice wasn't done is getting it for themselves. Any details you have could save her life."

Someone who thinks justice isn't done, Grayson thought. A cop like Newman? He decided not to voice that to Dorothy. Yet.

"Aye." Santiago waved a hand at Grayson. "Move, Fed. I'll hit the precinct now, with a life at stake. Coming with me, Lieutenant?"

"Depends," Grayson said. "That chop shop still in operation?"

"Maybe. Hard to tell with all the construction around the new convention center."

"What's the address?" Dorothy asked.

"There's row of three or four of the garages still there on that street. I'd have to look up the exact number," Santiago answered.

A lead. Finally. "We need to check that street," Grayson said.

"Be nice if we had a specific address and a search warrant," Dorothy said. "Santiago, I need those files ASAP."

"I'll go there now," he answered. "You coming with?"

"No," Grayson said. No more detours. To that street, now, however slim the chance that Patricia was there.

"We'll meet you at the 1-0 after we check that location." Dorothy rose. "And thank you."

"Thank me after you find the girl." Santiago wrote the street name down on a napkin and offered it. Grayson snatched it away, boiling with the need to get away from this lazy cop.

"Your girl who's missing," the sergeant said, stroking his beard again. "She wouldn't be the same punk-ass redheaded reporter who comes in here sometimes and beats me at pool and darts?"

Grayson blew out a breath. "Likely."

"You should've told me you were friends of Trisha right away, then, instead of blowing fire at me." He slapped a hand down on the old man at the bar. "C'mon, blockhead, Red's in trouble. We got work to do." He turned back to Grayson. "Find her. She's still got to pay off my bar tab this month."

Despite himself, Grayson smiled on the way out. Patricia made friends in the most unusual places. His humor quickly evaporated in the chilled night.

He stomped up the cement steps to the street. Winds blew around the drifting snow, cutting the visibility to maybe five feet. They escaped to the patrol car, still double-parked, and looked at the address on the cocktail napkin.

"Three blocks down, one block over," Dorothy said as she started the car. "It's a long street. And it'll be hard to see anything in this snow."

"Circle once in the car, then on foot?" Though the visibility might be just as bad on foot.

"Again, you and I are agreed." She grabbed a hat and scarf from the back of the black and white. "This is a true longshot, English. You might be better to help with the research at your office. That might lead us to this killer, not a wild goose chase."

"A longshot is all Patricia has right now, Dorothy. I'm going with you."

CHAPTER TWENTY-THREE

TRISHA SAT NEXT to the door, her head resting on her knees, waiting for her captor to come back. Go for the legs, she thought, and then run like hell. She'd tried the lock already but had nothing left to pick it with. Her cross had broken when she'd pried apart the handcuffs on her feet.

Blood pooled on the slab floor below the gouge in her leg. She'd peeled off her T-shirt and tied it around the leg above the bleeding. Seemed to help except now her teeth chattered from the cold.

Maybe she'd been left here to die. No, that made no sense. Whoever this was wanted her to pay. They'd spent time carving up the other victims. She hadn't been tortured yet. They'd be back.

Unless…they were watching her struggle.

There was a horrifying thought. Trisha looked around at the four gray walls for some sign of a camera. But she couldn't see any hiding places for one. God, if all this was some damn plan to draw out her torture, she was going to be pissed.

Trisha closed her eyes and concentrated on taking regular, steady breaths through her nose once more. The hyperventilating and panic subsided.

Impossible to judge how long she'd been in this endless gray space.

Patience. She let her thoughts ramble, let the memories come, let whatever swam to her mind appear.

Nicky came to mind first, clearer and sharper than in years. She remembered their wedding day, a bare-bones ceremony at City Hall, with her dressed in her favorite black leather jacket and a Springsteen "Born to Run" T-shirt, and Nicky in jeans and a black T-shirt, wearing the silver Claddagh necklace she'd given him. Basic gold-plated bands for rings. No engagement ring. They could barely afford rent, never mind diamonds.

Later, she'd dragged Nicky to a priest, and they'd had a church wedding because…well…she thought Father Mike would have liked it. Nicky had been a lapsed Catholic like her, so he had known the drill and hadn't complained.

He'd asked for last rites in the hospital just before he'd died.

Anger brought her back to the cold room. If there was a God, he sure as hell let some people have too much free will. Or maybe he'd thrown up his hands at the entire human race. Who wouldn't? Or maybe He had a personal grudge, and she was already damned.

No one is damned who chooses not to be, Patricia Mary Connell.

Shut up, Father Mike. You're just a hallucination brought on by blood loss and the smack.

God helps those who helps themselves.

Trisha snickered at the idea of Father Mike going to that old cliché.

The click of the deadbolt unlocking sounded. Trisha tensed and curled her hand around the cuffs she'd removed. They'd hurt, if she slammed them into someone.

The door handle turned. Trisha knelt, staying knee-high, to get one good, strong blow in on the side of the knee before her captor knew what hit them.

"Now, Connell, I'm going to get your damn confession." Detective Estelle Bricker walked through the door.

Bricker? Trisha's surprise cost her a few seconds, seconds in which Bricker noticed the empty blood-soaked bed. Bricker turned at the same time Trisha bashed the cuffs against her knee.

The metal slammed into Bricker's kneecap instead of the vulnerable side of the leg. Bricker wavered but caught her balance and reached for her gun in the side holster.

Trisha leapt and tackled her.

They went down in a heap, sideways, Trisha's injured leg on the bottom. She screamed, half in agony, half in frustration. They rolled. Bricker ended up on top.

Trisha fumbled for Bricker's side holster, found the gun, curled her fingers around it. The cop grabbed for it. Fuck, she didn't have the strength for a wrestling match with Bricker.

Trisha flung the weapon away. The gun skittered across the concrete and under the bed.

Bricker swore. She punched Trisha on the right side of her face. Pain bloomed from Trisha's chin to her cheekbones. She caught the collar of Bricker's blouse and pulled tight, almost choking the other woman.

"Shit!" Bricker bent back Trisha's fingers.

Her hold gone, Trisha let go and bucked, knocking the other woman off her. Trisha scrambled to her knees, eyeing the open door, even as she swayed. One step, two steps….

Bricker grabbed her ankle. Trisha slipped on the blood and hit hard on her butt.

Something sharp stabbed in between her toes. "Deal with that, junkie!" Bricker yelled.

Everything went cold. Trisha's shoulders slumped. Through a haze that descended over her, Trisha saw Bricker clutching a hypodermic needle in her hand.

Drugs again. Smack. Too slow, she'd acted too damn slow.

Still had to keep Bricker away from the gun. Trisha flailed, found Bricker's arm, curled her fingers around it, and bit down on her wrist.

Bricker screamed and punched Trisha again. Trisha teeth's lost hold and her head bounced off the concrete. The coopery taste of blood filled her mouth.

Bricker climbed on top of her, knee in Trisha's gut.

"You're not going anywhere until you give me a confession!"

Bricker's eyes were wide, bloodshot, her chest heaving. Weakening? Giving into the crazy?

Trisha spat the blood in her face. Bricker choked her, cutting off air. Trisha fought for breath, grabbed Bricker's thumb and twisted, just like Bricker had done to her.

Bricker released the stranglehold but remained on top of her. Trisha gasped for breath.

"That's enough for you!" Bricker wiped her face with her sleeve.

So tired. It probably was the smack was washing through her. Damn. Stall, stall. Bricker wanted to justify herself. Wanted to justify murder. This was her final strike, the one she'd been working up to.

Bricker wouldn't kill her until she had whatever she wanted.

Bricker drew a familiar switchblade out of the pocket of her wool coat. "You're going to give me that confession."

"That's *my* knife," Trisha said through clenched teeth.

"I know." Bricker grinned without mirth. "You just handed it over to me. What a nice, law-abiding citizen. And now I can use it as part of your confession."

Second time she'd mentioned confession. "What are you, a priest?" Trisha croaked out. She should hurt more. Why didn't she hurt more? An image of Richard Dawson pointing to a gameboard and saying "Survey says heroin!" flitted through Trisha's mind.

"I'm the hand of justice," Bricker responded in between breaths. "You will confess your murders."

"I confessed to those a long time ago," Trisha whispered. Breathe in, breathe out. Get strength back. Get her knife back. The knife Nicky had given her.

"No!" Bricker pressed the switchblade to Trisha's throat. "No more lies. Your confession is nothing but lies."

"I—" Trisha looked into Bricker eyes, ignoring the threat at her throat. What gnawed at Bricker? Play on it, find the key. C'mon, take a trip with me... Trisha almost began whistling.

"I didn't lie about killing them." That seemed the only safe response. The cold, sharp edge of the blade dug into her throat.

Bricker drew the knife back a few inches. Trisha felt a small trickle of blood roll down her neck. Every muscle twitched, wanting to run. Smart muscles.

"I'd intended to spend a long time hearing your confession and obtaining a record of the truth," Bricker said. "I got delayed. Too long, I see." She glanced at the bloody bed. "It's probably better this way. My appearance must have crushed all your hopes. Still, we have time to get to the truth of what you did."

"And just what did I do?" Trisha squeaked out.

"You lied about them!" Bricker pressed the sharp edge against Trisha's throat once more. "You lied about why. And now you're going to tell the real story."

"I—it's hard to concentrate. You drugged me." Her voice was so low that Trisha wasn't sure she'd spoken out loud.

"Oh, yes, how unfortunate for you," Bricker said, drawing back with a smile curled around her teeth. "Second wave's coming. Can't you feel it yet?"

The drug exploded into every nerve that Trisha had. Her head jerked back. Her chest heaved as she fought to breathe. Her body shuddered, equal parts pleasure and pain, euphoria and panic.

"*Sonofabitch.*"

And yet, agony receded to a small corner of her brain. That helped. If she could fight the lassitude, she had a chance again.

"There, better now?" Bricker leaned back on her heels, watching, less concerned now with being attacked.

Trisha stared at nothing, unblinking. Thoughts were coming in a disconnected haze. Her limbs felt heavy, impossible to move. Dammit.

"You didn't drug the other victims with smack. Why me?"

"They didn't lie about my brother forcing drugs on them," Bricker said. "Oh, you were high, but on purpose."

Trisha finally blinked. Her head lolled to the side. "Your brother?"

Bricker grabbed her hair. "My brother. Do you even remember his name?"

Something in Bricker's expression triggered memory.

"Jack. His name was Jack." *Hold her down, Jack. Man, she's fine isn't she, Jack? Hey, Jack, time for your turn. We got a few hours before we turn her over.*

Turn her over to whom?

Bricker slapped her face. "You don't get to say Jack's name."

Bricker's fingernails dug bloody groves into Trisha's cheeks. The blood trickled down her neck but she felt immune to the agony that should be accompanying it. Her eyes focused on the wolf's head of the switchblade that Bricker held tight in her hand.

"He was everything to me, my brother. And his friends pulled him into this. He was under orders!"

"Orders? What the hell are you talking about?" *Don't have to turn her over for a few hours yet...*

But Bricker ignored the question. "I've seen the crime scene photos. You pumped a whole clip into him." Tears fell down Bricker's cheeks, contrasting with the harsh anger in her voice.

"You think I—" Trisha swallowed.

Bricker's breath blew hot on her face.

"Partied with him? That I had sex with him voluntarily? Then how did I get the scars?"

Bricker released her face and slashed at Trisha's bare stomach. The edge of the blade caught her skin, and a red line appeared across her belly. She looked down at it in sick wonder. The cut had been directly along one of her scars. Bricker was doing exactly what her brother and his friends had done.

Doesn't hurt this time.

"You have a wild streak. It doesn't surprise me that you'd be a cutter. Why the hell else do you carry this damn switchblade?" Bricker said. "You either wanted them to cut you, or you did it to yourself." Bricker's heavy breathing slurred her words. "If your story was true, why didn't you turn them in right away? Why did you go to a public defender? You just wanted an easy out."

Hah, good questions. Bricker must be a cop or something. "I didn't trust the cops."

"Damn right, they'd have locked up your ass. If not for your public defender, the D.A. would have tried you as an adult, locked you up for good."

"But you killed him anyway."

"He did his job badly. Time he paid." Bricker clicked her tongue. "But this was ultimately on you. You wanted the drugs. You seduced them, partied with them, and murdered them. That's why I was planning to set you up for Martin and Brennan's murders. That's why you'll be blamed for them."

"Lt. Gilbert won't buy it."

"She won't have a choice, since I've got a nice neat case planned. With a confession."

Nice fairy tale, Trisha thought. Dorothy wouldn't buy it. Grayson sure as hell would never accept it. She hoped.

Her body started to float. She looked at the cut on her stomach. *Fly away on a red carpet this time, Father Mike....* She fought back a giggle.

"So why I did even bother with the public defender?" she said out loud. "Why did I even confess?"

"Probably ran out of smack and wanted into a program," Bricker said. "Get somebody to take care of you for a while. Sponge off the state. But it didn't go the way you expected."

"You have it all sorted out." Trisha licked her lips. "Jack, why—"

Another slap. A warm feeling pulsed through Trisha's cheek.

"I told you, you don't get to say his name."

Trisha licked her lips. "Your brother, why was he everything to you?"

Bricker lowered the blade. "You have no clue, do you? You really didn't care about your victim's families at all, did you?"

Um, that would be a "no," Trisha thought. Raping scum.

"Jack was my responsibility, my connection to my mother! After she died, my father took me, and Jack went to his father."

At least you had a parent, Trisha thought.

"So you missed him?" she asked.

"He was my responsibility and I couldn't help him." Again, tears fell down Bricker's cheeks. "My dad was good, my stepmom was okay. They took care of me. I had it fine. But Jack didn't. He was all stuck with his father, who was an ass. He had no choice! And *you* took him away. Seduced him. *Murdered* him, before I could help."

Survivor's guilt. Trisha blinked, remembering how she'd often wished Nicky had lived and she'd died. Trisha's breaths evened out. Her mind kicked into gear again. She might be able to move. Needed to pick her time.

"So you blamed yourself for your brother's choices?" Trisha asked.

"I blame you!" Bricker wiped tears away with the back of her hand.

"Lots of people have horrible parents and don't rape and torture teenagers." Nicky would never have done anything like that.

"More of your lies! Shut up!" Bricker pressed the knife to Trisha's throat again. "I became a cop, so I could eventually bring justice to Jack, expose your lies. I owed him that."

She'd have been better to go after Jack's father, maybe, expose the abuse. Once Trisha had become a reporter, she'd investigated Nicky's father. She had quite a file on him, almost enough to get him arrested, before he'd finally overdosed.

"So you came after me instead of the people who got your brother into the gang?"

Bricker froze for a second before she slapped Trisha. It hurt enough to make her teeth ache. Shit.

"It was your fault. You're the one who had to pay. But you vanished. Changed your name. But you screwed up, allowed a photo to be published during that museum case. I'd seen your byline before but not a photo. Once I saw it, I knew you. How I laughed when you were fired."

"The museum stories." Above the fold headline stories, those had been, especially with Grayson's takedown of the murderer and Kimba Sue's story of how the *Herald* had fired their reporter for no good cause.

Well, in fairness, Trisha had called the publisher/owner of the *Herald* an asshole. But in fairness, the publisher had actually been an asshole.

"Yes, your museum stories," Bricker echoed. The detective seemed to be relaxing, focused more on talking and getting a confession, unworried about Trisha fighting back now. How long had she been planning this? Years? Damn, Bricker had spent her entire adult life carrying this guilt because she had parents who loved and cherished her and her brother hadn't. Then she went after innocents instead of the people who'd really hurt Jack.

Talk about being illogical.

"You're still a murderer," Trisha said.

"It was righteous vengeance. For you and all those deceivers like you. Once you're done, your defense attorney is next. That'll close up the circle. Thanks for finding her for me."

"Killing her after I'm dead will mess with your frame."

"I don't care!" Bricker slashed at Trisha's stomach again. Another red line appeared.

Trisha giggled.

"You think this is funny?"

"Don't get me high and complain about my sense of humor."

Another slash. Another red line.

"I don't think Lt. Gilbert is going to be thrilled with your sense of justice, Detective."

"You dare criticize me? You're the one responsible for corrupting her, for fooling her. She fights me and Newman over such a neat case, she'll go down too. She's got enemies in the department, you know."

"All her enemies are assholes."

"It would be a shame for the department to lose such a good detective, I suppose." Bricker wiped sweat away from her forehead with her sleeve. "Save Lt. Gilbert the need to sacrifice her career. Show your true colors, murderer."

Another slash to the stomach. Cold metal on her skin, then warm blood. "Red's my color, I guess."

Bricker grabbed her hair again and stared into her eyes. "Confess now. If you've absorbed anything of value from Church, then make your peace with God and tell the truth. Tell me you lied about my brother and clear his name. He wasn't capable of that. Drugs, yes. Kidnapping because he had to follow orders, yes. But not rape. I know him! He was a sweet kid! He'd never do that! Clear his name, and maybe you'll have done something worthwhile with your worthless life."

Bricker wanted Old Testament justice but she'd chosen all the wrong targets. "'For now we see through a glass, darkly, but then face to face. Now I know in part; but then shall I know even as also I am known.'"

"What are you saying?" Bricker frowned.

"You like Bible quotes. That one's applicable."

Trisha's memories whisked her away, far from Bricker and knives and blood. The earthly smell of the leather-bound Bible. Father Mike's voice, thick with his Boston accent.

Forgive. Atone. Have faith.

"'And now abideth faith, hope, charity, these three; but the greatest of these is charity.'"

Bricker put the blade to her throat again. "Don't fucking quote forgiveness to me, sinner. The Bible is not for you."

"I always liked St. Paul's letter to the Corinthians, you know. Of course, it's the King James, not the approved Catholic version, but Father Mike always liked the language of the King James better—"

"Those words are defiled by your mouth." Bricker banged Trisha's head against the floor.

The wave of pain started small, and grew until it seemed her whole head became one throbbing mass.

"Confess your lies," Bricker demanded.

Trisha blinked away the tears, trying to focus. The world stopped spinning, at least for a second. Trisha could never give Bricker what she wanted. Might as well please the voices in her head instead.

"Forgive me, Father, for I have sinned. It's been, uh, forever since my last confession." The once-familiar refrain rolled off her tongue.

"Good, that's good. Speak the truth," Bricker whispered in her ear. "And I'll be quick after. You won't even feel it, as high as you are."

"Forgive me, for I killed with anger and hatred in my heart." Trisha's gaze flicked down to her cross, broken, lying on the bed, covered in blood.

Warmth flooded her. Father Mike's voice came again. *If you kill yourself, you can never atone.*

Atonement. Redemption?

Bricker didn't exist. The blood didn't exist; the gray walls didn't exist. It was only her and Father Mike. Father Mike would listen to her. Whatever happened now, she'd do what he would have done.

"I have sinned. I regret the pain those sins have caused. I will try to follow a different path," she said out loud but not to Bricker.

As the words flew into the air, the fear seemed to go with them.

Trisha raised her head to stare at Bricker. "For what you suffered, I'm sorry. I know you did your best for your brother but, Christ, you were just a kid. It was the adults around him who let him down. Let him rest in peace. I can't give you lies. If I have to stand before God with the truth, so do you. I accept my actions. But you…you killed two, maybe three, *innocent* people for your vengeance." Was Mrs. D. dead? "Mrs. D. has children, grandchildren. How do you think they feel right now after getting that goddamned knock on the door? How does it feel to be the one who caused their grief?"

"*You* judge *me*?" Bricker's words were a hiss, her eyes wide in disbelief.

"I don't judge. God does. How do you stand before him, Estelle Bricker? How do you judge yourself?"

"Vengeance. An eye for an eye," Bricker ground out, but her shoulders slumped.

"But Mrs. D. wasn't part of your vengeance," Trisha countered.

Bricker stood, almost backing away, unsure of herself? Could Trisha's words really be working?

"See your brother the way it was, Bricker. Know that he loved you and did his best for you, but he was also capable of horrible things. Same as you. You're a murderer, but you are also a damn fine police officer. Maybe you have time to atone."

"Atone?! I've done what is *necessary*." Bricker cut the air with the blade. "Those men allowed evil to flourish. The law couldn't touch them, but I knew what to do."

"You forgetting Mrs. D. again."

"No one who lives in Hell's Kitchen that long is innocent," Bricker hissed. "I wanted you to see, but you don't." Bricker pointed the knife at her. "Enough. Clearly, you're too far gone. Time to end this."

Bricker turned, looking at the bed, probably looking for her gun.

Trisha swallowed, trying to taste saliva and not fear. If Bricker got the gun, this was all over.

"I feel sorry for you, Bricker. You had so much, and you tossed it in the garbage."

"Fuck you!" Bricker lunged for her.

Trisha tackled her. They landed on the bed. Bricker slammed her head against the remains of the cuffs hooked to the iron bars of the bedframe. She moaned and flailed with the knife. Trisha rolled off her, grabbed the side of the mattress and covered Bricker's face, also trapping the hand that held the switchblade.

Muffled screams came from underneath. Trisha added her body weight to the mattress. Bricker's legs kicked out and went still. But her fingers still opened and closed. Down but not out, and Trisha was fast losing any strength she had. Trisha rolled off the bed to the cement, spotted Bricker's gun from under the bed, grabbed it, and half-stumbled, half-ran through the open doorway. She cut left, toward darkness. She could hide, hold on to the gun, and if Bricker came for her again, she'd have to shoot her. There was no reasoning with that insanity.

Her bare feet slapped against concrete. Trisha slammed her shin into concrete steps. She ignored the pain and scrambled up the steps, hit a landing, and crawled up the second set of stairs. The gun clinked every time it hit the floor. Shit.

When would Bricker came after her?

Thuds sounded below her. Trisha ducked, involuntary, and fell against the door at the top of the steps. She fumbled, found the door handle, and lunged through. She slammed the door shut behind her, kept running, and nearly ran face-first into a garage bay door

What?

The smell of grease, gas, and metal surrounded her. She was inside a mechanic's shop. She crouched low, put her hand flat against the door, and scooted on her butt until she was on the far side of it. She curled her hands around her knees, the gun braced loosely on top of them. A gun. She had a gun in her hand again. She curled her finger around the trigger guard. Huh. This time she prayed she wouldn't have to use it.

Maybe she had changed.

CHAPTER TWENTY-FOUR

DOROTHY CRUISED the street at a speed low enough to see in this damned blizzard. But it was far too slow for Grayson's taste. It'd been hours since Patricia was taken.

An absence of solid space appeared to his left. "Stop," he said.

She stopped. "What?"

"There's a free parking space. I want to check how long it's been empty."

He stepped out into the swirling snow. The parked cars had at least three inches piled on their hoods already. But this space had only a wisp of snow covering the empty pavement. Dorothy rolled down her window.

"What do you think?" she asked.

"Someone was parked here until recently." Please let this be a true lead.

"As good a place to start as any."

She parked the black and white in the empty space in front of a garage bay of a seemingly deserted mechanic's shop. The streetlamp far above provided pitiful illumination. They turned on their flashlights. All looked dark.

Dorothy checked the knob of the door at the side of garage bay. Locked. "No sign of activity."

Dead end? Likely. He checked the garage door. No handle on this side. "There may be a back entrance. There's an alley here at the side."

"Possible." She walked to the right side of the building. "Alley here too."

"You take that side, I'll take this one," he said.

"If we separate, we have no backup," she said.

"But we ensure no one gets past this way." He was willing to take the chance of confrontation on his own.

"One minute." She went back to the black and white and requested another unit.

"I'm not waiting for them," he said.

"Neither am I but I needed to know they're on the way."

It finally penetrated that she was risking her life as well. "Good idea."

Once he set down the alley, he pulled out his Berretta. He would take no chances. Whoever had Patricia deserved it.

He felt along the solid brick wall of the narrow alley. The wind died down as the buildings cut it off, leaving nothing but snowfall. Still, nothing but pavement ahead. He reached the corner, leaned down, and peaked around it. Clear. A light flashed on the other side. The flashlight clicked on and off. Dorothy. He answered the same way. He took a few steps toward her and immediately spotted a back door ajar. A sliver of light streamed through the opening from inside.

He waited precious seconds for Dorothy to approach.

"Open door is enough justification for a search," she said.

"I'll go first."

He kicked the door open wide with his foot and waited a few seconds for a reaction. Nothing. Weapon at the ready, he slipped inside. It took a moment for his eyes to adjust to brightness. A short corridor, leading to another open door.

His flashlight caught the edge of something dark smeared on the wall.

"Blood," Dorothy whispered.

Fear threatened to send Grayson to his knees.

"Stay with me, English," she said.

He kept ahead of her and, when he reached the half-open door, he rushed into the room, Dorothy on his heels.

A bed with a metal frame was wedged in the corner. Bright red blood covered the mattress and stained handcuffs dangled from the headboard. Splattered blood decorated the floor, along with bits of torn clothing.

"Jesus Christ," Dorothy muttered.

"There was a struggle." Grayson hung on to that idea for sanity. Patricia had fought. She'd escaped. But to where?

He backed out of the room and focused on the floor. "There's a blood trail here," he called.

Again, she backed him up as they crept down the corridor. He stumbled when they reached the steps and found a larger bloodstain.

"Shit," Dorothy said.

He gripped the Berretta tighter and held the flashlight in a death grip on his shoulder. Up one step, the next, to the door at the top. It was on a spring and shut automatically. He shut off his flashlight and slammed it open. He half expected to be struck down with a bullet. But only silence met them again. He risked turning on the flashlight and caught the flash of something to the far left of the bay door.

Movement!

"Police!" Dorothy called.

Something metal clinked against the floor. He and Dorothy rushed to the sound.

In the circle of the flashlights, Grayson caught a glimpse of bare shoulders, blood, and a shock of red hair. A gun lay next to the body. Oh, bloody hell, he'd been seconds from shooting her!

"Patricia!" He holstered his weapon in an instant and knelt next to her. He enclosed her with trembling hands. She lay limp in his arms. Oh, fuck, he could barely see her face through the blood on her cheek.

"Alive?" Dorothy asked.

Grayson could not answer. His throat was shut with grief. She was so still. He ripped off a glove and set cold hands against her blood-soaked neck. "A pulse!"

Alive!

Her mouth moved. He thought he heard "Teddy."

"Love, easy," he whispered. "I'm here."

"We're back to the front entrance of the shop," Dorothy said.

Through the window, he saw a patrol car pull up next to Dorothy's vehicle. She called to them through her radio.

"She needs an ambulance," he said.

"On the way. Follow me through this door. They're wary and expecting me first."

Grayson lifted Patricia, who weighed even less than usual, and followed. The cold, wind, and snow hit the minute he stepped outside. Patricia emitted a noise, half-cry, half-whimper, and his heart broke.

"She's freezing!" He rushed to the car, slipped Patricia in the back seat, and threw his coat over her, but her shivering threatened to shake her in half.

Dorothy slid into the front, locked the doors, and aimed the headlights on the front of the garage. She activated the lights and sirens. "That's to help the ambulance find the way through the storm," she said. "Keep her here until then." She took a moment to close her eyes and let her head rest on the back of the seat. "Stay here, it's a crime scene now."

Like he would leave Patricia now. But all he could do in answer was nod.

He stared into the blue of her eyes. "Dilated," he said out loud. Fear seized him. Drugged, maybe. Where was that damn ambulance?

He hugged Patricia as tight as he dared. Yes, they'd found her, but this blood-splattered, half-naked, shivering woman barely resembled the one he knew. She'd been handcuffed and held in that room, had confronted her captor, and somehow, she'd rescued herself. He'd been useless. All he'd done was find her in the aftermath of whatever she'd survived.

He curled her against him, vowing to never let her out of his sight again. She began to shake more violently, and he thought she was having a seizure until he recognized her laughter. Had she gone over the edge?

"I'm always…ruining your coats," she choked out.

The words pierced his heart. Tears ran down his cheeks. "Patricia, where are you hurt?"

But she didn't answer this time.

"We'll get you warm as soon as possible."

He checked her pulse again. Fast, too fast. But he noticed the needle mark this time.

Dorothy poked her head in. "How's she doing?"

"She's definitely been drugged at least once. Where's the bloody ambulance?"

"Almost here."

Grayson willed his warmth and life into Patricia. He heard the welcome sirens in the background.

Finally. "Help's coming, love." But if she heard him, she made no sign.

Red and blue lights cut through the dark and the snow.

"Broke the cross. My cross. All broken," she mumbled.

"But you're not."

"Always broken."

He stroked her hair. "Then now you're stronger in the broken places."

"Hemingway?" She burrowed her head against his sweatshirt, her matted hair bright red against the dark blue. "You real?"

"Yes, real." He nearly choked on the words.

"So…much blood."

Dorothy opened the door. "Ambulance is ready."

"Hate hospitals," Trisha muttered against his chest.

"Better than the coroner's van." Dorothy loomed over Patricia and brushed a hair back from her bloodshot eyes. "She talking?"

"Not anything sensible. Broke her cross, she said."

"Who was it who held you, Connell?"

"Dark mirror," she mumbled.

"Not helpful." Dorothy stepped away. "You stay with her, English. I want someone with her at all times to get that name. I'll be on scene."

"Where she goes, I go," Grayson said.

Trisha waved her bare arm around again, almost hitting Dorothy in the face.

"Pretty lights. All sparkly."

Dorothy patted her shoulder. "Hang in there, Sparkles."

CHAPTER TWENTY-FIVE

NOTHING MADE SENSE TO TRISHA. Teddy stayed with her but was he real or a figment of her imagination? Perhaps she was still cuffed to the bed in that cold, cold room. Perhaps she'd never left it, all those years ago, and everything since had been her vision before dying.

She saw the ambulance, heard the voices and sirens, but she'd no way to distinguish reality from hallucinations. She wanted to talk but it seemed like too much effort.

Was that Father Mike hovering near the hospital bed? David bursting in? She fought when they first tried to put the IV needle in, swore at Teddy when he held her, got distracted by the cool, clear taste of water going down her throat.

She flew over Hell's Kitchen and saw the big ugly cement convention center crushing the apartment houses under it. She floated above the Hudson, swam under it, saw the fish and the dead bodies attached to anchors, heard the cries of seagulls.

A hand grasped hers, pulling her up from the depths. A soothing voice with a slight English accent told her everything would be okay.

Broken, she thought. Stronger in the broken places said the voice. A Hemingway quote, she vaguely remembered.

More images. Nicky, hugging her like he'd never let go on that day they'd let her out of juvie. Finally, Father Mike again, saying it was never too late to have faith.

She closed her eyes and slept.

———

Grayson's fury rekindled the minute Newman walked into his sight outside the X-ray facility. He blocked the detective's path in the hallway, fists clenched.

"Are you satisfied now?" Grayson threw the words at the detective, uncaring that his anger spilled out to those in the area.

"You won't sucker punch me this time." But Newman put up his hands in surrender. "I'm not here to fight. I'm here to gather information on her injuries. I'm collecting blood and tissue samples to compare what was found at the scene."

"Who was it?" Grayson ground out.

"Unclear yet. But there's a second set of fingerprints at the scene that we're running."

"If you'd been in charge of this case and not Dorothy, Patricia would be dead," Grayson said.

Newman stood close to him, almost chest to chest. He had a new bruise blooming around his eye. "That's been pointed out."

"Where's your shadow?" He would have expected Bricker to be with her mentor.

"Bricker's off-duty. She pulled almost a twenty-four-hour shift." A pause. "Now, Grayson, move and let me do my job and find the person who did this to your girl."

Grayson shifted and let Newman pass but kept a wary eye on the detective as he talked with the nurses at the their station. David returned with a cup of coffee.

"Any word?" David asked, eyeing Newman.

"No, they wouldn't let me inside during her X-rays. But her pulse is stable now. The fluids are doing her some good." Grayson sipped the coffee. Terrible. Acrid liquid burned his throat. He welcomed it.

"She's got to be in a lot of pain."

"Once they get the blood work back, they'll know what's safe to give her for the pain." He finished the awful coffee. "You're a good friend to her, David." Better than he himself had been.

"She's been a good friend to me," David answered.

So much unsaid. Grayson pushed all that down. "Did you find anything useful at the *Herald*'s morgue files earlier?"

"Yeah, I put the copies with what you gave me from Mrs. D.'s apartment. Kimba Sue found an article about the massacre at the chop shop where you found her, plus a bunch of stuff about unsolved murders in Hell's Kitchen that might be related, including that 1956 arson. Tony's looking them all over." A pause. "One of the victims at the chop shop scene resembles the father who supposedly died in the 1956 arson. Tony and the police are looking into whether the resemblance could be connected. After all, they only identified the mother's body in the fire."

"All Irish look alike in Hell's Kitchen." Grayson shook his head. "That's what she would say."

"I know. But it's a lead. Gives us something to do."

"A good lead," Grayson conceded. "Do we think Patricia's intruder and her attacker were one and the same? Or are we dealing with multiple assailants?"

"Unclear." David said. "When she's coherent, maybe she can tell us?"

"Maybe. She spent some time raving about someone who stole her knife. Nicky's knife, she called it. She seemed incensed it was used to hurt her."

"Her assailant hurt her with it?" David paled.

"What's wrong? Is that important?" Grayson asked.

"Detective Bricker took Trisha's switchblade. She demanded the knife as evidence after the break-in and she never gave it back. Um, so unless Trisha is hallucinating that her own knife was used to hurt her...."

"*Bricker.*" A cop. Someone who could create a frame. *Of course.*

Grayson curled his hand around David's forearm. "Patricia's switchblade was found inside the room she was held in the garage. If Bricker had it last, then only she could have brought it there."

"Oh, fuck." David tossed the remains of his coffee in the nearby garbage. "Bricker was also at the scene of the fire, but not until after Trisha disappeared."

"Right under our noses." He'd failed to see. Not even suspected. "And then she couldn't get back to the chop shop sooner because Dorothy left her on duty at Gray Associates."

"Yeah, she hated that too. Damn, I never thought—" David cut himself off. "I'll call Tony and tell him to start digging on her right now."

"Tell him to send a team to watch her home as well. And inform Dorothy."

"ASAP. I'll use my car phone." David took off at a sprint.

Grayson let the acid coffee burn his tongue as he swallowed the rest. It was all a neat setup for Bricker, wasn't it? Make Patricia a suspect in the murders, get Newman to agree with the theory, then have her supposedly commit suicide. Even Patricia had seen how she was being set up, though she'd laughed it off.

He'd let Bricker into his conference room. Welcomed her help even.

Stop, he thought. Bricker being at his office meant she'd been delayed getting back to the garage. Assigning Bricker had been Dorothy's idea. Had she had a glimmer of suspicion?

Grayson stared at his bruised knuckles. He'd struck the wrong cop.

———

Pastel walls. Blessed warmth. Trisha blinked. The world solidified. Wonder of wonders, no spinning.

Something encased her left leg. Bandages covered her wrists. Her cheekbones throbbed, a bone-deep ache. She closed her eyes against the headache that announced its presence with a roar.

"Ouch." She hissed.

"Understatement. You should see your face, Trish," David said.

She blinked, and he came into focus. "Are you real?"

"That must be the fifth time you've asked that." He smiled and patted her hand. "Usually, Grayson answers. One time, the 'what is reality' question devolved into a philosophy discussion that mentioned Aristotle, plus some of your dead white guy writers. Damn, you can ramble."

"I had to suffer through English lit classes. Had to find a way to survive. I had…" She shook her head, and her face hurt. "Ouch. Hurts to talk."

"Easy."

"Grayson's real, right? I didn't just, like, dream the last two months?"

"He's real but human. The doctors said you were stable, so I came on shift while he went to shower and work the case. He looked like hell. Never seen him with a five o'clock shadow before."

"Need photos of that." She cleared her throat and closed her eyes again, pulling at memories. Fire, she thought. So much fire. Then so cold. Bricker. Jack? Cold cement, gun in her hand… Teddy's arm around her.

"Mrs. D!" Her eyes flew open once more.

"That tough old lady is still hanging on," David answered.

Trisha let her hand fall back into the pillow. An image of Bricker dismissing Mrs. D. came to mind. "Did you get her? Bricker?"

"Here, have a sip of this." David held a glass of water up to her mouth. She drank, more than she expected.

"I take it that means Bricker is still out there." Ah, that was better. Not so scratchy when she talked this time.

"No, she's in the wind. Lt. Gilbert's pretty pissed about that. Even Newman is angry that he was snowed by her. But there's no doubt it was her."

"I *know* that."

"Considering you weren't coherent, we had to rely on the physical evidence. Fingerprints on her hypodermic needle match hers on file with the department. Plus, so does the blood type on the blood samples we took from under your nails. You must have dug grooves into her."

"I hope to hell I did."

David offered her more water. This time, she took the glass from him and drank it down in two gulps. "Ah. Good. Thanks."

"Damn glad to see you talking like yourself."

"Damn glad to be talking at all." She stared at him, half expecting him to vanish like the ghosts in her memory. "What else is going on?

"Other than the manhunt for Bricker? Gray Associates is still protecting Taylor. Newman's been apologetic. Dorothy is walking around with quiet fury."

And Grayson had sat at her bedside. So maybe some of that had been true.

"We've all been hoping for more information from you, but you were—"

"Flying high," she finished and looked at the IV. "What are they giving me?"

"A little bit of painkillers but mostly fluids. At first, we didn't know how much smack was in your system and they told us an overdose might be a possibility, so we kept you talking. Well, Grayson did."

"Damage?"

"Brace yourself." He rubbed his forehead. "Doctors gave it all to me because I'm your emergency contact. Pissed Grayson off they wouldn't talk to him. You probably should switch us and fix that."

"I should fix a lot of things."

He ruffled her hair. "Anyway, you're worse than the time with the snake and the biker bar." He shifted from the chair to the side of her bed. "You fractured the shin bone." He tapped the cast on her leg. "Cheekbone isn't broken, but your face is cut and badly bruised." A pause. "You might have a scar."

"Come in handy if I'm in a biker bar again. Though I guess it's a while until I ride my Indian." She licked her lips. Broken leg. She'd run away on a broken leg. Or else broke it when she'd hit the concrete steps. Another scar? Whatever.

"The concussion worried them. They said to avoid excitement."

"Ha! But it explains the headache."

"You should have mentioned that right away."

He went to the wall and turned off the light.

"Better thanks," she said.

He returned and gripped her hand. "We were scared. You're a damn mess."

She took in David's two-day stubble, his sweaty T-shirt, and bloodshot eyes. *It's real. I'm safe.*

"I'd say you should see the other guy, but I'm pretty sure she got me worse." She set her hand on her stomach. "Bandages here too?"

He winced. "Yeah. Stitches, so probably new scars too, but I guess you're used to that." He squeezed her hand tight. "Can't believe you walked around for years carrying all that inside."

"Nah, I gave it to the whiskey to carry. God, I need a drink. Need a smoke even worse." She reached reflexively at her neck, but nothing was around her neck. "Shit. I broke Father Mike's cross."

"I know. You've been ranting about that. But, fuck, that was clever, using it as shim."

Still, her neck felt bare. Wrong. "I miss anything else?"

"Grayson smacked around Newman. You should've seen it." He rose, throwing shadow punches. "Newman said you'd run off after the fire, accused you of setting it, and Grayson sucker-punched him. Got one in the gut too."

"Holy shit." She closed her eyes, picturing the scene.

"Yeah, it was beautiful," he said. "More water?"

"Yeah."

She sipped this one before putting it aside. After, she was silent. Not much else to say, was there? She almost wished to float away on the smack again, felt a craving begin to stir. Dammit.

What the hell do I do now?

An attendant walked in, carrying a vase of black roses.

David took it from him and set it on the bedside table. "Well, that's cheerful."

But she snapped her fingers, delighted. "I bet I know who it's from. Read the card."

"'Since your funeral would be too late for you to appreciate the roses, we thought we'd send them now.'" David tapped the card against his palm. "It's signed 'Kimba Sue & the *Herald* staff.'"

She laughed. It hurt, and she didn't care. "Reporter humor. Or writer humor."

"I'll take your word for it."

"I love them," she said.

"The roses or the *Herald* staff?"

"Both."

The door opened again. Grayson walked in with a bouquet of colorful flowers in his hand.

Trisha's throat tightened. She stared at him. Whatever he'd looked like at her bedside, he was clean-shaven now and dressed immaculately in one of his gray tailored suits. Hell, even a pocket square that matched his tie.

He looked like the proverbial million bucks. And she, well, looked like a mess, which worked, because her whole damn life was a mess right now.

He stared back at her. Neither one spoke.

"Well, I'm headed home finally. Be back later, Trish." David kissed her on the forehead. "Take it easy."

"No choice," she whispered. "Thank you. I love you, you know."

He squeezed her hand again. "I know."

David left. Grayson walked closer. He fingered one of the black roses. "I see someone beat me to flowers."

She nodded because she wasn't sure how to respond. "I like flowers. I like the dark humor even better."

He sat at her bedside. So close, but yet so far. "You're, um, making more sense than last night."

"Semi-coherent now, I guess." Memories before, just before oblivion, flitted through her brain. "Ruined a coat again, didn't I?"

"Coats are easy to replace."

"Yeah."

She looked down at her hand. Empty. "I lost the ring," she whispered.

"We found it. Our clue to that you'd been taken."

She closed her eyes. It hurt to look at him. "Bricker shoved a needle in my neck." Another memory flashed. She sat up in the bed. "Dammit, wait, she got me when I was distracted. The intruder, the man who broke into my place, he was there, at the fire. Dressed as a paramedic."

"Easy, love, you're safe now. I have a twenty-four-hour guard outside. Are you sure you want to talk about everything right now? You just woke up."

"It's important! This was the guy who broke into my place! Maybe he's in it with Bricker. Besides, I need to give a statement, don't I?"

"I agree that we need to start looking for the man you saw, but are you sure you want to relive that right now?" He stroked her uninjured cheek with the back of his hand. "I'm so sorry, love."

"I don't need pity." She pushed his hand away. "Don't coddle me."

"All right." He took off his jacket, tossed it over the chair, and rolled up his sleeves.

"Woo! Take it all off," she called.

He sat in the chair this time and leaned forward, taking her hand once more. "On the coddling, guilty. I hate to see you hurt. But I don't pity you, love. I care for you, and I'm sorry for what you suffered."

"Pity pisses me off, it does." She closed her eyes. She smelled Grayson's aftershave over the faint, fresh aroma of his soap. Pissed her off she cared what he thought. Pissed her off that he'd screwed things up. Pissed her off even more that she had too.

"What else pisses you off?" He asked in a low voice.

"Want a list?" She held up her bandaged hand. "That I was careless enough to be grabbed. That I thought I could leave the past behind. That I took that attack and shoved it into a box and never looked back, but instead let it ooze out like fungus and poison everything."

"Not everything." He stroked the back of her hand.

She felt the flush heat her cheeks. "C'mon. Why were we so angry at each other before Bricker nabbed me?" She finally met his gaze. "I killed them, Teddy. I killed the guys who raped and tortured me. I was glad they were dead. And even seeing how Bricker suffered, even knowing I killed her brother Jack and that she saw that as a failure to protect her little brother, I'd probably make the same choice to kill again. I remember what I felt then. I can't get rid of it. I'm glad they're dead even now. So Bricker has a fucking grievance."

"You can't *agree* with her?"

"I did, though. I heard her. I could feel the pain she was in because he was torn from her life. She wasn't responsible for it but she felt responsible for not helping him, even though it's hard to tell what she could have done." Trisha shook her head. The room spun. She blew out a breath. "He was her half-brother. When their mom died, she went to a nice home with her dad and stepmom, and he got tossed into his dysfunctional father's mess. I figure she became a cop to save others like she couldn't save him. Then she discovered I was out there, living my best life, and she couldn't bear it. Seeing her grief was like looking into a fucking mirror."

"Patricia."

He drew her name out, as he did when he wanted her full attention.

"Yeah?"

"It's not a sin to be alive, to quote your Springsteen."

"Maybe, maybe not." She curled her hand around his tie and pulled him closer. "Give me a kiss. Make it better."

His lips touched hers, tentatively, full of life and warmth. She lost herself in it. He returned the fierceness, as he had during his homecoming.

She desired love, redemption, and… acceptance, something he might not be able to give.

After, he pressed his forehead against her. "Is that better?"

God, his eyes were so brown. And those crow's feet around them were adorable. "For the moment, yeah."

"Are we better?"

"Seems we got a bunch to resolve still, don't we?"

He straightened. "Likely."

Everything hurt again. "But we also need to find Bricker, so get Dorothy in here. I'll make a statement, especially about the fake paramedic. Maybe he helped her."

"She's in the waiting room. I wanted to see you first." A smile broke out on his face, the first since he'd walked in.

She felt herself smiling in return. "Why are you looking at me like that?" She was so stupid goofy for him. That was why this hurt so much. "And what are you smiling about?"

"Because I buried the lead: they're going to let you go home in a few hours. You'll come to my place where—"

"I can get a hotel or something."

"You'll come to my place, which is properly secured, where you'll stay until such time as Bricker is in custody," he repeated, "I've gathered all the information we have about Bricker and the history of your initial attack for *your* insight and study." A pause. "You can sleep in my bedroom. I'll take the couch. And after all this is over, we'll talk and sort this. All right?"

Talk? So much talking. And her without the words.

"Yeah, that's good." She relaxed the smile because it pulled at the stitches on her cheek. "You really know how to appeal to a girl."

CHAPTER TWENTY-SIX

GRAYSON SIPPED HIS SCOTCH, no ice, while standing over the Christmas tree in his living room. His hand shook, nearly spilling the drink.

He set the glass down on the coffee table.

Patricia had settled in the bedroom and seemed to be finally asleep. For all that she seemed near death only forty-eight hours ago, she'd recovered quickly.

He winced, thinking of the statement to Dorothy she'd given at the hospital. He'd been appalled at what she'd suffered yet her statement had been a matter-of-fact recitation of her ordeal. What bothered him—she'd been alone, cold, injured, drugged—was not what bothered Patricia.

She'd shrugged off the physical pain and viewed escaping from the cuffs and the resulting injuries as par for the course. The potential scars produced another shrug. But her eyes had blazed fury as she'd recounted what weapon Bricker had used to cut her.

She stole my knife!

Eventually, he worried her anger would give way to something else. Fear? Resignation? He wished he could predict her. She had his number, but he didn't have hers, not the way he'd thought. He closed his fist around the engagement ring resting in his hand.

How much did the killings of her rapists bother him? She'd claimed to have kept the secret because it would change his view of her.

Knowing what she'd done *had* changed his perspective. He'd killed in the line of duty once. He'd had no choice and done the job, but still, it'd taken time to put the guilt aside. Trisha's killings hadn't been in the line of duty, and she'd admitted she felt guilty because she didn't feel guilty. That made sense to him. He'd read the damn police report of her attack, he'd wanted to murder them himself.

Oh, he didn't condemn her fury. But she'd been driven into a dark place and some part of her still lived there. Did some part of her *want* to live there? The day they'd met, Dorothy had called her a loose cannon. And he'd had to pull her off one of the neo-Nazis she'd been beating after he'd gone down. So would the urge to kill come out again? And if it did, could he accept it without reservation?

He believed so but he *needed* to be absolutely certain. She'd know if he wasn't.

If her account of the confrontation with Bricker was accurate, she'd had *compassion* for Bricker. That spoke of the fury dissipating for good.

He didn't share her compassion this time, however. Maybe tapping into his fury could lead to the certainty he needed. No, that she needed.

He picked up the Scotch and drank it down.

Enough. Bricker was out there. They'd have no peace until they found her and the mysterious intruder who'd also been at the scene of the fire.

He knew this: when he'd thought about Patricia being dead or near-dead, his world had gone gray.

He contemplated Detective Estelle Bricker. An intelligent, tough woman, one who'd been able to rise to detective in a sexist department. A police officer with a clean record. Commendations even, enough for Newman to mentor her. She'd done much good in her time on the force. Yet she'd become a murderer who'd methodically plotted to kill and frame Patricia.

Did everyone possess that murderous rage under the surface? Did he? Before yesterday, he'd have said no. But today, he craved to kill Bricker and didn't much care how. If he knew where to find her, he'd be out there, in the aftermath of yesterday's blizzard, not caring what the law said about his actions. That brought him closer to Patricia's thinking. So, a silver lining?

Grayson poured a second Scotch. First, call his daughter. Call his anchor to normality. Find out how she was coming along with the college applications, double-check the date of her event this week. Share a bit of his life with her.

There had been enough blood spilled for this week.

———

Trisha hobbled out of Grayson's bedroom on crutches, wearing a pair of his black boxers, one of his T-shirts, and a robe. She wanted pants, too, but even if his pants fit, the leg cast nixed those. She wanted her clothes but going up the four flights of her apartment building to get them wouldn't happen and asking for someone to fetch them seemed a little much after all everyone had done for her.

She struggled with the short distance to the dining room, the crutches digging into her armpits. By the time she maneuvered into a chair, the pain in her wrists had gone from a dull ache to stabbing agony. She could take the prescription painkillers, but she'd rather not experience any more drugs right now, thankyouverymuch. She knew pain. She'd handle it.

A bottle of Irish Whiskey and a pack of Marlboro Reds, though, those would have been perfect right now.

Work would be the next best thing.

Grayson, as promised, had the case research on the table divided into three neat piles. One with clippings from Mrs. D. and the *Herald*'s morgue files, one with police files from fourteen years ago, and one marked "present day" with a typed report on top. She scanned that first and realized Grayson had summarized the current case (her) with up-to-date information about her rescue.

Such a cop.

She wondered what it cost him emotionally to put together the report. How much had he allowed himself to feel? Oh, forget that. He probably didn't acknowledge feeling anything right now.

She could understand the not-feeling. The interview with Dorothy

Gilbert had emptied her well, for certain, save for the need to get justice for Mrs. D.

Trisha wondered how the loved ones of Brennan and Martin, Bricker's other victims, were doing right now. Getting used to life on the other side of grief? Or not there yet? She should reach out to them. But that might make it worse, not better, because if she didn't exist, their loved ones would be alive.

Finding Bricker would make it better. Maybe. It wouldn't fill the well of grief. Nothing would. No fucking closure. She knew that.

Another deep breath and she started with Grayson's report, keeping a pad on the side for her notes. (Naturally, he'd left out sharpened pencils and empty pads for her.)

Interesting. They'd just missed Bricker at the chopo shopo. Also interesting, Dorothy said she'd caught a glimpse of movement in the alley when casing the place before entering. Grayson hadn't mentioned that. Maybe Bricker had seen the police car and ran instead of finishing her off. But Bricker had seemed unconscious when Trisha fled. Had enough time had passed for her to wake up? Maybe the movement had been Bricker's co-conspirator, the fake paramedic.

Part of Trisha had wondered for a split second if she'd killed Bricker. She was kind of glad she hadn't, at least she'd be okay with Bricker being alive once they caught her.

Trisha fiddled with the pencil, rhythmically turning it over and over, hoping to remember something that would help in the search for Bricker.

Jack was under orders.

Grayson had mentioned his theory that she'd been a specific target the day before her kidnapping. He'd obviously found evidence to back that up. She closed her eyes and rubbed her forehead. *The past is never past. It's not even past.*

When she opened her eyes again, she pulled the clippings in front of her and began reading.

She handled the yellowed, brittle clippings with care. Hard to read, given they'd been dried out, but Grayson had left a magnifying glass on the table.

November 16, 1970: The chop shop massacre where seven men had killed each other, with an article buried in the bottom corner of the full page.

Fuck, that was the same day as her attack. So, Mrs. D. had found something after all, and Trisha hadn't gotten to her in time to hear it.

The other clippings were far older.

April 1, 1956. Mrs. D. had circled the birth announcements.

May 4, 1956. A full-page clipping headlined "Hell's Kitchen Inferno" that wrote of a fire that allegedly killed a family of four. That was the one Mrs. D. had posted to her refrigerator.

Father, Mother, toddler son, and baby daughter. Trisha frowned, then backtracked to the April 1st story. Yes, one of the babies in the birth announcements had died in the fire.

Fiona May Riordan. Seven pounds, nine ounces. Trisha's throat thickened.

What did a family dead in a fire have to do with the chop shop massacre fourteen long years later? Perhaps Mrs. D. had been pointing to an arsonist who might still be active after over twenty years. No, wait. Mrs. D. had pulled the earlier clipping *before* a fire had destroyed her home.

There was a handwritten note at the bottom of the May 4th page: *Connected to chop shop massacre!*

Grayson had said there was a resemblance of one of the chop shop victims to the father from the arson. A relative?

Trisha brushed the fading newsprint off on the T-shirt. If they'd lived, the baby would have been about the same age as she was. She looked at the date of the arson again. The day before she'd been dumped on Father Mike's doorstep. The one she celebrated as her birthday.

A chill crept up Trisha's spine.

She flipped to the next clipping. This one had a handwritten note from Kimba Sue.

Wow, this was buried deep in the microfiche, but David said the 1956 arson was relevant. Damn, Trish, sure you're not a time traveler because this woman looks so much like you. A lost cousin, maybe? In any case, I hope you like the flowers, and you're back to raising hell soon.

• • •

A long-ago *Herald* article about the arson included a photo of the murdered family. The woman, the mother holding the baby in the photo, could have been her twin.

Jesus, Mary, and Joseph.

Trisha's hand shook.

No, it didn't mean anything. Most of the Irish in Hell's Kitchen were related. This woman could've easily been a second or third cousin or whatever. None of this—the baby, the date she'd been dropped at Father Mike's—meant this long-dead woman was her mother.

Fiona May Riordan. That had been the baby's name.

Her birth name?

"You were dropped at the doorstep of the Church one night while I was working late inside that day. But someone must have loved you because you were a month old, healthy, and wrapped in a hand-knit blanket."

That had been Father Mike's never-changing story every time she'd asked. It never much mattered who her birth parents were because she knew Father Mike loved her. She'd suspected *he* was her birth father. Why wouldn't she? Everyone knew he acted more as her father than to the rest of the kids.

She'd known that she'd had parents at some point. But…

Oh, God, I had a brother?

An image of the man posing as the paramedic the night of the fire danced in front of her eyes. He'd looked familiar. He looked like *her*. And he resembled one of the victims of the chop shop massacre.

Grayson had a note about the fire in his report. Only the body of the mother had been recovered. There had been a memorial service for the other Riordans.

Three bodies missing.

Trisha laid her head in her hands and blocked it all out, concentrating on the throbbing ache from the stitches in her stomach. The next step was to find out if Father Mike had a connection with this murdered family.

But that would require moving from the chair.

"Patricia?" A quiet question.

She rested her head on her arm. "Not now, Grayson."

"I have coffee. Black. Fresh-brewed."

She rolled her shoulders and raised her head. "Well," she drawled, "so long as you have coffee."

She waited until he came back with a mug, waited until after she had two long swallows before speaking again. "You saw these already. You came to the same conclusion I just did."

"I saw them briefly. Long enough to give Tony and Dorothy the details to pursue leads."

He'd dressed for work today: pinstriped blue suit, blue silk tie, matching pocket square, white dress shirt, and his ever-present cufflinks.

It was as much armor as her black leather and jeans. To ward off her? Ouch.

No, he wanted to be calm himself. Grayson being all business helped her do the same. She hoped.

"Are you researching possible connections to Father Mike and this supposedly dead Riordan family?" she asked.

He stayed in business mode, his expression blank. "It's slow work, especially since Michael O'Connell is a common name." A pause. "Kieran Riordan, the father of the doomed family, has a somewhat more unique name, as does his wife, Moira, though we still need her maiden name. The son was named James Murphy Riordan, so we're checking Moira Murphy. Did you ever look into this yourself?"

He said the last sentence in a near whisper, worried about setting her off.

Way past that, Grayson.

"No. I told you before, I considered Father Mike my father. Hell, you know I believed he *was* my birth father. Even the nuns found that story of his finding a foundling on the church steps fishy. I overheard them talking about it once." And one of the nuns that she'd met again last Christmas had confirmed it. Trisha pushed the haunting photos away from her. "Church records. Did you check the records of Father Mike's parish for any Moiras?"

He raised an eyebrow and wrote that down. "No. I'll have Tony get on that as well."

"Okay. All this is speculation unless we have blood samples to compare between me and this family." She rubbed the bridge of her nose. "And, given they're dead, I don't see how we ever can."

"Unfortunately, you are likely right," he said.

"Well, we might have had some samples, since my intruder's blood was on my knife. But given Bricker stole it…" Fury rose again.

"The sample would be corrupted, yes. It's possible DNA might be advanced enough now for a comparison but…" He cleared his throat. "Are you saying your intruder was your *brother*?"

"I thought he looked familiar that night at the fire. He looks like…me."

"That…"

Grayson let his words trail off.

"I know, not definitive. Still, he could have hurt me both times and didn't, so far as I know. But, dammit, I want to know!"

Grayson stayed all business. "Completely understandable."

He worried about triggering her rage. But rage had been burned out of her when she'd looked into Bricker's soul. About damn time she stopped being freaked out and started behaving like an investigative reporter.

She grabbed Grayson's report and waved it at him. "You sure have been busy."

"I dictated the report into a tape recorder while you were sleeping. Lois typed it."

Right. He'd put the full resources of Gray Associates behind her case. "Everybody there knows as much or more about me than I do, then."

He winced. "I didn't think we could waste time while you were missing. Bricker is still out there."

"Efficient. That is very like you. The part of you I like." She finished the coffee. "Let's take a huge leap of logic and assume Mrs. D. was pointing to me being related to this murdered family, perhaps as the supposedly dead baby, and thought the chop shop massacre was revenge for the fire fourteen years before. That means someone in the Kitchen came after me when I was fourteen because they noticed my resemblance to a dead woman."

"A working theory." He refilled her coffee and sat across from her, hands folded in front of him.

"A theory full of holes. The adults in this family were dead. Why stir that up by coming after someone who looks like one of them? And what was the fight about in the chop shop?"

"All good questions, yes. But I'll point out that if we believe the theory of you being the baby, then an adult had to deliver you to Father Mike."

"Another survivor of the fire?"

"Stands to reason, perhaps the father, given the resemblance to one of the victims in 1970. Or a cousin or uncle."

"Us Irish have big families. Right. Dammit." She couldn't argue with that. "Go on."

"Bricker held you at the scene of the massacre. That's how Dorothy and I found you. We were desperate and decided it was worth checking on the theory that a person out for revenge would take you there. We got lucky there and, still, we were too late. You'd saved yourself."

"Yeah, but you wrapped me in a coat." She held up a hand. "The police file on the chop shop murders is in the third pile, right? Fine, let me finish this second cup of coffee first."

He fiddled around in the kitchen.

The black coffee gave her a jolt. Perfect. She picked up the pad and pencil. "First, you fill me in. It'll give me an overview before digging through the reports myself."

It'd also buy her time to compose herself. Grayson probably knew that.

He flipped through the old police file. She took notes. Seven dead. Gruesome crime scene. Half the leadership of the West Side Gang gone in one night.

"West Side is suspected in that long-ago arson that killed that family?" she cut in.

"Unclear, but if not them, perhaps someone who later became one of them."

Barely connected, she thought. If this was a story, the *Herald* would never run it. Joe would toss it back to her with a note saying, "FACTS NOT SPECULATION. SLOPPY WORK CONNELL."

"Which victim looks like the Riordan dad?"

"The one who died of a gunshot near the door, not grouped with the others. Tony traced the name this man was using. His identity was fake."

"Shit!" She stood up, intending to pace, but remembered the cast around her foot and thigh. "First, he's murdered in a fire, and he might be my father, but, wait, he's still alive and killing people, and now he's dead again. 'Seems to resemble' just isn't good enough. I need facts. What did Sherlock Holmes say? 'Can't make bricks without clay?'"

"We're following all those leads. It takes time."

She glared at him. "Don't you dare tell me to rest when all this is to be determined."

"I'm looking at a woman who fought through a punctured lung for a story. I wouldn't dream of telling you to rest."

Her frustration deflated without a target. "Okay."

"None of these puzzle pieces fits yet, Patricia, and some of them may not fit in the end. If Mrs. D. recovers, she may have answers, especially since she put these three incidents together."

"*If* Mrs. D. recovers. I don't suppose there's an evidence file somewhere in police custody that contains the blood of my supposed dad?"

"It's an open case, so there is an evidence file. The file is currently MIA, however. The precinct's filing system leaves much to be desired."

"Or someone dumped it long ago, through carelessness or negligence or corruption."

"Yes." He winced. "I hate corrupt law enforcement. I'd thought the NYPD had improved. Bricker was supposed to be the exception, at least in these times. But, in any case, it's suggestive this man died separate from the others. If police officers were in the pay of the West Side Gang, then they could have killed the man when they arrived on scene. I would have liked to have worked that crime scene. It would have told us a great deal."

"Bricker might know. She seemed to know a lot about this. She taunted me with it." Bricker. Her twisted metaphorical twin. "No word on her?"

"Nothing, save that Dorothy found evidence at Bricker's home confirming her obsession with you. Also, your injuries contained skin and tissue samples matched to Bricker, completely corroborating your story." He frowned. "But Bricker herself seems to have utterly vanished. It's frustrating," he admitted with a sigh. "Taylor's security detail reports no sign of suspicious activity. Perhaps you did seriously injure Bricker that night. She could be dead somewhere."

"Nah, I knocked her out temporarily but…she likely got up and out on her own. I figure she was afraid of me because I stole her gun." Trisha twirled a pencil in her fingers. "She was so good at hiding her obsession. I never suspected anything when I spoke to her that day in my apartment. But even if we never find her, she's already done what she wanted. She blew up my life."

Trisha hobbled over to the entranceway to the living room to stare at the Christmas tree, remembered the joy when she'd dragged it up here to surprise Grayson, the happiness when they'd made love on the carpet.

A lie. A beautiful lie but a lie, nonetheless.

She spotted the engagement ring sitting on the coffee table. No, she could not carry any more in her heart right now. Perhaps Grayson couldn't either, which explained why he hadn't given it back to her.

"Bricker," she said with her back to Grayson. "She said her brother Jack was under orders to hand me over."

"I read that in your statement."

"I should have kept her talking."

Grayson laughed softly. "Love, you fought off an armed woman while drugged and injured. You then escaped without any help. You could hardly have done better."

She rolled her eyes where he couldn't see. "Flattery, Grayson?"

"Truth."

"Truth. There's a lot of that going around, all of it uncomfortable."

"For now," he allowed. "And better than lies."

Unexpectedly, her stomach rumbled.

"Let's eat." He stood next to her. "I have bagels and cream cheese. Or I can make you something else."

That was it for personal talk, she thought. "I'll eat, then see if I'm some supposedly dead or missing baby and what the hell the West Side wanted from me."

"To hurt you." He lent her his shoulder as she hobbled to the kitchen.

"Lot of that going around too."

"You hurt Bricker worse than she did you. Your statement said she hesitated when you told her she was just like them."

"She hated the truth, at least long enough for me to escape. She's probably gone back to justifying herself now."

Grayson settled her on the kitchen stool at his island.

"Can we skip the bagels? I'm not sure my cheek is up to chewing."

"How do you like your eggs?" he asked.

"Over easy."

"Easily accomplished." Grayson cracked the eggs with one hand, straight into the pan, without breaking the yolks. The eggs started to sizzle.

"I wonder if Bricker ever made her little brother breakfast?"

"She coolly plotted the murder of three people, including you, killed two of them," Grayson snapped. "And critically injured another. And not under duress. She was perfectly calm and sane when she did these things."

"Oh, she's not quite sane. That much came through. But I've been told I'm crazy too." She inhaled deeply. "Damn, those smell good."

"Thank you." Grayson flipped the eggs. "You're not her. What she did was wrong. Evil. You are not."

"Evil? God, Grayson, you sound like a priest."

He slipped the eggs onto a plate. "I sincerely hope not, given Catholic priests are celibate."

That made her laugh, finally, and she even tolerated the pain caused by the mirth as the movement pulled at her stitches. He added toast to the eggs and presented her with breakfast. She settled onto the kitchen stool just as the phone rang.

Grayson answered it and, from what she could tell, it was his daughter. Poor kid. What could he say to her about his girlfriend? *Hey, daughter, seems like my new girlfriend has a homicidal past and she was kidnapped and tortured by someone who wanted revenge. Think you could accept her anyway?*

What Eleanor wanted was her parents back together. *Fat chance, kid,* Trisha thought. *I saw your parents together a couple of months ago. Your mom might want him again but there's no spark on his side.* And there were too many sparks between her and Grayson. Following the metaphor, that might leave them both in ashes.

"Yes, of course, I'll make your basketball game tonight. I know it's important," Grayson said.

That made Trisha wonder how many of Eleanor's games he'd missed while working. Hopefully not too many.

"Yes, I'm fine." His voice rose. Uh-oh. That had to be a complaint about her.

"No, she's not trouble." This time, Grayson lowered his voice, probably worried about being overheard. "I want you to meet her. We're…serious."

Trisha bet he'd been about to say "engaged." Yeah, best not to torture herself listening to any more of this. She tuned out the conversation and spotted a pile of mail with her name on it. Someone had cleared out her mailbox, likely David.

She flipped through them. Bills, bills, bills. She might have to hustle pool to come up with her rent next month. Hell, maybe she could put her injuries to work and seem more helpless for the hustle.

Aha. One freelance check. Numerous magazines she had ordered for research. A couple of rejections of her queries.

Oh. Wow. She held the letter in her hand, tactile proof it existed.

The New York Times Magazine wanted her article about the juvenile justice system. The acceptance she'd been hoping for the day she opened the razor blade letter. Only a week ago. She'd hoped it would give a huge boost to her freelance career.

And now?

Now she lacked the brain cells to even answer the editor and the physical stamina to do the research. She set it aside, wondering if there was a future when she wrote and published that piece.

She picked up *Sports Illustrated* out of the magazine stack, attracted by the Giants cover. Out of the pages fell a business-size envelope without a stamp and with a typewritten address.

Another one of Bricker's letters?

Trisha picked up the envelope with a napkin to preserve any fingerprints and sliced it open with her butter knife.

No razor blades. Only a single slip of paper. On it was written "Jimmy Riordan" and a telephone number.

Her supposedly dead brother.

CHAPTER TWENTY-SEVEN

GRAYSON HAD JUST ENDED the call with Eleanor when the phone rang again.

"Good news," Dorothy said. "Anne-Marie Donohue's been moved out of ICU."

Tension eased from his shoulders. "That is very good news."

"You're smiling. Is Bricker caught?" Patricia called to him.

"Mrs. D. is better, out of ICU."

"That's good." Patricia put her head in her hands. "Very good," she whispered.

"Patricia says 'thank you' for letting us know," Grayson told Dorothy.

"It's a relief to me as well. I thought you'd want to know right away. Also, a full search of Bricker's place provided enough evidence for a slam dunk at trial, given we find her."

"You're worried she's running?"

"She won't run," Patricia called.

"It's a concern," Dorothy said. "Stay alert. Keep me updated on any progress you and the reporter make."

When he hung up the phone, Patricia's face had gone almost sheet white, emphasizing the small freckles on her cheeks and the bruise that had bloomed into a black eye. Her hand sat atop the stack of mail David had dropped off last night.

"You found another letter from Bricker in there!" He reached for the stack.

"No." A sharp denial. "Don't."

He stopped and shoved his hands into his pockets. "What is it then? You look…as if you're not all here. Too much activity? Are you in pain? Should I—"

She leaned forward, elbows on the black marble. "You're cute when you're get panicky, which isn't often, and it usually means you've no idea what to do with me. Turns out, I have no idea what to do with me, either. Give me a sec."

"All right." Bide his time. She'd just been through an ordeal. He'd promised himself not to push.

He busied himself with cleaning up and making another pot of coffee. When that was done, he gave her another mug of black coffee and sipped his own while watching her.

Color had returned to her face, though that shiner would take a few weeks to heal. But the dark circle somehow made the blue eye seem larger, like it was peering into his soul. "Secrets and lies and truth," she finally said. "I've got a thing I need to handle. I'm wrestling with myself about it."

"Tell me," he said in a near whisper.

"Yeah, but do I want to risk you disagreeing with me and storming off?" A deep sigh. "There's a limit to how much heartbreak I can take right now."

She wanted him to push at him again. Already. "I want to help."

She smiled, wistful. "This fucking note." She tapped the envelope. "I liked your plan of waiting to talk about us until this was over. I liked your plan of not exploring our mess until I had some perspective, but here it is again."

"Very little sounds less appealing right now than excavating our unique relationship." He should have taken her with him for Thanksgiving. They would be in a much different place now if he had. "How about we go sailing instead? I'll pay for the flight to Miami."

She laughed. "You'd have to tie me to the boat mast or whatever you call it so I don't fall overboard."

"That's basically the metaphorical equivalent of what I'd like to do right now."

"Yeah." She looked down at her wrists. No one would be tying her up for a while yet. "What if, instead, we go overboard together?"

She held out the paper to him with trembling fingers. The name, Jimmy Riordan, and a phone number. He was real, then.

"Your intruder?" he asked.

"Potentially my older brother, since James was the name of the toddler killed in the fire."

"Yes." He sat next to her, their shoulders nearly touching. "You want to talk to him. You want to know. You want the truth."

"All of that."

"And you were debating about doing that behind my back because you thought I would stop you."

"Because I *feared* you might stop me. I'm not sure I intend to tell what I find out to the cops. I don't know this Jimmy's story. I'm not sure you'd agree to not tell the cops."

That statement felt like a knife to his heart. "Because we have no trust."

"Because I don't know *what* we have." She laid her hand flat on his countertop and jerked her head to the living room. "I saw the ring over there on the coffee table."

Everything depended on what he said at this moment, and yet he lacked the words. "At least we have the truth of things."

"And where did that get us?" She snorted. "And now we've got another crossroad."

"Your first instinct was to handle this on your own." He kept his voice low and refused to let anger into it. Not helpful, anger. "But you showed me the note anyway."

"Since Nicky died, I handle things on my own. But that's not been working so well." She rubbed the bridge of her nose. "I see the aftermath of my decisions. I'm lucky to be alive. You and Dorothy saved me."

"You saved yourself."

She shrugged.

"And now you want to walk into danger again."

"Because I'm finally tired of hiding from everyone, including myself." Her voice gained strength. "I'm going to call this guy because I have to know. I've been driven to follow the truth since I got out of juvie. But it was never my own truth. It's past time to have that piece of me."

"I understand." Yes. She wanted to change, to go forward. The ball of fear and anger nearly closing his throat began to dissipate.

"Yeah, well, I'm also scared."

"You want me to be with you?"

"I don't know if I can do it alone," she confessed in a whisper. "But… I'm a killer. You know that now. I'm also contemplating breaking the law again. Do you…will you…?"

He pulled her into his arms. She remained there, against his chest, for a while, silent. He searched for words. "I'm sorting through whether I was angrier with you for lying to me or if I'm…judging you for what…happened."

Deliberately killing someone, no matter the provocation, changed a person. But maybe it had turned her into the person she was now, that he'd fallen in love with?

"Fair," she whispered.

"I'm…I'm not good at knowing how I feel." He cleared his throat. Shutting down was what had ended his marriage or, at least, part of what had caused it to fail.

"Ah." She closed her eyes. "You're a cop, deep down, and have that way of viewing things. Plus, Dorothy is your friend and choosing to help me means hurting that friendship, especially if we look up Riordan without telling her. And God knows what your kid thinks of me right now, and this feels like a bridge too far in our mess and—"

"Now who's rambling and sounding panicky?"

She stared up at him, blue eyes bright. "I usually just do what I damn well please."

"I think," he said and took a deep breath, "we both do."

"Teddy," she whispered. "Will you help with this?"

Taylor had said that Patricia craved his approval. But that was not correct. What she needed was his *acceptance*.

"Yes."

"Oh. Okay. Let's stop there for now." She put a hand over her heart. "You might regret it."

"I regret going behind your back to investigate your past. I regret not protecting you better." He rose and put their empty coffee cups in the sink. "I've made a few bad mistakes in my life. I'm sure I'll make more." He finally smiled and his stomach settled. "But I've never regretted time spent with you, Patricia, not for an instant. And that's my truth."

"Not even when you're furious?"

"Especially not even then. Dorothy told me once I need people around me who piss me off or I go cold." He smiled. "She was right, as usual."

Patricia smiled and it brought sunshine into the room. She set the note on the counter. "Let's call and see what happens."

But as he handed her the receiver, a call came in through the intercom. "Mr. Grayson?" Kevin said through static.

Grayson pushed the button and answered. "Yes?"

"Sir, two police detectives are on their way up. They pushed past me. I couldn't stop them."

Dorothy? "Is it Lt. Gilbert?"

"No, sir, I'd have recognized her. I didn't know them. One plainclothes man, one in uniform."

"Thank you for the warning, Kevin."

"Shit," Trisha said. "Are they here for payback about your tagging Newman?"

"I have no idea why they're here." Grayson flexed his fingers. His Beretta was locked in his safe.

A hard knock at the door. "NYPD!" a voice called.

"Patricia," he said. "Act as helpless as you can."

She set her jaw and curled an arm around the crutches. "Right." But she grabbed the knife he'd used to slice the bread and slid it out of sight.

Grayson rolled his shoulders, took the few steps to his entranceway, and opened the door. The two men pushed inside. One older, balding, dressed in a badly tailored suit. The second, a hulking uniform.

"Gentleman," he said, leaving the door open.

"You're coming with us, Grayson," growled the suit.

Grayson crossed his arms. "Why?"

"We don't have to tell you." The hulking uniform drew out a pair of handcuffs.

A thud against the floor. Patricia's crutches.

Both men's hands flew to their weapons.

Patricia appeared in the doorway. "Hey, Teddy, I can't open the—" Her eyes went wide. She slumped against the crutches. "Oh my God, what's going on? Did you find Bricker?"

Her voice broke. She sagged into the crutches. Even he might have been fooled by the show of weakness.

The men relaxed, hands falling away from the service weapons. "Miss Connell," the plainclothes detective said roughly. "It's not your concern."

"But he's taking care of me! If he goes somewhere, I can't even… I mean, I can hardly stand upright, Captain."

Captain? Patricia knew him.

The captain frowned. "Can you call someone?"

"I…maybe, but the hospital said to have someone watch over me in case there…in case there were any complications."

Tears welled in Patricia's eyes. She was scared for *him*, Grayson thought.

The captain's hostility dropped a notch. "You, Grayson, call someone for her. Then we go to the precinct."

"Thank you," Patricia whispered.

Grayson made a show of helping her back to a kitchen stool and picked up the receiver.

"Call David," she said. "Let me talk."

He dialed and handed her the phone. "Hey, David," she said in a voice far more tired than only a few minutes ago. "Can you come to Grayson's place?"

A pause. "No, David, I'm okay but Captain Bennitti and another detective from Midtown South's precinct are here. They have information for Grayson. He's going to the precinct with them."

With those short three sentences, Patricia had informed a third party of who was in his apartment. A witness, in case something went wrong.

She nodded vigorously as David said something. Playacting, Grayson decided.

"Yep," she finally said, and hung up.

"Done," Captain Bennitti said. "Let's go, Grayson."

It might be some time before Grayson saw her again, if he judged the police correctly. He leaned over and kissed Patricia on the cheek.

She grabbed his tie, pulled him closer, and kissed him properly. Thoroughly.

Oh, bloody hell, this was not the time to be aroused.

"Don't talk to them. Be careful," she whispered.

The captain cleared his throat. "Now, Grayson."

The two men framed him as they went out the door of his home.

"I love you," Patricia called after him.

Grayson closed his eyes for a brief second, absorbing the words he'd wanted to hear since the day they'd met.

Whatever happened next, he had that.

CHAPTER TWENTY-EIGHT

THE SECOND THE door to Grayson's home shut, Trisha dialed up Gray Associates. Lois answered, Trisha told her it was an emergency, and Tony's voice came on.

"Is Edmund all right?" he asked, no preamble.

She explained the cops taking Grayson into custody.

"I hope Captain Bennitti took him to the precinct, but...I don't know, Tony. They oozed hostility. He's being taken in for questioning, if not being arrested outright, or, worse case, they're taking him to a site where they won't be disturbed. Grayson only left with them because he was worried I might get hurt in a confrontation."

"You did all the right things. They know they're being watched. And the fact they left you unharmed, as a potential witness, probably means he'll be safe, at least until they get him to the precinct."

"I bet anything Dorothy knows nothing about this."

"You'd be right," Tony said. "I'll call our lawyers. Hopefully, one is available ASAP."

"Call Taylor. She owes Grayson, and I bet she's available, and she knows the case."

"Good idea."

"But, damn, Tony, I hate the idea of them tossing him into a cell. They don't have cameras back there, and they could do what they wanted with him, Tony, they could—"

Real panic crept in.

"I will do *everything* in my power to protect my friend," Tony said. "Trust me."

Tony was former NSA. He had connections everywhere. She knew that.

"This is my fault."

"The fault lies with the assholes who are fucking with my partner," Tony said. "And they're gonna fucking regret it."

Mild-mannered Tony, swearing. Good.

"I'm calling Kimba Sue too," Trisha said. "Letting her know what's up. You make sure Taylor is aware the press has the story."

"I will. Now stay safe and stay with David. We can handle this, Trisha." Tony hung up.

Trisha took another deep breath and dialed Kimba Sue. No answer. Fuck. She dialed again, this time Tony Borelli's direct line at the *Herald*.

Borelli was at his desk.

"It's Trisha. Cops from Midtown South just took Grayson into custody for who knows what. Make sure Kimba Sue knows."

"Right," Borelli said. "You okay, Trish?"

"Remains to be seen. Loved the flowers." And she hung up again.

She slumped over, let her hands and head rest on the counter, took deep breaths, fought the fear and grief about to take over.

The lock to the front door turned. She reached for the bread knife.

"Hey, Trish," David called.

"Kitchen," she yelled back.

He rushed over and hugged her. She hung on tight. Breaking down would not help Grayson. Deep breaths, deep breaths.

He held her out. "You okay? You look like hell."

"You already said that yesterday." But it made her smile, however weakly. "You got here fast."

"I was on duty across the street. We have a detail watching in case Bricker shows. Your call got sent to my car phone," he said. "I watched them put Grayson in a black and white. I sent the detail to follow them. What the hell?"

"I don't know." She outlined calling Tony and the *Herald*.

He slipped onto a stool next to her. "He'll be okay, Trish. You know he's tough."

She closed her eyes. The fear burst forth. "He wouldn't be in trouble if not for me!" She slapped her hand on the marble counter, and immediately, her wrist erupted in pain.

"Shit." She drew back her wrist and rubbed it. "Just shit."

"Look, pull yourself together, and we'll figure out what to do next because I know damn well you're no good at waiting."

She rested her head on David's shoulder for a minute. "You're my family, you know that?"

"Yeah, I know. And you're as much trouble as any of my sisters. So, what's next?"

"My past is the key to the truth. Bricker knew it but she's out of reach. But this guy isn't."

She showed the note from Jimmy Riordan and explained that she'd been about to make that call.

"Dangerous," David drawled.

She twirled the bread knife. "So am I."

"Not with that dull blade." He took it from her with a laugh. "That's the Trish I know."

He dialed Riordan's number and handed her the receiver. She held it so they both could listen.

Someone answered.

"Who?" he asked.

A man's voice. "Trisha Connell."

"Shamrock's at Anderson and 90th. Today. No police."

"No." The word came out impulsively.

A pause. Static on the line. "You are stubborn." Another pause. She held up the receiver so David could listen.

"Yeah, I'm a bitch. But you left me the number, Jimmy Riordan. What the hell do you want from me?"

"To talk to you."

"I'm listening."

"In person," said the voice.

"I'd be a fucking idiot to meet you somewhere at your choosing."

"Dammit. Fine. So, you pick the place."

She closed her eyes. Another risk. Had to be taken.

"Parking lot on 35th Street across from the convention center construc-tion. Two hours." Mostly in the open. Hard to spring a trap that way. Plus, this had all started near the convention center. The right place to end it.

"No cops," Riordan said.

"No cops. But I won't be alone, and I can't promise I won't hurt you."

A sarcastic laugh. "We'll see."

CHAPTER TWENTY-NINE

TWO HOURS. Not much time to prepare herself for whatever this Riordan would say. Hell, he might spout a bunch of lies. He might try to kill her. Trisha would take that chance. Besides, at this point, she felt indestructible. What could hurt more than the past few days?

"You don't have to come with," she said to David. "I can take a taxi."

"You think I'm not curious as hell as to what he wants?" David smacked his chest. "Family, right?"

"Family."

"Now, to solve the logistical problems," Trisha said, "I need outside clothes and a long winter coat."

"I'll have Lois send over some stuff, ASAP," David said.

"Okay." Now what? "Let's assume things go badly with Riordan in the parking lot. Someone needs to know the truth."

"Agreed. What did you have in mind?"

"A story." A deep breath, and she dared call Kimba Sue again.

"Oh. My. God!" Kimba exclaimed. "TRISHA! Are you okay? What's going on? What's the story? Was it really a cop who nabbed you? Are the Westies involved? What the what is up with Grayson being taken into custody by Captain Bennitti personally? Talk to me!"

Trisha laughed. "You're quite a mix of worry for your friend and wanting a lead on the story."

"Well. I'm both things, right?"

Trisha could practically hear the long hair swish in the background.

"Det. Estelle Bricker was the cop who kidnapped and tortured me. She's on the run, which is probably why the NYPD isn't releasing her name."

"I heard that much. Good to have confirmation to run with. But are you okay?"

"Not nearly, not yet. But I'm about to do something stupid and dangerous, so I'm sending you over a typed story. If I don't call by tonight, run it. If I do call, you give it back. It's my story, my words, and I want it under my byline if I'm still here."

"Trish." A pause. "You going to do this alone?"

"No. I got back-up. I'll send this via bike messenger. Probably an hour or so."

"If Grayson is in custody, who's going with you?"

"David."

"Good. Then be careful!"

"Never."

David made his own calls then. He arranged for clothes and a security detail to shadow them during the meeting with Riordan. "Just in case," he said.

She agreed. Mrs. D. almost died because of this. David was risking his life. This would protect him.

Kevin the doorman alerted them through the intercom that the clothes from Lois had arrived. He delivered the Macy's bags a few minutes later. She tipped him with cash from Grayson's wallet and thanked him for the warning about the cops.

"Mr. Grayson will be all right?" Kevin asked.

"Absolutely," she assured him, with more confidence than she felt.

She sat on the living room couch with the clothes, careful to ignore the engagement ring resting on the coffee table. David remained in the kitchen, making more calls.

The contents of the bags amused and appalled her.

"How the fuck does Lois know my underwear sizes?" she said.

"She orders undercover clothes for our teams, so she developed a good eye," David called from the kitchen. "I gave them your shoe size. I remembered from that time we bought Converse high tops together. I figured you'd like the Nike Air Force 1s."

"I think I want to marry Lois."

"We all do," David said.

She checked the clock on the wall. An hour and fifteen minutes to get ready. An hour and fifteen minutes Grayson would spend in police custody.

David ambled in. "Nice tree."

"Thanks."

She displayed the bandaged wrists and tapped the cast. "I can get the underwear and shirt on but…." She took a deep breath. "I'll need help with getting the sweatpants over the cast."

"I've seen you in your shorts, so I'm fine with seeing you in your underwear if you are," David said. "While you do the first bit, I'll be in the kitchen, chugging the last of the pot of coffee. Call when you need me."

Dressing forced Trisha to pay attention to the full damage from Bricker's attack. The bruises on her arms and legs were in full colorful bloom, while her torso was mostly bandaged to cover the stitches.

It looked like someone had stomped all over her.

But she'd gotten up again.

The blue cotton T-shirt went on easily enough. Next came an oversize New York Giants hoodie. David wordlessly helped her with the sweatpants, easing the pant leg over the cast. She cursed as she grabbed the crutches to stand. "I can already tell I'll hate them. Six weeks. Fuck."

She bent to put a sock on her healthy foot and pain lanced through her wrists. David grabbed the sock and sneaker and did that for her.

"You never said why you like the Giants over the Jets," he said.

"Father Mike was a Giants fan. Y. A. Tittle. Frank Gifford."

"Ah."

Finally, David helped her into the long coat. It hung all the way down to her toes, but the wool would keep her warm. Temperatures had dropped to below fifteen degrees.

Another coat of Grayson's for her to ruin. *You better be okay, you arrogant pain in the ass.*

She leaned on the crutches. "I've been thinking?"

"Uh-oh."

"Nicky. He must have heard about the chop shop massacre. It had to be the talk of Hell's Kitchen. But I can't remember if we ever talked about it."

"You think he knew something about why you were taken?"

"I think he heard stuff. We used to exchange letters when I was in juvie. I'm wondering if he hinted at…whatever this is."

"How do we find out if he did?"

"I kept his letters. I meant to read them when this first started, but then we found Taylor and things went to shit."

"Are you sure you need to go there?"

She shook her head. "Whatever he knew or didn't know, he did it to protect me. Besides, I told him over and over I didn't want to deal with it anymore. Hell, we didn't even live in the Kitchen until I graduated from college because my attack was too raw. Then the rent on that place was too good to ignore…. Anyway." She rolled her shoulders and slipped on the Ray-Ban sunglasses Lois had included with the clothes. "Let's pull off all the scabs now. Besides, my typewriter is there."

"I don't want to see you bleed any further," David said.

"Way past that."

————

Grayson said nothing on the ride to the precinct, nothing as the Captain led him inside, nothing as they searched him and took his watch and his belt, and nothing as they brought him to the dingy police interrogation room. He settled himself in the off-balance plastic chair, stretched his feet out, and wondered what was the purpose of all this.

Intimidation because he'd struck Newman? Or was this some sort of internal strike at Dorothy because she'd stepped on Newman's toes? Bloody hell, for all he knew, Bricker had friends in the department who had somehow twisted what happened into Patricia's fault.

He'd half-expected to be thrown into a cell, forgotten, off-the-books. If he'd been alone at his home, he'd have refused to leave without seeing an arrest warrant. If they'd tried to haul in Patricia, he'd have confronted them.

But cooperating had been safest for her.

In any case, that they'd let Patricia make a call, that they'd put him in interrogation rather than a cell, meant this was likely something besides payback or revenge. He planned to say nothing. Not about his investigation, not about the research done by the *Herald*, and not anything about Patricia. Especially not the note from Jimmy Riordan.

He'd made a grave mistake in digging into Patricia's past without her permission. He would not reveal her new secrets now, not for anyone.

What worried him was what she might do about Riordan while he was locked in here. At least she'd called David. And her injuries should prevent her from leaving the apartment without help. He closed his eyes, crossed his hands over his chest, and settled in to wait, ignoring the smells of sweat and urine. He'd dealt with worse on stakeouts.

At the moment he was nearly asleep, the door flew open.

This time, the captain brought a plainclothes detective with him. The younger man resembled a clerk with a wide, innocent face. That probably fooled many people into believing he was harmless. Neither one of them would be fools.

The captain introduced the detective. Grayson ignored them. The detective slapped a folder on the table. Grayson merely tilted his head.

"Yes?" he inquired.

"Name. For the record."

"Edmund Marshal Grayson." He rattled off his society security number, his place of residence, and his age.

The captain loomed over him. "You know why you're here."

"I voluntarily came when requested," Grayson said. "Am I being charged with something?"

"Not yet." The detective sat on the table, next to him.

Grayson braced himself. It was going to be a long session. "I request a lawyer, as is my right." Tony would already be working on that.

"That makes me think you have something to hide, Mr. Grayson." The captain made a show of flicking through the binder and slapped two photographs on the table. "Explain this."

His eyes widened, though he managed to control his surprise otherwise. Estelle Bricker. Dead. The first photo showed her body in a dumpster.

The second, the gunshot wound to the back of her head that had killed her. Double-tap, he thought. Mob execution. Bloody hell.

Riordan? Patricia, be careful!

"Grayson? Where were you in the last two days?" the captain asked.

They suspected he'd murdered Bricker. *If I did it, you'd never have found the body.* That's why Dorothy had been kept away from the case and why the captain was personally sitting in on the interrogation. A cop, whatever else she'd been, was murdered. And they'd want to arrest the killer. Nothing he said in here would work in his favor.

"Lawyer," he said.

"According to Lt. Gilbert's report, you and her were alone for a time when you approached that building that night."

Dorothy had simply told the truth. He said nothing.

"You arrived on scene perhaps around the time Bricker fled. You encountered her and killed her while you and Lt. Gilbert were separated."

An eerily possible scenario, except it hadn't happened. "Lawyer," he repeated.

The younger detective kicked Grayson's feet. "Sit up straight when you're talking to the captain."

"No."

The detective pulled out handcuffs. One went around Grayson's left wrist, the other on the table leg. Cold, he thought, and his mind pictured Patricia, cuffed to that awful bed in that freezing room in the garage. She had found the strength to break free. He could endure this.

"You need to take this seriously," the captain said.

Tony would have called the law firm they kept on retainer. This would only be a matter of time. Unless they hid him from the lawyer.

A knock sounded at the door. The captain jerked his head at the detective, who opened the door a crack. A hushed conversation followed. The captain was called over.

The door shut, and Grayson was left alone again, still handcuffed. He rolled his shoulders, contemplating his few options. They'd taken his belt, but he still wore the cufflinks. He could use one as a shim to unlock the cuffs. He'd had the cufflinks made especially for emergencies like this. Well, not this. He hadn't expected to be held by police.

But he'd wait and see if that would be necessary. Best not tweak the grim-faced captain too much. Grayson rearranged the chair so he could rest the cuffed hand on the table and let his mind drift through his relationship with Patricia.

The day they'd first met, when she'd challenged him, the search in the dark tunnels for the museum thieves, the discovery of the bomb, her dogged refusal to leave and save herself. The look on her face when he offered her the ring. The terror of finding her so damaged only three nights ago. He'd seen the outer pain caused by Bricker. But he wished he knew the inner damage.

I love you. She'd called that after him this morning. The *first time* she'd said it. He held on to that like a freezing man drawn to a fire.

CHAPTER THIRTY

DAVID DROVE Trisha crosstown to the empty lot that offered a view of the rising cement hulk that would become the new convention center. Rumor had it that the topping ceremony, where the final roof beams would be put in place, would happen later in December, or so Trisha had heard through the grapevine.

Too bad that ass Trump was getting a finder's fee on the site. But then, the construction was lining a lot of pockets. That was New York and if you dealt in construction, you dealt with the mob.

The tires crunched over snow half-turned to ice once they pulled alongside the vacant lot. No cars but plenty of construction debris.

"Progress." Trisha shrugged. "Just like Hell's Kitchen is supposed to be Clinton now. But it doesn't seem better to me."

"Wait inside the car or out?" David asked.

"Out in the open."

He helped her out and steadied her on the crutches.

"Thanks." She looked around. On the far side of the corner, pedestrians walked past. "Where's the security detail?"

"Homeless person, with the cart, sitting next to the empty building over there. The rise gives him a clear view of the whole lot. There's another in the window of the fast-food place behind us."

"Your guys are good."

He steadied her as she navigated a patch of snow. "Yeah, I know."

She leaned forward on the crutches, stared into the lot, and resisted the urge to check her watch. Riordan would either show or he wouldn't.

"Chances of Bricker out there, waiting to pounce?" she asked.

"Close to nil." David ran a hand through his hair before jamming his watch cap down again. "No way she'd get past our security details."

She hoped David was right. She stared out over the lot and could just barely glimpse the Hudson River. "This setup makes me think of that time when you insisted on coming with me while I met a source over blackmail of that real estate magnet."

"He set a trap."

"I knew it was a trap. That's why I told you about it."

David let her lean on him for balance. "We've had quite a run."

"We're not the type of people who are supposed to be only friends." She stared at the mess around them. "Does Darlene resent me? She's great, and she's made you happy, but, hell, even Grayson has a twinge of jealousy about us, David."

"Darlene knows me." He slipped an arm around her waist. "Besides, she's used to me being pulled into things by my sisters. My mom, though, she took some convincing." He waved a hand. "Quiet, I hear something."

Footsteps crunched over the ice. David tensed and slid his hand into his coat pocket, over the .45 he'd hidden in there for easy access. Trisha straightened and braced herself.

A red-haired man, backlit against the sun, appeared from around a ten-foot-tall stack of pipes.

The paramedic the night of the fire. He possessed the same hair color as hers, red with dark highlights. His jeans displayed a rip where she'd sliced them open. His hands were shoved into the pockets of an Army jacket. Huh. She had a jacket like that too.

"Hands," David called.

Slowly, Riordan displayed his empty hands. "Helluva protector you have."

"You can see why he's worried," she said, leaning forward on the crutches.

"Yeah." He stopped about six feet from them. Blue eyes. She'd noticed them the night of the fire too.

Like mine.

"Damn." Something caught in his throat. "You really look like Mom, even accounting for the bruises."

She dug her fingers into the pads of the crutches. "How would you know what that woman looked like anyway? You were supposedly three when she died."

"So, you've put the Riordan family history together. That's good, makes this faster and time is short," he said. "Dad had photos of her. I stared at them a lot growing up, wondering what my life would be like if not for that night."

So many questions flared in her mind. Was her mother the only one to die in the fire? Why had her father taken her to Father Mike and kept her brother? Most of all, how much of this was true?

"If you're trying to create a bond here, it's not working," she said. "If you wanted to tell me any of this, the time was *before* you broke into my home."

"Yeah, that was a mistake. I'm too impulsive, Dad always said. And I'm used to doing stuff without asking. You got me good, though." He pointed at the rip in his jeans. "I needed stitches."

"Good," she snapped. "Now say what you come here to say. My patience is fucking gone."

"Okay." He ran his hand through his hair. "So, I'll start at the beginning. Some rival gang member wanted to take out Dad and the family way back when. He was out that night with me because I wanted to catch fireflies." He looked up at the cloudy sky. "Came home to the house in flames. He ran in. Found Mom near the door, you in her arms. He grabbed you first, turned to run back in, the place exploded." A pause. "Mom died."

Trisha shoved that information way down, refusing to let it bubble over. "He was West Side Gang."

"Yeah."

"You remember the fire?" she asked.

Riordan paled, and his freckles became more prominent. "Flashes of flames. That's it." He cleared his throat and looked around. "You sure there are no cops?"

"No cops." Was he a criminal, just like her supposed father? Probably. He'd had no problems holding a gun on her. But, then, she was a killer too.

"So, Dad had no idea what to do with a baby, no supplies, and only the cash in his pocket, with people still out to murder him. He told me later—much later—that he took you to Father Mike because he wanted you safe and far away from his mess."

"How did he know about Father Mike or the orphanage on the Lower East Side?"

"They were Army buddies."

A fact she could check. She didn't react. He was silent a moment.

"Go on," she prodded.

"Dad said he kept me because a child is easier to identify, and I'd be spotted at an orphanage. We ran to Florida. He changed our name. That's where I grew up."

A rueful smile, one Trisha'd seen in her mirror more than once.

"If you can call it growing up," Riordan continued. "Dad never recovered from that night. He used to wake up with nightmares and crawl into bed with me."

Trisha tried to imagine a man seeing his home, his love, destroyed. And what had this man done to call such carnage on himself and his family?

"We had a good life down there. But he couldn't let it go."

"The chop shop massacre." Realization dawned. "That was his revenge."

"Yeah, like I said, he never moved on." He jerked his thumb at himself. "*I* had a good life. I had a *football scholarship* offer. Instead, we came back up here when I was, like, seventeen. He reconnected with his old buddies. Planned to take back the West Side Gang for his own. Said everything would be fine once he took care of this business. And he'd get me into college. He knew a guy."

Bet he knew lots of guys, Trisha thought. "He got his revenge, but they killed him."

"Yeah. He got them, they got him." Tears welled in Riordan's eyes. "I should have been with him that night, but I was seventeen, it was New York City, and I was pissed at him, so I was out painting the town. I blew him off instead of helping him."

Uncertainly laced Riordan's voice. A lie? Trisha set her jaw.

"Why didn't you find me then?" she asked.

"I didn't know where you were," he whispered. "Please believe that."

When people begged you to believe something, it usually meant they were lying. But given Riordan had been seventeen and his father had just been murdered…

"How the fuck did they know to grab me, Riordan? And *why*?" A pawn in a game she'd never known existed.

He held his hands out, palms up. "Never had a clear answer as to how they stumbled across you but, damn, you look *just like her*. And he'd just reappeared in the Kitchen, and it was all full of rumors about him. I figure it was just damn unlucky you happened to be there at the wrong place, wrong time, where someone who knew Mom spotted you."

"She was leverage." David finally spoke. "They thought his worry for you would pull Riordan into the open, Trish."

A father she'd never known had wrecked her life. Great. Just great. Assuming what this guy said was true.

The younger Riordan shoved his hands back into his pockets. "Fat lot of good it did them. They died anyway."

"So, did he go into the chop shop to get me back or because he wanted revenge?" Trisha channeled Grayson. Ice cold. Keep the anger or despair at a distance.

"Revenge," Riordan said in disgust. "He wanted to win a war. He'd have done that without you in the picture. He sure as hell didn't care about *me* in the picture."

Big resentment there. Whatever love Jimmy had gotten from this father, it wasn't the same as what she'd gotten from Father Mike.

"You never once tried to contact her after you knew all this?" David ground out.

Trisha waved a hand. "Let him talk." Lance the wound.

Riordan stared at the ground. "Look, after he died, all I wanted was fucking out."

"You were seventeen, a kid raised by a man obsessed," she said carefully. "After he died, you were clear, though. You could do whatever you want. Where did you go?"

"I went back to Florida at first. Took the football scholarship. Blew out my knee. Found work eventually as a paramedic in Jersey. I thought the past was past."

"Why come back *now*?" she asked.

"I read your museum stories and saw your photo. And I *knew*."

That was the same way Bricker had caught on to her. "So instead of writing and saying 'hey, sis, long time, no see, let's catch up,' you broke into my home."

"Guilty," he agreed.

"You pointed a gun at me."

"You slashed my leg!"

Silence hung in the air for a few minutes. Fog from their breaths filled the air.

"Look, time's running short." Riordan glanced behind him. "Whatever questions you have left, ask them fast."

"Did you set the fire that injured Mrs. D?" she spat out.

"No!"

"You threatened her that day you broke in."

"Christ, I just wanted you to back off. I knew I'd screwed up." He took a few steps sideways, like he wanted to pace. "I made sure you were okay right after the fire. But you knew something was off, so I cut out of there before you could have me arrested." He ran both hands through his thick hair this time. "Wish I'd stuck around that night because…."

"Bricker grabbed me."

Another nod.

"So why bother telling me all this now? Why not just vanish again? I'd never know."

He smiled, and again, she felt like she was looking into a mirror. "I had to meet you, sis. I couldn't resist."

"Or maybe you want something from me, *brother*," she snarled.

"Moi? Never." He put a hand on his chest, exaggerating.

She almost laughed, despite herself.

"Besides, you're as broke as I am and your Fed is too sharp to give me funds. Ship's sailed on that." In the distance, sirens sounded. He slid a hand inside his coat.

"If you're reaching for a gun, don't." David drew his weapon.

Riordan paled again. "Easy." He pulled out and displayed a creased photo. "I've got this memorized. I figure you should have it."

He held it out. She hobbled forward. He handed over the photo. She stuffed it into a pocket without looking.

"I know I've been a lousy brother," he said. "But I had your back this time. Just know you'll be safe from now on. Feud's done. No one's left to carry it."

"What the hell is that supposed to mean?" Her hands tightened on the crutches.

"You'll find out soon enough." He turned and disappeared around the pipes.

David rushed to follow him. Trisha blocked his path with a crutch. He slipped on the icy ground and knelt on one knee.

"What the hell, Trish?"

"He's armed. I saw the outline of the gun in a waist holster when I got close. Grabbing him isn't worth risking your life."

"And what if he's working with Bricker? What if everything he told us was bullshit?"

"I'm sure he lied to us. He was too nervous about some of the things he said. But he told the truth too. He's no threat to me."

David straightened. "You sure?"

A deep fatigue swept through her. "I wouldn't risk you." She reached out and gripped his forearm. "Besides, what right do we have to hold him? We're not cops."

"All right but, damn, he confessed to the break-in."

"But he didn't steal anything. And I got him good, anyway."

"Fine, fine." David rested his arm around her shoulders. "What now?"

"We find out what's up with Grayson. I have a horrible, sinking feeling about why the cops dragged him off this morning."

"Shit," David said. "You think *Riordan* did something to Bricker?"

"Yep. That's the only way his having my back would make sense. Plus, Riordan knew where the chop shop massacre was. He could have made it there before Dorothy and Grayson and grabbed her."

"And now, if the cops found Bricker's body, Grayson would be the best suspect in her death," David said. "Shit."

She shuffled toward the car. "C'mon, help me in. We can use this info to help him."

David held on tight as she half-fell, half-slid into the car. He passed her the crutches, requiring yet more adjustment. She cursed.

"Not the crutches' fault." David started the car.

Trisha closed her eyes and let the heat flow into her frozen hands. "I know."

"Where to? The precinct so you can tell Dorothy what you heard?"

"No, if Bricker's been murdered and Grayson's a suspect, they'll keep Dorothy away from the case. We need to arm Taylor with what we know."

CHAPTER THIRTY-ONE

BRICKER WAS DEAD. Murdered. One problem solved, one problem created. They'd keep him here for hours, Grayson knew, hoping he'd confess to the crime. Logical enough. No one else had as strong a motive to kill the woman. He possessed opportunity too, as he'd left Patricia's side at the hospital and had driven home alone several times to shower and change. He lacked an alibi. As for method? He owned plenty of handguns.

When Patricia had been accused of murder, he'd attacked her as being unconcerned and detached from the consequences. But, like her, he found it difficult to take this accusation seriously when he was innocent.

Would he have done it, if he could?

I don't know.

That was a lie. He would. And he now understood Trisha's murderous rage a little better.

His mind drifted again, remembering Patricia's "I love you," remembering the night in front of the tree, remembering the initial joy on her face when he'd asked her to marry him.

He smiled, bringing back the memory of the first sight of her, all attitude and black leather, insisting she knew exactly how to solve the museum murder.

She'd smashed into his life. Wrecked all his careful plans. Disrupted his existence. Brought life to it. And he'd not trusted her. Pushed her to prove she loved him. Rejected her over what she'd done after being tortured. Yet, still, she'd called out, "I love you."

The door opened again. The hulking uniformed cop this time, with another cop accompanying him. Frick and Frack.

"Doing okay, suit?" Frick said.

He ignored them, staring straight ahead at the mirror. Frack came around and pulled the chair out from under him. Having anticipated the move, Grayson kept his balance. But now, he watched them more carefully. They intended violence.

"Fancy suit won't protect you," Frick said.

"Neither will your police uniform protect you," Grayson said. Dammit, he'd broken his rule about speaking to them. But he doubted that would matter now. They didn't want a confession. They wanted to intimidate. To hurt.

They bracketed him. With his hand cuffed, he couldn't move away. Adrenaline spiked. He forced his breathing to stay deep and even. Patricia had endured Bricker's torture. He would endure this. He would channel her insolence and use it as fuel.

Frick glared, face only inches from Grayson's. "I hear you like smacking cops around."

"If they deserve it."

A hard object smashed into his kidneys. He caught the table for balance. A police baton, perfectly aimed. He palmed a cufflink. He might have to fight. They could be here to kill him. For that, he needed his hands free.

"You deserve it," Frack said.

Another blow came, sending Grayson to his knees. But he uttered not a sound. Gah. He'd expected this. But he hadn't expected it to hurt so much.

"You think because you're the Lieutenant's friend, you get a pass?" Frick peered down at him. "She's on thin ice, you know. Like the rest of her people."

Lovely. Add racism to the rest of their sins. Grayson struggled to his feet, glaring at them, allowing the rage to show in his face. Frick took a step back.

Frack punched him in the gut. Grayson doubled over, fighting the urge to toss his breakfast.

"Not so tough now. English are always pussies," Frack said.

Pain spiked through Grayson's back and stomach.

"Lawyer," he said through gritted teeth.

"You sonofabitch." Frack raised his baton. "You ain't getting squat."

The door opened, admitting Captain Bennitti, the younger detective, and attorney Taylor.

"What the hell do you think you're doing?" the captain growled.

"Checking on the suspect," Frack said with a straight face.

"Is that what you're calling it now?" Grayson laced his words with the contempt that he felt. With them distracted, he used the cufflink to unlock the cuffs. He moaned to cover the sound of the lock opening, but also because it hurt like hell. Taylor stepped between him and Frick and Frack. An unlikely knight, given she was dressed in a flowing floral skirt, a pink blouse, and a scarf that matched the skirt. But her black work boots thudded on the concrete, making a statement, as she blocked the police from him.

"Get those handcuffs off my client," she ordered the captain.

"It's for our safety," Frick said.

Grayson dropped the empty cuffs on the table with a dramatic crash. "They're off, counselor."

Taylor tilted her head. She had the strangest expression, perhaps holding back a laugh. "Thank you, that removes that obstacle. Now, Captain." She turned to the highest ranking man. "Unless you're charging my client with something, we are leaving."

The captain crossed his arms over his chest. Frick pulled his service weapon. Grayson's lawyer ignored it.

"Oh, I almost forgot, Captain. I have a statement for you." Taylor dramatically pulled out a folder from her attaché case. "I believe it answers all the questions you had as to Estelle Bricker's fate."

What? Grayson almost grabbed for the folder, but Taylor put a hand in front of him.

"We're leaving now. I'll consider any contact with my client without me present to be harassment and will take legal action as necessary." She focused on the cop who'd pulled his gun. "Put that toy away before you hurt someone."

She swept out of the room. Grayson kept a wary eye on the weapon as he followed in her wake, all the way to the outer reception area. He caught a glimpse of Newman headed for the interrogation room. Dorothy spotted him, but there was no reaction. She had to be careful, as so many in the department wanted to see her fail. Had she been the one who alerted her captain to the beating? Cleared the way for Taylor to see him? Likely, and Dorothy might suffer for that. Dammit.

Ginny Lawrence, who'd been assigned to Taylor's security detail, awaited them in the reception area. Grayson narrowed his eyes and pushed aside the agony blooming in his back.

"I appreciate the rescue but what the hell is going on?"

Ginny merely stared back, no expression on her dark face, imperturbable as ever in a man's dark suit. "That's a question for your attorney, Boss."

"Not here," Taylor said as she hooked her arm through his. "Let's blow this pop stand."

She was right. Not in front of the police. Grayson followed her outside where Ginny led them to one of Gray Associates' specially designed security cars, a luxury Lincoln fortified like a tank.

Ginny held the back door open for them, and Grayson flashed to Patricia picking him up at the airport last week.

"Explain," he said again.

"I'm simply the driver today," Ginny said. "Ask your attorney. But I believe the redhead is involved."

"So she is." Taylor settled in next to Grayson as Ginny shut the door behind him. She patted the soft seats and leaned back with a sigh as the car pulled away from the precinct.

"They hit you," she said. "Where?"

"Two shots to the kidney with the baton, one punch to the stomach." He winced. He'd been hit harder but not for a long while. "I have a feeling it's only going to hurt worse in a few hours."

"Their usual M.O."

She sounded resigned to bad cops. Grayson hated that she was right.

"Ginny, take us to the ER. Make it the Mercy branch in the Village. I know the ER nurse."

"Right, ma'am."

"I'm fine," he ground out.

"I want those injuries documented. I want the police abuse documented."

He wished she wasn't correct on all of it. "All right."

"Good." And she finally relaxed. "I have to say, I'm going to miss being driven around, Mr. Grayson. You were right, Ms. Lawrence and I get on splendidly."

"Ginny is an impressive person. She should be moving up the ranks in Navy intelligence," Grayson said. "Save the Navy had discovered that she was a lesbian and pushed her out. I'm very lucky to have her with Gray Associates."

"I like the size of my paycheck better now," Ginny said.

"You're an interesting man, Mr. Grayson." Taylor looked at him over her dark-rimmed glasses. "To look at you, I'd assume you were the average moderately wealthy white man in a suit. Yet you surround your-self with people like Dorothy Gilbert, Ginny, and Trisha Connell. And you take beatings without a qualm."

"Are you asking me if I murdered Estelle Bricker, counselor? Because I did not," he snapped.

"Of course you didn't do it. I just gave them the person who did."

"*What?*" He almost growled the word. "Surely, Patricia didn't confess. She's incapable of having done it."

"No, not her; she's got quite an alibi, what with being in a hospital bed at the pronounced time of death. She said if you want the full story of what happened, come talk to her when you're ready."

The full story? "She called Riordan." He closed his eyes.

"She *met* with Riordan."

"That was damned dangerous."

"She didn't seem to care. Though she did bring Mr. Valesquez with her as protection."

"Something Riordan said made him a suspect. That's what was in your document."

"Trisha typed it up herself, had it ready when I swung by her apartment on my way to the precinct," Taylor said.

His anger flowed away. Patricia had anticipated he'd refuse to talk and that his refusal wouldn't shield him from the cops if things went sideways. Which they nearly had. She'd put her supposed blood brother in jeopardy. For him.

"I'm surprised Patricia didn't insist on coming with you."

"That precinct is not exactly handicapped accessible, to say the least. I refused her request to come," Taylor said. "I suspect she's remained awake and alert only on a thread and collapsed once I'd gone. For her first day out, it's been a long one."

They pulled up to the hospital ER. "Ginny, let Patricia know I'm free. Don't mention the injuries."

"Will do," Ginny agreed. "And David's with her, if you're worried about her safety."

"Thank you."

"If Lt. Gilbert helped you, could she get blowback for this?" Grayson asked the attorney.

"Oh, no doubt, even if she didn't help, some will think she did," Taylor replied.

And a formal complaint would only make Dorothy's situation worse.

"Counselor, how averse are you to calling in my full resources to back us up?"

Her eyebrows rose. "What resources?"

He told her about prominent clients he'd protected. He'd saved several of their lives and prevented threats against others.

She whistled. "They'll put pressure on the NYPD?"

"As will some people I know in the FBI, once the word gets out that I was nearly railroaded."

Her eyes gleamed. "Do it. Use your rich white guy power for good. About time they picked the wrong person to screw with. But first, let's get evidence."

As promised, Taylor knew the nurse on duty, who quickly brought Grayson to be examined. They gave him some painkillers, did blood and urine samples, and told him to rest and watch for blood in his urine or for nausea and vomiting. He took the painkillers before leaving, as his back was erupting in agony.

His attorney helped him to the security car. "I'll walk home from here. It's only a couple of blocks," she said. "Ginny, you see him home safe."

"Of course."

Grayson lay down in the back of the limo.

"Do you want me to drop you off at home, Boss?" Ginny asked.

Patricia was in Hell's Kitchen. He thought of the four flights, the narrow steps. He thought of Patricia's "I love you" and wondered where they now stood. Had that been out of desperation or fear?

He checked his watch. Already late afternoon. He'd be no good to her right now, in pain and angry. And she'd be upset about the beating he'd taken. He also had a concert recital to attend for Eleanor tonight, an event he'd promised to attend. And there were calls to make. Dorothy first, to strategize. Then to Tony and others to pull down whatever wrath he could on the NYPD.

"Take me home," he said to Ginny.

When he felt better. When she'd rested.

He could give her back the ring then.

If she'd accept.

CHAPTER THIRTY-TWO

GRAYSON TOOK a taxi to Patricia's apartment the next day. He moved gingerly, each step pulling at the purpling bruises on his lower back. Everything internally seemed to be functioning, but each spasm of pain increased his fury at Frick and Frack.

He stopped at the bottom of the steps of her apartment building to catch his breath and winced at the open maw that used to be Anne-Marie Donohue's window. Black streaks of soot bled out from the hole, like spider threads. A collection of cut flowers sat below the ruined window. An impromptu planter made of snow surrounded them.

Life among the cold winter? Grayson took it as a good sign. Still, he felt the weight of the engagement ring in his blazer pocket as he took careful, deliberate steps to the entranceway.

The four flights exhausted him and made him glad he'd taken the painkillers. He rested at the top, regaining his equilibrium, before knocking on her door.

"It's Grayson," he called, to warn her, in case she was jumpy.

"Come in."

He found her sitting at the rickety kitchen table, typewriter in front of her, half-hidden behind the tabletop Christmas tree. Several chocolate ornament wrappers were crumbled on the table. He sniffed. Faint smell of tobacco. A dirty ashtray sat below the open kitchen window. She'd gotten into her cigarettes.

Patricia held up a finger, asking him to wait, finished off the page, and set it on a stack next to the typewriter.

"Thanks for waiting. I'll be glad when I can afford my own computer. I'm so tired of Wite-Out."

"You have only to ask for a computer, Patricia."

"This works." She tapped her typewriter. "Besides, I owe you so much already." She hobbled over to her sink and washed out the ashtray. "I already dumped it. Then I cleaned up in the bathroom. I'd say 'showered,' but given the stitches and cast, let's just say I did the best I could."

"You needed the cigarettes?" He sat across from her on a rickety chair that he'd also offered to replace.

"I got on a roll. They helped. Sensory memory, I'm told. That's what makes it hard for smokers to quit." She dried off the ashtray. "But it was only two."

"I understand." And he did. "And you owe me nothing. We shouldn't keep score and even if we did, I'd say we were even, especially after what you did for me yesterday."

"I did nothing except make sure the truth is told." She studied him with a frown. "Christ, Grayson, you're moving stiffly, and you very carefully lowered yourself onto that chair." She moved to his side. "Shit. The cops got to you. Dammit."

"Easy." He held up a hand to prevent her from touching sensitive areas. "It's nothing."

"Bullshit," she snapped as she sat back down. "Tell me what happened. Tell me what cops are going down."

He couldn't answer at first, struck by her fierceness. Still injured, still nursing a black eye, and she'd have stormed the police precinct on her crutches.

"I'm not without resources." He allowed himself a wince. "Wheels are already in motion."

And he told her the whole story.

"I think I love Heather Taylor," Patricia said when he finished.

"I will join you in that admiration society. I suspect I'm not the first of her clients to suffer in police custody."

"But probably the first with the pull to hit back where it hurts." She adjusted a tiny ornament on the tree. "What made you decide to play back-room politics with the NYPD?"

"Dorothy's advice. Mostly, it was her plan. Who should hear about it, who had the power to act, who should be targeted," he said. "Results should be in within a few days. Your Kimba Sue may play a part once heads roll."

Patricia's eyes sparkled. "Excellent." But she frowned. "Why didn't you tell me any of this last night? Why did you stay away?"

"Why did you come here instead of staying at my place?"

"Pain in the ass," she muttered and rubbed her wrists.

He snorted. "Truthfully, I felt incapable of your steps and also needed to attend a concert for my daughter."

"Fair."

"How do *you* feel today?" he asked.

"Oh, sure, circle back to the loaded question." She held her wrist up against her chest. "The typing probably set me back a bit. Damn, they ache. Leg feels okay, though. But don't make me laugh. It pulls my stomach stitches. On the other hand, I've totally forgotten the slice on my finger."

"Your black eye is fading," he noted. The slash across her cheek had faded and was healing too. It would leave a scar. Not that she cared.

"What were you typing?"

"The story." She laid her hands over it. "That's what I do, right? Report. Who, what, when, where, and how. The 'why,' though, is the killer. But it's got everything. Arson, murder, torture, long-lost family, corrupt cops."

She stared off into space at something only she could see.

"What will you do with it?" he finally asked.

"There's the $20,000 question." She pointed to her cabinet. "I need a drink. Please tell me I still have whiskey in my cabinet. And no lectures, Grayson. I'm not on painkillers today. It's either whiskey or more cigarettes."

"No lectures." He wouldn't join her, however, because *he* was on painkillers. He also wanted a clear head around her today.

As for Patricia, she should be resting in bed, not excavating her emotional pain. She should take the painkillers and recover as the doctors had ordered. She never would do that. And, he admitted, neither would he if he'd been in her position.

He found the full whiskey bottle in the cabinet above the refrigerator. He sipped water while she downed the drink in two swallows.

If all the assumptions about his life had been blown apart, how would he feel? Shaken, yes. Selfishly, his first thought was disappointment that now was not the time to ask her to marry him again. Not helpful.

This was her life. She had to decide what pieces to pick up. But the thought she might do it without him made him sick enough to throw up what little breakfast he'd eaten. Still, she'd said "I love you."

She saluted him with her empty glass. "More."

He poured less than the last time.

She pulled a creased photo out from under her typed story and handed it to him. "My supposed mother. This time a color photo."

He stared at the photo of a long-dead woman, almost struck dumb. "That's a striking resemblance. Kimba Sue was right. You might be a time traveler."

"It's like a fucking mirror. Can we prove or disprove my relationship to her? Them?"

She needed him to be dispassionate.

"Possibly, perhaps if we had blood samples to compare, but those can only rule out a relationship or provide probabilities. There's DNA but that's not completely accurate yet and even if it were, the lab work might take months. Confirmation has to come from long way around, with research. We should corroborate Jimmy Riordan's story, as a start. I know it's not what you wanted to hear…"

She held the photo up.

"I've no clue what I wanted to hear." She slammed her empty glass on the table and stood, using her crutches. She hobbled over and collapsed into her favorite chair. She splayed her hand over the battered lockbox that contained the remnants of her life. "I locked my past up. I could hardly bear to look inside this the other night. But it's time."

He laid his hand on her knee. "This has waited for years, Patricia. It can wait longer when you're—"

"When I'm not such a mess? No, this is like a sword over my head. I need to get it done. Especially since I found this last night." She flipped open the box and pulled out a letter. "This is from Nicky."

Her eyes filled with unshed tears. He put his arm around her. She hesitated but finally leaned on him, thank God.

"The envelope is addressed and stamped but there's no sign it was mailed," he said.

"It wasn't." She straightened. "When Nicky died, I tossed all our letters to each other in this box. Couldn't bear to look at them. I didn't notice he'd never mailed this one. When I found it last night, I lacked the courage to open it."

He clasped her hand. "You could give it to me. I'll read it for you and—"

"And spare me whatever evil things are in it? Maybe it's more lies. Maybe it's a confession of a crime I know nothing about. Maybe I should rip it up without reading. But no. He wrote it to me. He didn't throw it in the garbage, either. I have to read it."

Every instinct screamed at Grayson to take this burden from her. But if he'd learned anything in the past week, it was that while he could share her burden, he couldn't make it vanish. She slid the letter open and unfolded it with shaking hands. Regular lined paper, not stationary. Nicky had not been a pretentious man.

The letter was dated 12/5/1980 and addressed to "Tic."

"*Tic*?"

"A play on 'Trisha Connell.' Trisha Infuriating Connell, he called me. Later, he changed 'infuriating' to 'irresistible.' Always Tic, though. He said we could rhyme. Nick and Tic." Her voice lowered to a whisper. "This was written a week before he died."

"I could read it to you."

She cleared her throat. "You can read it with me."

He enclosed her fingers. "Of course."

Hey Tic,

You're probably going to be pissed at me for not giving you this letter right away. Maybe I should rewrite it since I was dumb enough to date it. Maybe not. Anyway, I should've told you all this a long time ago, but I didn't want to mess up your head in prison, and then we were so happy when you got out, and I didn't want to mess that up either.

Yeah, I'm delaying. That's OK, you read fast. You'll get to the good stuff in a minute.

Patricia snorted out a laugh. At least her hands had stopped shaking.

I want to joke about this secret, tell you that you're a long-lost space princess or a shapeshifting Skrull or the heiress to a big fortune. But the secret's too ugly, really, for jokes, and I've delayed long enough.

So, the truth is, I have a clue as to who dropped you at the church that night when you were a baby, a guess about your blood family. But I can't prove anything, just tell you what I know. None of it's pretty, but then, we haven't had much pretty in our lives, have we?

OK, I'll set the scene, back to that day we both wish never happened. We went to Hell's Kitchen so I could grab something from my cousin while you hit up the convenience store for dinner. Next thing I know, you're snatched, and I have no clue where to find you. I smelled a rat in my cousin. (He's not a close cousin, he's like something, something on my drunk father's side. Should never have trusted him.) Anyway, he was a fucking coward like everyone on that side, and after I spent some time punching him out, he let slip it had been a setup.

Here's the insane part. He said you'd been nabbed to get at your father, some asshole named Riordan who they'd thought was dead but had come back after almost 15 years to take over the West Side Mob. Riordan was gathering loyalists to his side. This scared the guys who'd supposedly killed him. The story was that one of Riordan's enemies spotted you the day when we came to Hell's Kitchen so I could grab some transpo, remember?

Patricia shuffled to the next page.

"Transpo?" Grayson asked.

"Our code for his lifting a car. When we got really short of cash, he'd boost one, take it over to Jersey, and sell it to a guy there, no questions asked." She looked at the model cars on a shelf in her kitchen. "That's how I learned how to drive. On stolen cars."

"That explains so much about your driving," he said drily.

"It does. Look, he stopped stealing after I got out. Said it wasn't worth the risk of getting tossed in prison and being without me again."

"I'm not judging him, Patricia. You had to live and had few other options. How old was he when this happened? Fifteen? Sixteen??"

"Sixteen."

Grayson schooled his face to have no reaction. Children, they'd both been children. Yet they'd kept each other alive.

"And now I'm the one procrastinating. Back to reading," she said.

OK, wait, I should put the facts in order like one of your headlines. Back when you were a baby, in 1956, some of the West Side Mob wanted to kidnap this Riordan guy for ransom. But, instead, his house was torched, and everyone thought the whole family was dead. If the story is true—and I've got no proof it is—Riordan dropped you on Father Mike's doorstep to hide you. Don't know why he picked Father Mike Connell. Maybe because his church wasn't in the Kitchen. You'll have to research it. I know you'll find a reason.

"Why would gangsters kidnap a whole family?" Grayson asked. What a twisted environment.

"Kidnapping was a tactic of Mickey Spillane's gang," Patricia said. "The gangster, not the writer. Spillane's people would kidnap people for ransom. Usually, nobody got hurt, the money was paid, and it had the added benefit of making everyone afraid to cross the gang."

"Charming," Grayson said.

She shrugged. "My generation just kills you if they're pissed at you."

Anyway, fast forward to when those fucking assholes took you in 1970. You looked so much like Riordan's dead wife, and they snatched you as leverage against him. You're the right age to be the supposedly dead baby, but I don't think they cared if you actually were. Just that you looked enough like the dead wife. Riordan was hitting the gang hard. Double-taps to the back of the head, hard. They figured to use you to draw Riordan out. Figured messing you up would be good revenge on this Riordan.

"That's what Bricker meant about her brother Jack acting on orders." Trisha looked away from the words for a moment.

"It's confirmation of what young Riordan told you," Grayson said, "including the story about Father Mike."

"Yeah. Jimmy said Riordan and Father Mike were Army buddies." Her voice had lost that edge as she became engaged in the story.

I'd been pounding the streets looking for a clue for almost two days. Got a tip about where you might be from a lead the asshole cousin gave me. (I might have threatened to break his arm this time.) That's how I found you after your escape, thank God. I heard later about the chop shop murders. Riordan got taken down with his enemies. Bloodbath, everyone said. Nobody won. Word was sent out in the Kitchen to let the whole revenge thing die. But there were rumors of a man who was seen fleeing that scene. Some said he was more a kid than a man. Maybe it was Riordan's kid.

"He was there. I *knew* Jimmy lied about it," Patricia said.

"There's no statute of limitations on murder. He wouldn't want to confess."

"He practically confessed to Bricker's murder," she snapped.

"To protect you." Though Grayson hated to admit it, that seemed to be the truth. "And while it's a strong implication, he stopped short of a full confession in Bricker's murder."

"What a fucking mess." She shook her head. "Nicky should have told me all this right away. Let's see what else he has to say for himself."

Yeah, yeah, yeah, I know what you're thinking. I should have told you all this. But I didn't because you were so fucked up right then. I couldn't see how it could help you to know your maybe-father and maybe-brother were murderers. By the way, good thing the ones who ordered your kidnapping died in the chop shop. Saved me the trouble of doing it. Anyway, I wanted you far away from Hell's Kitchen then. I deliberately shifted over to Alphabet City when you got sprung. It was a fresh start.

"We stayed down in Alphabet City a few months in '73." Trisha picked up the model of an old Corvette from her shelf. "I got out at seventeen for good behavior. Place was a pit but, well, there were some good clubs back then, when punk was new. He bought this for me as a present. Well, after we took a joy ride in a real one. Sort of a way to remember. We moved uptown to around Columbia when my scholarship came through."

"How did you end up back here, love?" Grayson asked in a low voice. Had Nicky been drawn into something else he hadn't told her?

"This place was close to my new job at the *Herald*, plus the rent was dirt cheap. Nicky said Mrs. Donohue gave him the lead." She held the last page of the letter. "Hah. Here, he explains it himself."

I know, if I knew all this, why did we come back to the Kitchen? Yeah, maybe we should've stayed in that closet-sized apartment with the lousy heat near Columbia. But this was a much better place, and, fuck, it'd been years since you were snatched, your kidnappers were dead, and Riordan and his enemies were dead. Fresh start, right? That was the time to tell you, but…fuck, I can say I was trying to protect you, but mostly, I didn't want you pissed at me. And you would be. You probably are, reading this.

Tears began to roll down Trisha's cheeks. "You idiot," she muttered.

So here we are today. It's been a good place. I think we've been happy here. I know I have. I also know I don't have much time left. I wrote this all down so you'd know. I figure after Christmas, I'll tell you. Give you this letter and let it all loose. I figure you can't be too mad at a dying man, right?

Love you, Tic.

Nicky

The letter floated to the floor as Patricia dissolved into heaving sobs that broke Grayson's heart. He held her tight, it was all he could do. Her sobs ran down to tears, and finally, quiet breaths. He offered her his pocket square.

"You are the one of the few men I know who has a pocket square handy and the only one I know who'd let me get snot all over it."

He smiled. "I'll wash it first before refolding it back into the square."

"Hah!" She smoothed out the letter and set it on top of the lockbox.

"Are you angry with him?"

She shook her head. "I want to be so pissed. If he were here, I'd let him have it. He knew it too. But I just…I can't find the rage. That letter was so him, to the life. It's like I could have one last talk with him. I think I'm grateful."

She stood, waved off his offer of support, and hobbled to the bathroom. "Be back in a second."

He heard water running and assumed she was cleaning up. When she came out, she seemed clear-eyed. He poured two glasses of whiskey this time. He held his glass up.

"To Nicky and Tic," he said.

A single tear ran down her cheek. She clinked their glasses and downed the shot in one swallow. He held her after that as they stood in her little kitchen. Finally, he stepped back to look at her.

"That's most of the answers," he said. "Perhaps it's over now?"

"Is it? Truth, justice, and the law is a Venn diagram. Sometimes they overlap." She drew circles in the air with her hand. "More often, there's no justice in the law. Sometimes, you get justice in the truth. Today, all that remains is bitter truth: everyone involved in this is dead."

"But you're alive," he said. "There's justice in that."

"I'm not worth all the blood."

"It not about being worth it. It's about being alive and moving forward. Why did you become a reporter?"

"Excuse me?"

Ah, he welcomed that sharp tone, so much like her usual self. "You're a born writer, that's clear, but there must have been some inspiration for you to become a reporter."

She pointed at her television. "The 51st State. A PBS news show that ran until 1976. We were allowed to watch it in juvie. It was considered educational. Selwyn Raab did a lengthy investigation of the injustice in the George Whitmore case. The Black guy they sent up for a double homicide in which he had an ironclad alibi."

"Whitmore was finally exonerated. I thought, damn, that's what I wanted to do. Right some wrongs. Get the bastards who think they're immune." She settled on the couch again. "But there are more bastards than I ever dreamed existed, including my supposed blood family."

"Is there anything comforting in knowing that Father Mike did his best for you?" he asked.

She closed her eyes. "I got the impression from Riordan that my eight years with Father Mike was a damn sight better than his seventeen with Kieran Riordan. That man kept that photo of his dead wife to fuel his hatred. All he wanted was more blood. It destroyed him and probably his son too."

"You think James Riordan, if he's who he says he is, is lost?"

"Damned. Oh, yeah. He knows it too."

She rolled the empty whiskey glass in her hands. "Nicky's letter proves that Jimmy Riordan was at the chop shop. But there's another thread to pull here. I read the police report on the chop shop murders you found for me. I know cop-speak. There's a lot between the lines in that report."

"You mean the fact that Kieran Riordan was killed on his way out of the garage, maybe after the others were dead?"

"You have done your homework."

"Always."

"I like that about you. I believe the cops who responded to the chop shop killings took Riordan senior out, either because he was a threat or because they were in bed with the men who were killed." She leaned forward. "Jimmy got away but knew he was seen. That's why he stayed away. I wonder what he was really doing here, at the same time Bricker started sending the letters. He implied he was protecting me, but I wonder if he still had an axe to grind."

"Did he hold others responsible for killing his father, you mean?" Grayson asked quietly.

"I believe he did. I believe Bricker's not the only one he killed this time. But the East and Hudson Rivers are deep. They don't give up secrets easily."

"Do you want to find those responsible for Riordan senior's death too? Get revenge?"

Silence reigned for a bit.

"No," she finally whispered. "I should feel something for the Riordans. But they're assholes, especially the older one for dragging a kid into his revenge scheme. I'm glad to be out of it. I killed my rapists. Far as I'm concerned, it's done. The rest of it has nothing to do with me."

"You feel what you feel," he said. "I think it's a healthy reaction."

"Then why do I still feel like everything's broken?" She waved a hand at the apartment. "I thought I'd be able to relax once I came home. But it's not the same. *I'm* not the same."

"Change doesn't necessarily mean something is broken. We moved around every year or two when I was growing up. It's the life of a military brat," he said, choosing his words carefully. "My mother used to say home didn't mean a place; it meant people, the ones you loved."

She choked, almost a sob. "And when the people you love or should have loved you are all horrible or dead?"

He winced. "Not all of them."

"Oh, Jesus, Teddy. I'm sorry." She looked down at her ring finger.

Teddy. She'd called him Teddy for the first time since she'd woken up in the hospital.

"Come closer, love."

"All right."

She curled next to him again. He kept his arm around her, closed his eyes, and let them just be.

Yes, this was good. Very good.

A tap came at the door. "Trish?"

"Come in, David," she called.

The younger man, carrying a grocery bag, sauntered over and gave Patricia a kiss on the cheek. She smiled. Again, Grayson envied their easy relationship.

"Feeling okay, Boss?" David asked.

Grayson grunted. Just when he'd gotten Patricia to relax with him, now they had company.

"That good, huh?" David set the bag on the coffee table and pulled out the daily newspapers: *The Herald, the Daily News, The New York Times, The New York Post.*

"Awesome," Trisha said. "What else?"

"Cookies, beer, and a couple of subs from the deli."

"Perfect. Thanks, David."

"Hey, it's only because I wanted a beer too. It's afternoon already."

David served himself and sat on the couch, across from Grayson while Patricia flicked through the newspapers.

"Bricker is big news," she said.

"So are you," David added. "You plug your phone cord back in, and it's going to start ringing off the hook. Reporters are after you, Trish. Lois said she's even been fielding calls for you at Gray Associates."

Grayson frowned. "Why don't I know that?"

"You were resting," David said.

"Gotta admit, it's a smart idea," Trisha broke in. "People know I'm connected to Grayson, they get nothing at my number, but Gray Associates' phone is public. Is Lois annoyed?"

"It takes a lot to rattle her. The callers are probably coming out on the short end of the stick," David answered. "What else did you set in motion yesterday, Boss? Tony looked very pleased with himself."

"We'll see," he said.

Another knock at the door. David answered it this time. Grayson kept his hand near his weapon. But it was Dorothy, dressed in her full uniform. She walked in and shut the door behind her.

"Gang's all here. Good."

Grayson leaned forward to rest his hand on Patricia's arm. "You see? You have people who care, Patricia," he whispered.

Patricia's eyes lit up. "Not sure Dorothy is going to like being considered part of *my* family." And she laughed, but that devolved into a gasp of pain.

"What's going on?" Dorothy said. "What did I miss?"

"I have the same question," Patricia said. "What's with the full dress blues?"

"I see an empty glass. Where's the rest of the whiskey you're drinking?" Dorothy asked. "Because I have news that calls for a drink."

"Kitchen," Grayson, David, and Patricia answered.

Dorothy made a show of pouring the whiskey, tasting it, pronouncing it excellent—which produced a "damn right it is" from Patricia—before facing them.

"Well?" Grayson asked.

Dorothy actually grinned. "The plan worked. Frick and Frack are suspended immediately, and I fully expect them to be fired after an IAB hearing."

"Good," Grayson snapped. "Is that all?"

"Nope." She took a dramatic sip of the whiskey. "Ever since David was driven out of the force for reporting corruption, I've been watching, learning, and gathering allies." Her eyes narrowed. "Sorry, I couldn't help you then, David."

"You did. You prevented charges against me. I appreciate that," he said.

"It wasn't enough. But I was waiting on the right time and the right push."

Patricia straightened. "Do go on."

"Edmund's assault was the right time and the right incident to push. They're embarrassed by Bricker and that you were even considered a suspect, Trisha. Edmund calling in the dogs of war sealed the deal. Captain Bennitti took the fall. Officially, he's taking an early retirement."

"Who's replacing him?" Patricia asked.

Grayson knew the answer before Dorothy spoke.

"I am. I've been promoted. The precinct is to staff as I see fit." She finished the whiskey.

"Congratulations." Grayson stood and kissed her on the cheek. "You've earned this!"

"Damn right I have."

She actually hugged him. He winced at the back spasm that produced.

"Sorry."

"All in a good cause," he said.

"Woo-hoo!" David called. "Outstanding. Here's to Captain Dorothy Gilbert!"

They all raised their glasses.

"So, what's next?" Patricia asked.

"I go home and give my family the news." Her eyes gleamed. "Then it's back to work. What about you?" She jerked her head at the typewriter. "You back to work?"

"I'm taking a break," Patricia said. "Gonna figure some stuff out."

"Good. You do that. David," she asked, "Can you walk with me? I want to toss a few names at you for possible reassignment to my precinct."

"My pleasure." David finished his beer and grabbed his coat. "Later. Trish, figure this"—he pointed at Grayson—"out before he drives us nuts at the office."

She flipped him the bird. David laughed as they left.

Patricia relaxed on the couch. "Dorothy will still have to continue to watch her back."

"She knows."

Grayson slipped his hand into his pocket, fingered the ring. "Patricia, your words the other day when the police escorted me—"

"I remember." She closed her eyes. "All true."

"I need to hear you say it again, love."

He closed his hand around the ring, seemingly waiting forever for a response.

Please don't let her pull away.

Instead, she took his face in her hands. "I love you, you arrogant pain-in-the-ass. You've known that for a long time. But still…"

"Is it Nicky?"

"Not the way you mean. I'll always love him. That doesn't change. But it also doesn't change how I feel about you."

A deep breath. But she didn't pull away.

"But…you said you don't always know how you feel about something right away," Patricia said.

"I was angry."

"You're not angry now, and it's been a few days or maybe a lifetime since you said it, but…how do you feel now that you know what I did?"

And then she did pull away. Defensive. Worried for his answer. Their future depended on him finding the right words.

"I thought back to everything since we'd met, but especially that day at the museum when you charged an armed man with nothing but a wooden spear."

She mimed holding the spear. "Not one of my brighter moves. I should have tossed it at him, distracted him, and then—"

"Bloody hell, Patricia, would you let me finish?"

She made a zip motion over her lips. "Okay."

"You saved my life that day."

He held up a hand to forestall another interruption. She waved her fingers in a "do go on" gesture.

"If you hadn't been the person you are, I would be dead. And all the things that you've experienced—good and bad, horrible and wonderful— make you who are. I either love the whole person, or I don't love you at all."

He swallowed hard. Tears welled in her eyes.

"I love you. All of you."

She simply stared at him for what seemed like forever, blue eyes filled with unshed tears. Finally, she cleared her throat.

"That's a…damn good declaration." Her voice broke. "But don't you dare investigate me again without my asking."

"And don't you dare keep secrets."

"Deal."

He kissed her, long and slow, as each nerve inside him relaxed even while other parts of him stirred. When they broke apart, he pulled out the ring from his pocket.

"Will you marry me, Patricia?"

The tears flowed again. Happy ones, he hoped.

"Yes," she croaked out.

This time, he slid the ring on her finger.

"We don't have to rush to City Hall, do we?" Her voice was still thick. She squeezed his hand. "There's so many logistics to figure out. Like, I'd like a chance to have your kid not hate me. And where will we live? And, hell, I need to figure out how to make a living now that—"

He laid his hand on her cheek. "I accept any timing less than 'when hell freezes over.'"

She flung her arms around him and laughed.

EPILOGUE

TRISHA LEANED against the door frame of Mrs. D.'s now empty apartment. It kept her from having to use the hated cane for balance.

Inside, Mrs. D. stood, rotating in a full circle in the home she'd lived in for thirty years. No longer. Outside, an old Ford sedan owned by one of her burly grandsons stood waiting to whisk her to her new home in the suburbs. The landlord would invest in renovating the apartment now that it wasn't rent-controlled any longer.

"End of an era," Trisha said to her.

"For all of us, eventually," Mrs. D. said.

"True. The landlord can't wait to get the rest of us out and convert the whole thing to condos," Trisha said.

"Not what I meant, dear, though that's true enough." She looked out over the windows. "I look out at this street and see ghosts. Past time to let them go."

Trisha joined her at the window, her cane thumping on the wood floor. "When did you know?"

"Know? That's a funny word. Who really knows? But I guessed."

"When?" Trisha persisted.

She touched a strand of Trisha's hair. "Moira Murphy went to catechism with my eldest daughter. I thought you looked just like her when you moved in. But then, the Irish all tend to look like each other. I thought nothing of it."

"Until?" The old lady was enjoying drawing this out.

"Until I saw young Jimmy Riordan on the street a week before the fire. Spitting image of his father, much the same as you with your mother." She smiled. "Brought me back. His father was a charmer. Memorable to everyone. That's when I started looking for the clips."

Trisha's fingernails dug into the window frame. "And you kept silent?"

Outside, her grandson gestured for her to come out. Mrs. D. held up one finger to ask for more time.

"I was *guessing*. I thought about telling you the day you fixed my fan, but I'm an old lady, and sometimes I see ghosts, as I said. What good does it do to bring them into the light?" Her face hardened. "Then I saw him that day he broke into your place."

"You didn't tell me when you brought the casserole?" Trisha asked. "Why not?"

"If you *remember*, I told you to come see me that morning. But you didn't." She pointed a finger at Trisha.

"You're right, I surrender. And then there was the fire."

"Yes, the fire. I saw her, that Bricker, when she was here that day. Called to her, like an idiot, because she looked like someone I knew."

"You couldn't know she was a killer."

Mrs. D. shrugged. "Anyway, thanks to you, I'll get to dance at my grandson's wedding."

Silence for a bit, like Mrs. D. was waiting on her.

"What do you remember about them?" Trisha asked, almost afraid of the answer.

"Moira Murphy was a sweetheart. But him! He could be charming. But, oh, he was ambitious. The West Side wanted to use him."

"And he stepped over a line?"

"So, we all guessed. You've pieced that fire together?"

"Yes," Trisha said.

Mrs. D. arched an eyebrow. "Tell me, how did young Jimmy get out?"

"He didn't. He was never in the house. He was out with his father, catching fireflies."

"A flight of fancy? That describes his father, no doubt." A sigh. "But you were there. It was your mother who saved you, wasn't it? She'd have done anything for her children."

"Yes, my mother saved me." What odd words to say.

"I always wondered." Mrs. D. turned from the window.

"What can you tell me about her?" Trisha asked again.

"She was a good girl, Moira. She came to church every Sunday, even after she was married. A bright light. She comforted those grieving and laughed with those celebrating." She smiled. "I went to your baptism. You cried."

"I don't remember."

Mrs. D. chuckled. "Likely not. Your father flashed money around that day, all great smiles and plans." A pause. "My daughter and Moira were friends, as I said. I could arrange for you to talk to her."

Would that be wonderful or terrible? She'd no idea how she was supposed to feel about Riordan, or her supposed brother. They felt unreal. David. Kimba Sue. Grayson. Even Dorothy. They were real. But Moira Murphy had given her life for her daughter. That was something.

"I'll let you know," Trisha said.

"Good." Mrs. D. patted Trisha's arm. "Time for me to go."

Trisha waved to her from the stoop as the car pulled away. Grayson came up to her from behind, carrying her suitcase.

"She tell you anything?" Grayson asked.

"Nothing I didn't already know, mostly that I was a dead ringer for my mother. And that my father was apparently a charming asshole. Sounds like my mother was a sweetheart, I guess." Mother? Strange word.

Grayson put his arm around her shoulders.

"Thanks for carrying the suitcase," she said.

"Thanks for agreeing to move in with me." He'd said that over and over.

"I'm still worried about what your kid will say."

"She has agreed to meet for brunch next week, all three of us."

Oh, won't that be fun. "It's a start," she said. "Just like moving in. It's temporary, until we find a place together," she answered. "I don't want to sponge off you. I can support myself."

"Then we should start looking for a place of our own in earnest," Grayson said.

"Yeah." He was good at deflecting when she was nervous. They still had to work out the cost. He could afford more but the unequal split bugged her. "That'll be interesting."

"Any word on Jimmy Riordan?" She knew she was stalling leaving the Kitchen. This building had a hold on her.

"No, he's still in the wind," Grayson said.

Good, she thought. Let him vanish. She hoped he found whatever he was looking for, now that all his enemies were dead. "Okay, let's go."

Grayson offered her his arm as they walked down the steps. Around her, car horns beeped. Demolition two buildings down sent dust into the street.

This fucking city. But it was hers.

"Let's go home, Teddy."

———

Thank you for reading! Did you enjoy? Please add your review because nothing helps an author more and encourages readers to take a chance on a book than a review.

And don't miss the next book of the *Trisha & Grayson Mysteries* coming soon!

Until then read BAD PRESS, by City Owl Author, Rachel Mucha. Turn the page for a sneak peek!

Also be sure to sign up for the City Owl Press newsletter to receive notice of all book releases!

SNEAK PEEK OF BAD PRESS

BY RACHEL MUCHA

When asked to describe his music, instead of an adjective or two, Dave Austin just lets out a laugh.

"It's practically indescribable," he shares with a grin. "People want to stick me in the Country category, but that's not quite right. My songs can be folk-y, but a little rock and roll, too. And some of them have such a stripped-down indie feel. In case you can't tell, I don't like labels."

When pressed for one all-encompassing word, Austin finally takes the bait.

"Unique," he says. "Just completely, one-hundred-percent, uniquely me."

I continued typing up my story, eyes darting to reference my notes, even though local singer/songwriter Dave Austin's interview reads nearly word for word as his peers' I've covered recently.

Just keep typing, Evie.

I tried to banish any cynical thoughts from my head, reminding myself that I was fortunate to have this job — even if writing puff pieces about wannabe country music stars wasn't my first choice. Or second choice. Or sixth choice.

You're lucky to be employed as a writer at all, I thought, more forcefully this time to get the message to stick. I always liked to look on the positive side, but when you write enough of these stories, you just sort of want to scream.

"You okay? You're making that face again."

I looked across my desk at my colleague and best friend, Grace Lee. She knew all too well how soul-crushing I found the Arts and Culture beat.

"How can I be making a face when I'm writing about the *unique* Dave Austin?" I flashed her a grin.

"I heard him at open mic night at The Ranch a few weeks ago," Grace said. "He's unique in the sense that he's not that great, but still lands gigs."

"What are you working on? Something more exciting?"

"Eh, the hardware store down the street got into the habit of not paying people overtime, and they just settled a pretty big lawsuit," she said. "The details are boring, though."

"I'd kill to write about that," I said, slumping in my chair. Grace covered the business beat, which had been my third choice—hypothetically, of course. I didn't get a vote in my assigned beat. It was either Arts and Culture, or no job—and man, did I need a job.

I opened my mouth to ask Grace if she wanted to procrastinate our assignments by grabbing an early lunch, but shouting from our editor's office made both our heads snap towards it.

"…is *unbelievable*," Shelly yelled. She brought her voice down a tick, but I managed to catch an additional, "…should absolutely know better!"

I looked back to Grace, eyes wide. "What's that all about? Who's in there?"

Looking just as bewildered as me, she quickly surveyed the newsroom, noting whose desk was empty. "Jeff?"

Grace's suspicion was confirmed a few seconds later when Jeff Borelli burst out of Shelly's office, swinging the door open with so much force it collided with the wall. Every reporter's eyes followed his movements as he marched to his desk and began tossing various possessions inside the cardboard box he carried.

"Whoa," Grace murmured as we all continued to watch him. Another minute later, a security guard I didn't even know we had wandered over to Jeff's desk, hands on his hips, legs widened into an intimidating stance.

"Seriously?" Jeff yelled over his shoulder towards Shelly's office.

"Sir, you need to leave," the guard said, voice deep as the ocean. "You can't take anything except personal effects."

"This is *bullshit*," Jeff muttered not-so-quietly. He tossed two framed photos into his box, the surface of his desk cluttered with folders and legal pads he had to leave behind.

"Well, show's over, folks!" Jeff said, already halfway to the door.

The security guard brought up the rear, disappearing with Jeff into the hallway.

The hush amongst us all remained for a solid thirty seconds.

"*What* just happened?" It had all gone down so quickly, I needed verbal confirmation everyone else had seen it too.

"It's about time," Maggie shouted from across the office. "I never liked him."

"It's gotta be porn," Phil chimed in. "When that happens, it's always porn."

"Did you hear what the guard said about not taking anything?" Alyssa asked. "Was Jeff stealing stuff from here?"

"What's there to steal?" Grace gave her monitor a hearty smack. "My nine-year-old nephew has a nicer computer than I do."

Murmurs of agreement filled the newsroom, and more people shouted out wild theories about what Jeff could've done.

"Wait," I said to Grace, tearing her attention away from the gossip. "Wasn't Jeff working on an update on the serial rapist?"

"I think he was."

"Well, who's going to write it now?" I asked.

She shrugged. "Beats me. Something tells me this firing wasn't planned."

I turned once more towards Shelly's office, wondering if she'd thought this through yet. She couldn't just not have someone covering the crime beat. Surely, she'd be reassigning it soon—and if I pounced now, I could throw my hat in the ring.

I sprung out of my chair.

"Shelly?"

Lingering outside her office, I gently knocked on her half-open door. She held a phone receiver to her ear, but when she noticed me, she whispered something quickly and hung up.

"Evie, now's not a good time," she said. "I have to meet with HR in a few minutes. I'll answer your questions about Jeff as soon as I can."

"Well, I actually wanted to ask about Jeff's story." I dared to step inside. "His piece on the serial rapist."

"Oh, *shit*." Shelly closed her eyes and massaged her temples. "That was supposed to run tomorrow."

"I know." I took a breath. "I was going to offer to finish it up."

Shelly stared at me like I'd spoken a different language. "But you have your own assignments already."

"I'm almost done the Austin piece," I said, even though I'd only just started. "I could spend the rest of the afternoon on Jeff's story."

"Hmm." Shelly drummed her fingers on her desk.

"You know," I settled into the seat across from her desk, "I have experience covering the crime beat. I did that in D.C. for two years. I would love to do it again."

I held my breath as Shelly considered this. My kind but tough editor had a really good poker face, and it was impossible to tell which way she was leaning.

"Evie, you know I think you're a very capable writer, but, if I remember correctly, you had some…issues on the crime beat?"

I tried not to sigh. The "issues" she was referring to were a series of ethical missteps that had cost me my job at the *Post* and my professional reputation. The backlash had been so severe I'd had to move six hours away to Podunk, Virginia to find a paper that would take me. Shelly didn't know the details of my slip-up, but my lack of a reference from my previous editor spoke volumes.

I was grateful for this job, but I couldn't help but feel a sense of ownership when it came to the crime beat. It was what I was supposed to do. And now that the opportunity was hanging right in front of me, I couldn't not reach out and grab it.

"That's right, I did have a bit of trouble back there," I said. "But I promise you, I've learned my lesson. I always do everything completely by the book now. You've never had one complaint about my work."

Shelly's mouth quirked to the side. "It's just, with what happened with Jeff, we can't afford to have any more scandals—especially with our crime reporter. It's an important section to get right."

Even more curiosity gnawed at me about what scandalous thing Jeff had done, but I forced myself to focus on the task at hand.

"Absolutely." I paused before continuing. "Why don't you let me just try this one story? And if you're satisfied with it, maybe I could take on the beat on a more permanent basis?"

"Okay." She gave me a weak smile. "I'm in a bind here, so if you deliver on this, we can talk."

"Thank you," I said, leaping out of my chair. "Don't worry. I'm on it."

Shelly had already turned back to her phone, too distracted to bask in my victory with me.

I hustled to my desk. "Grace! Shelly says I can do Jeff's story."

"That's great," she said. "But what about Dave Austin?"

"Oh, who cares about Dave Austin!"

Fifteen minutes later, I'd swiped every notepad from Jeff's desk and started poring over his scribblings. The man had atrocious handwriting, but I finally found what I was looking for.

Four attacks now, same M.O., no suspects announced by PD. Call Delaney for quote and update.

My heart slowly began to sink. This wasn't much to go on. I'd been following the story of the serial rapist, of course—what woman in town wouldn't be? But based on previous articles, it appeared little was known about him, and Jeff seemingly had planned to write an entire story based off information from this Delaney person.

A quick Google search brought me to the Bristol PD's website, gifting me Detective Tom Delaney's extension. I eagerly dialed.

"Delaney," a gruff voice answered after three rings.

"Hi," I said, tone chipper. "This is Evie Hartley from *Bristol Daily News*. I was hoping I could talk to you for a few minutes about the serial rapist."

There was a long pause. "What happened to Jeff? I normally talk to him."

"Jeff is…no longer with the paper," I said. "But I'm taking over for him. So would you be able to give me a quick update on the investigation?"

"Look, lady. I don't know you, and I sure as hell don't have time to chat. I've got a case to solve."

With that, Delaney hung up on me. I stared at my receiver for a moment, a little stunned by his shortness. It was true that cops didn't love talking with reporters, but Delaney seemed to be punishing me for the simple crime of not being Jeff.

"Okay…" I refused to let myself get discouraged. I'd been out of the crime game for a bit. I'd forgotten how tough it could be to get sources to spill. Budding country music singers aren't as tight-lipped as cops working a serial rapist case.

Scrolling through Bristol PD's list of officers, I learned our tiny town only had three bona fide detectives, counting Delaney. Two chances left.

I called Nicole Zimmerman next. A female detective would be all too familiar with handling sexism at work—she might throw me a bone.

"Detective Zimmerman."

"Hi, this is Evie Hartley from *Bristol Daily News*. I—"

A loud click cut off my spiel. Again, I was surprised. How was she ruder than Delaney? What happened to girl power?

Starting to panic now, I dialed number three on the list, Marcus Pennington. The call went straight to voicemail, and I didn't bother with a message. I wondered if he wasn't there, or if his colleagues had warned him not to answer. Didn't really matter, either way.

"Everything okay?" Grace asked as she sat, having returned from a fast-food run.

I threw down my pen. "The cops aren't talking, and Jeff left me nothing." I threw down my pen.

She offered me sympathy fries, and I took a few. "Sorry. It's tough coming into it last minute like this. You might need to get creative."

I shoved the fries into my mouth and tried not to panic. Back in D.C. I'd started from scratch as a crime reporter once, with no connections. Sure, I was a little crunched for time this go around, but I could do it again.

Opening a new tab, I brought up Facebook and searched for Delaney, since he was the only one who'd actually talked to me. I easily found his profile and was pleased to see he posted *a lot*. If I could bump into him somewhere, it'd be harder for him to blow me off.

Scrolling through his page, I looked for any usual haunts. A few weeks ago, he "checked into" Last Call, a local dive bar so seedy looking, I'd never set foot inside. I read the comments, an exchange between Delaney and someone named Paul—the owner.

Thanks for stopping by tonight, Tom. Come back soon!

Those wings are KILLER. Glad Marcus dragged me along.

Haha, he should be our poster boy for wing night. Can't remember the last time he missed one.

Marcus. Could that be detective number three, Marcus Pennington? It would make sense. Excitement rushed through me as I realized it was Wing Wednesday. Would Pennington be there tonight? The owner's comment made me think yes.

I did a quick search for Pennington. He had a Facebook page, but his privacy settings were on. All I could see was a thumbnail of his profile picture, which told me two vague things: brown hair, youngish. Showing up at Last Call in the hopes he'd be there was hit or miss, but if I couldn't get in contact with a source soon, it'd be my only option.

I spent the rest of the afternoon alternating between writing more about Dave Austin's *unique* music and trying Bristol's elusive detectives again, getting nothing but voicemails.

Grace was right—it was time to get creative.

* * *

Don't stop now. Keep reading with your copy of BAD PRESS

Don't miss the next book of the *Trisha & Grayson Mysteries* coming soon, and find more from Corrina Lawson at www.corrina-lawson.com

Until then, discover BAD PRESS, by City Owl Author, Rachel Mucha.

———

Crime reporter Evie Hartley was at the height of her career, but a series of ethical missteps cost her everything. Now, she's working for a small-town newspaper's culture section, trying to prove to everyone, especially herself, that she's able to do her job by the book.

When there's an opening for the crime beat, Evie jumps at the chance. And while she manages to impress her boss, she makes an enemy of the detective she played to get the inside scoop. Her methods may straddle the line between professional and underhanded, but they work, and Evie solves a case the police haven't been able to crack. Detective Marcus "Penn" Pennington reluctantly calls a truce and becomes her go-to police source as she investigates more crimes for the paper.

Evie's thirst for the truth sets her on a dangerous path, and poking around in a cold case results in sinister anonymous threats. When she forms an alliance with someone who seems to know far more about the missing person's disappearance than he should, Penn sticks to Evie like glue, blurring the lines between protection and possession. But even with a cop watching her back, Evie's willingness to do anything to get the story might just get her killed.

———

Please sign up for the City Owl Press newsletter for chances to win special subscriber-only contests and giveaways as well as receiving information on upcoming releases and special excerpts.

All reviews are **welcome** and **appreciated**. Please consider leaving one on your favorite social media and book buying sites.

For books in the world of romance and speculative fiction that embody Innovation, Creativity, and Affordability, check out City Owl Press at www.cityowlpress.com.

ACKNOWLEDGMENTS

The Trisha & Grayson stories have been over two decades in the making, in various forms. During that time, I've had continued support from my fabulous husband and the backing of all four of my kids (one of whom actually wrote some Trisha & Grayson fanfic as teen). Thank you more than I can say. And to my mom, who when she read the final version of "Above the Fold," said "Hey! You've got something there."

I've also been blessed with the incredible friendship of so many writers at various levels of publication, cheering me on and hoping these books would see life. Thank you.

In a way, these stories are about a lost type of journalism, a world that no longer exists. It's one that many of my readers likely don't remember. But there was a time when we trusted journalists to tell the truth and put that truth and facts above all. To all those journalists who still consider the truth and facts above all, this is also for you. You are needed more than ever.

ABOUT THE AUTHOR

CORRINA LAWSON is an award-winning reporter, pop culture blogger, and the author of steampunk mysteries, paranormal and fantasy romance, and erotic romance. (And now, her first mystery!) She lives in rural New England next to a hiking preserve and occasionally bears wander through her yard. She can often be found walking the neighborhood with her young adult twins, chatting about pop culture. She lives with her twins, her husband, the dog, and four cats, including Buster, Lord Floofy Tail.

She is a certified superhero geek and loves attending comic book conventions, especially in New York City and Comic Con in San Diego. And, yes, Lois Lane originally inspired her to become a reporter.

www.corrina-lawson.com

X x.com/CorrinaLawson

◯ instagram.com/corrinalawson

f facebook.com/corrinalawsonwriter